THREE ANNIVERSARIES

Stacy Conway married Janine because it seemed expected of him. Their first year was difficult and Janine's baby was stillborn. On an impulse she agrees to adopt an unwanted baby, although it is unattractive and she feels little affection for it. Through a misunderstanding, Stacy and Janine part abruptly and she and the baby's mother join forces to share a flat. Stacy gets involved with a nurse and Janine meets an old flame. How this unhappy couple sort out their problems makes a moving and warm-hearted story.

THREE
ANNIVERSARIES

Kathleen Treves

A Lythway Book

CHIVERS PRESS
BATH

First published 1950
by Ward Lock Ltd
First published in Large Print 1975
Reissued 1982 by Chivers Press
by arrangement with the author

ISBN 0 85046 614 8

Printed and bound in Great Britain by
REDWOOD BURN LIMITED
Trowbridge, Wiltshire

THREE ANNIVERSARIES

CHAPTER I

"IT was a boy."

The walls of the corridor were pale green and buff. Here and there the paint was peeling. There was the faint rustle of nurses' aprons as in ones and twos they went off duty. Somewhere outside in the street a hurdy-gurdy jangled out a tune that he and Janine had danced to, on their honeymoon. He listened to it, with a dead, blank expression in his eyes, as he tried to recall the words. But the only words that fitted were the ones just uttered by the little ginger nurse with the compassionate brown eyes.

"It was a boy."

He licked his lips, and tried to speak, but his voice had gone, and left in its place a hoarse whisper.

"*Was?*"

The nurse nodded, with infinite kindness. "Would you like to see your wife now, Mr. Conway?"

He found himself following her, down a darkened corridor to a little room at the end. It was quiet, isolated, yet the hurdy-gurdy tune managed to penetrate even

1

here, beating at the senses with nostalgic memories. Janine lay in a high iron bed, listening. She was by herself, but he knew she wasn't thinking of close, personal things, so much as dipping back in the past. Listening to that tune, and going back, away from the frightening present. There was a taut, hurt expression on her little heart-shaped face, and there was the agonized look of unshed tears in her wide blue eyes.

"Stacy!" she gasped, suddenly looking across at him, over the wide space of polished wood floor. "Oh, Stacy, make them stop that tune!"

The little nurse was still behind him. "Don't excite her," she cautioned, in a whisper, and rustled out.

He stood there stupidly. That whispered warning suggested that Janine was very ill. His mother had warned him too, before he came, that Janine would probably be unconscious, or at least unable to speak or move. His sister muttered something about taking it easy, on this first visit. All had seemed to expect that Janine would have little to say, and that he would not be long with her.

Janine herself shattered that illusion.

"What's the matter, Stacy?" and as he didn't immediately answer, she asked in an urgent voice, "Did they tell you?"

He forced his legs to move. He was a very tall young man, whose long thin face was almost always pallid, and his eyes a startling, live blue by vivid contrast. His hair, fair and thickly wavy, added to the illusion of frail physique, as did his long, thin white hands.

"Yes, they told me," he heard himself saying, as he bent to kiss her. The action was awkward. They had never been demonstrative, either of them. She from lack of inclination, due mostly to her narrow upbringing, in an old-fashioned country town with two starchy great-aunts. He from the instinctive feeling that she wouldn't like it, and would probably snub him. He kissed her now, partly from the need of a greeting, partly because he felt husbands did so on this occasion, and he made the action suitably decorous. A glance at Janine's face told him she accepted it without anger, but his heart clamoured to take her violently in his arms, kiss her hungrily, bury his face on her shoulder, and give way to hard, hurt tears for the loss of the son he had lived for.

3

Janine said, with bitterness, "Five other women gave birth to boys to-day. Mine was the only one born dead." Her voice was hard, and now that the hurdy-gurdy had swung into a different, and less personal tune, there was no longer the taut look on her face. It settled into hard lines, and she had whitened as the memory of this morning came back to her.

"Why did they put you in here, all alone?" he asked, for the sake of something to say. It wasn't easy to make conversation, sitting stiffly on a hospital chair by that hard, white-covered bed. Janine, in her newly-made blue wool bed-jacket, her thick black hair falling loosely round her face in soft, large waves, was the only familiar thing in all the room. It was all harshly, austerely hospital. Even the smell of it.

"So I shouldn't see the other babies," she said.

"I would have brought you some flowers, Janine, only the shop was shut by the time I left the office. Overtime, and I couldn't refuse to stay." He was conscious of the stiffness of everything he said, yet he could do nothing about it.

"It's all right, Stacy."

4

"Mother's sending you some things—magazines and fruit. She wanted to know what you needed."

"It's all right," she said again. "Tell her not to bother."

"Are you all right, Janine? You look—all right."

She looked quickly at him, catching the surprise in his voice. "It's funny, isn't it?" she agreed. "I thought I'd be half dead, but I just feel a bit tired, that's all. Nothing else. Just tired. Everyone feels all right soon after, so it seems. Except one, and she had anaesthetic. She had twins...boys!"

Again the bitterness, and this time she started to cry. Hard, dry sobs that brought the little ginger nurse in with a rush.

"You mustn't, Mrs. Conway. You've to be quiet!"

"She's..going to be all right, isn't she, nurse?"

"Yes, yes. Make her stop crying, Sister's coming!"

Janine herself made the required effort, and mopped her eyes. "I don't want another lecture on being brave," she said, tartly.

He tried to hold her hand, with the

5

intention of being comforting, but Janine snatched it away. The ginger nurse pretended not to see, and busily straightened the bed.

Sister O'Neill waddled in, bristling with efficiency, her bright eyes birdlike behind gleaming spectacles. She was a dumpy little woman, and secretly nursed a grudge against all tall people, because of the dignity she could never bring to her position through her shortness of stature and not quite straight legs. It was difficult, too, to maintain discipline among the junior nurses, who, by an unlucky streak of fate, all seemed to be tall and slim.

Stacy Conway got up. "She's all right," he said, apologetically, as the older woman's searching glance spotted his wife's tears. "She'll be all right."

"You've told your husband, Mrs. Conway?"

Janine said, "No, he knew." It was obvious that she didn't like the Sister. The little nurse bit her lip.

"I told Mr. Conway, Sister. I thought it might upset Mrs. Conway to have to tell him."

"You have no right to do any such thing, nurse! You take unpardonable liberties!

6

You should have brought Mr. Conway to me at once, and *I* would have told him!"

There was a tight little scene, and Stacy found himself being shown to the door, and details of visiting hours being given to him in a brittle, angry voice. Janine was leaning over the side of the bed, staring fixedly at him.

He hesitated. She wanted to say something. Something was trying to push itself forward in his numbed brain, something he ought to remember. He passed a hand over his forehead.

"What is it?" the Sister asked briskly, pausing a little behind him. He had the feeling that she meant to be kind but didn't know how to show kindness, and there was a kinship between them for a split second, because of his own clumsy and thwarted attempts to show Janine affection.

"Nothing," Janine muttered, lying back in bed with a sullen look.

"Did you want me, dear?" he asked, going back to her, and hoping the Sister and nurse would go, leaving them to say their good-byes in privacy. That, however, wasn't to be. He had upset his wife once; they weren't taking chances again. They

7

waited, watching.

Janine said, carefully, "What's to-day?"

"Thursday," he said, puzzled.

"No, I mean the date. The first, isn't it?"

The Sister broke in, in a heavily soothing voice. "That's right, Mrs. Conway. The first of April. All Fools' Day."

Janine flushed, and closed her eyes. Her face was set and hard again. That illusive something tantalized his brain again, but refused to be pinned down.

"Try not to think about anything, Mrs. Conway," the Sister said, again. "Nurse will make you comfortable, and I'll send you a sedative. Good night! Come, Mr. Conway, you mustn't upset your wife again."

He was definitely and finally shown out, and he was in the street. There were lights in the cinema entrances, and people jostled past on the pavements. Buses whirled by and their lights seemed brighter than usual. They hurt his eyes after the dimly-hit hospital. He walked without direction, and it came to him that soon after leaving Janine's room, he had heard (without its significance registering at the time) the raucous continuous squawking

8

din from the nursery. The wails of the babies who had not been born dead.

His throat was tight. He stopped and looked at the stills outside a theatre, without taking in what he saw. All Fools' Day. The words repeated themselves nonsensically, until they stopped jumbling in a wild heap, suddenly made sense. Terrific sense. He opened his eyes wide in horror. That was why Janine was acting so queerly. The first of April. The anniversary of their wedding... and he hadn't even remembered. She had always said he would be the sort of husband who forgot such things. And *now,* now he would remember it for ever, because on that day their boy had come.

They hadn't had much of a married life, he and Janine. One year, started in a furnished room and finished in uneasy chasing after flats, and finally taking in desperation a basement in an old-fashioned house round the corner from his mother's place. A year of frustration, a mad keeping-up with time against the coming of this child. Janine hadn't wanted the baby at first, then she had suddenly changed and wanted it so badly that the thought of its coming had taken

9

possession of her to the exclusion of everything else. He supposed all women were the same. He didn't know; she had been the only woman he had known, and it came to him now that he didn't know even her really well. The thought made him cold for a second, and hurriedly he switched his thoughts back to the first moment they had met. In a small side-street church in a country town.

He had been in digs, because of a temporary job in his firm's branch of that town. Another clerk in the office had found him the room, but there it had ended. He had been alone, and bored; so bored that on the first Sunday he had wandered into the church for evening service, and sat beside Janine and her aunts.

When he had gone back to his mother's house, at the end of that month, Merrill had said, laughing: "Mother, I do believe your only son's got himself a girl-friend!"

He had grinned, and said, to cover his confusion, "I'm not the first fellow to have said that all sisters should be painlessly exterminated for the pests they are!" but the damage had been done. Both women were hot on the scent.

"Is it true, Stacy?" his mother had asked, gently.

"Yes, as it happens, it is."

Merrill whooped joyfully. "Where — and how—did you meet her?" she asked, curiously.

"I was introduced to her," he said, briefly and rather stiffly. Quite untruthfully, too. He had knocked Janine's prayer-book from her hand, just for the opportunity of saying something to her without the aunts having the opportunity of suggesting that he had engineered a "pick-up". They would have done so, he felt sure, if he had given them the chance.

He came to a bus shelter, and sat in a corner, closing his eyes, and placing one hand over them, hiding; he had a dread that someone would speak to him—ask him the way or the time or some other damn fool thing that would necessitate an answer, and for the moment, his throat had attained such proportions that he would never be able to voice the words. An aching for those lost days flooded over him. He wanted to go back, back, to Bletchbury, and that evening in St. Jude's, and start all over again. Somewhere, along the route of those two years since he had met Janine, something had gone wrong. Somehow they had lost something, that spark which had once been (or seemed to be) so vital, and which had been the indirect result of this day, their first anniversary, and its attendant misery.

Janine was twenty-two at the time. Everyone in Bletchbury dressed in a circumspect fashion, which suggested to him that they wished to be moving with the times just enough to escape being old-fashioned, yet they deemed it vulgar to be too up-to-the-minute. Janine's clothes and hair-style struck him as just "missing the boat". He wanted to tell her so. But he never did. Not only because she would have been offended, but because he suddenly realized how pretty she was, and forgot the clothes. Afterwards he remembered, but by then he was too committed to say anything about it.

"I say, how clumsy of me!"

"Oh, no, you couldn't help it!"

That was their first attempt at conversation. Sitting in the corner of the bus shelter, his lips twisted into a sad smile at the memory of that piece of hypocrisy on the part of them both. It was so obviously a ruse, and a not very subtle one, but

Janine accepted it. She had wanted him to speak to her. Whether the aunts knew what had happened or not, he could never decide, but he suspected that they guessed.

He walked home with them, along the tree-bordered streets of the little town, until they reached the straight tall house where the Misses Stanhope had lived since their youth. A thin, angular, middle-aged servant opened the door for them, and looked curiously at him, sniffing a little as she stepped back to let them file in. He sat down to supper under the woman's curious, faintly disapproving stare, and listened to an occasional sniff from her each time he contributed to the conversation, and that was often. The Misses Stanhope asked the questions, in turn, and he gave the required answers. It was beautifully done. In the space of an hour they had found out all about him.

"You are perhaps a stranger to the town, Mr. Conway?" This was from Miss Bee, acidular of face, and grey of hair. Thin, faded old Miss Bee, who was reputed to have had a tragic love affair at nineteen, of which all the town knew, and still spoke.

He admitted he was, and added that he

13

lived in London.

"On your own, no doubt, being a bachelor?" Miss Agnes contributed, smiling tightly and making her round white fat face crease so that an additional chin appeared. Miss Agnes had no reputed love affair, but was still very arch in her manner, and still wore pastel shades of velvet in the summer and purples and dark greens in winter. Her questions got double information; he told her he lived at home with his mother and sister (thus establishing his family background) and admitted, to her apparent relief, that he was indeed unmarried.

From then onwards it was easy work to get from him the fact that he was a clerk in a large manufacturing company's office, that he was occasionally sent to distant towns as on this occasion, that he would no doubt be here for a matter of months; he had no other friends in the town, he was lonely and would appreciate the opportunity of visiting their house, and keeping Janine company (as well as her aunts) and that his respectability and financial position were acceptable to the Misses Stanhope. He left their house that first night with the uneasy feeling that

14

somehow he had conveyed the impression that he wanted to marry that nice girl he had met in church, and that her aunts had considered him and approved. He wasn't sure he wanted to be married, nor that he wanted a girl like Janine Stanhope for a wife. He wasn't sure about anything that first night, but the aunts soon made up his mind for him . . . the aunts and Janine.

Their courtship followed the pattern of Bletchbury courtships. Sedate walks by the canal tow-path, and in the best of the town's two parks (the one with the laid-out gardens), and there was, of course, the regular attendance at church. Janine, he noticed, had a new look, a look of pride mixed with possession. He did not realize that as young men went, he had most of the desired ingredients; height, waving hair, no unpleasant characteristics such as a limp, squint or spectacles, nor did he attempt to grow a moustache. He was an ordinary nice young man, and in the jargon of the aunts, "quite desirable."

Tea at the Stanhope house on Sunday completed the picture, and when his firm transferred him from Bletchbury, there were regular weekly letters passing to and fro, and alternate week-ends spent at the

15

Stanhope and Conway houses. Mrs. Conway graciously accepted Janine, and Merrill "sounded" her future sister-in-law with her usual joyous enthusiasm, and decided she was pretty but wet. Week by week, Stacy Conway was pushed towards marriage, and didn't mind a bit, until one week-end when Janine mentioned the subject of children.

"My Aunt Agnes says I ought not to consider having children. It's beastly, getting them."

Stacy was shocked, and reasoned with Janine, but she refused to discuss the subject further. She had shot her bolt, and fled, leaving him with the uneasy conviction that she knew nothing of the facts of life, and that she was entirely unwilling to learn from anyone.

He realized now, sitting cold and alone in the corner of the bus shelter, that that was where he should have made a firm stand. It was a warning, one that he didn't take.

All through the hectic period of pre-marriage, when both camps were busily preparing, and enjoying the preparation, Stacy was aware of yet another change in Janine. She became more aloof as she awaited marriage with him. If she had been undemonstrative before, she was icy now. He couldn't understand it, and assumed that it was maidenly reserve. He didn't appreciate that it was part of her upbringing, this cooling off just before marriage. Part of the elaborate facade of conventionality rife in Bletchbury "nice" society. People of the Stanhope background expected this sort of behaviour, and if it wasn't forthcoming, a girl was considered fast, over-eager. It was this standard of life which caused Janine to spend the whole of the small legacy from her parents' estate on the trappings of a white wedding, because such a thing was "done" in that town. Stacy urged her to save her money for later, but she angrily refused, and sulked for two days.

Her standards floored him again and again. She didn't mind living in a furnished room in London, but told him that if they had been going to live in Bletchbury, she couldn't have considered such a thing. When he pressed her for an explanation, the best she could give him was that no one would know them in London, no one, that was, who mattered, by which he inferred that she meant her friends in Bletchbury. She bluntly and hurtfully refused to share his mother's house until they found a flat of their own.

Marriage with Janine was difficult from the start. She was heavily domesticated, and insisted on being shut away (or at least, left strictly alone) while at the stove or sink. Stacy, brought up to help in the kitchen, felt shut out when his young wife told him tartly that no man could give her any help. Even when she knew the baby was coming, and could eventually scarcely drag about, she would not let him do a thing for her.

"Last bus, guv'nor!" a harsh Cockney voice reminded him, and reluctantly he dragged himself to his feet. He had, he realized, been sitting in that shelter for close on three hours. He was chilled and stiff. His excursion into the past had done no good, yet he had funked going back to that basement flat, to the sight of the line of new nappies, freshly washed by Janine yesterday, in preparation for the child. That child who hadn't been due to arrive for another six weeks.

"What happened?" he had asked the landlady, who had summoned him by telephone that morning from the office.

"Dunno, ducks. Seems funny ter me. One minute she was all right. Next, she was down on the floor, dead out. I sent fer the ambulance, an' they whisked 'er off, like one-o'clock. Never seen nuthink like it. It's my belief she 'ad a fall. . . ."

The woman was garrulous, but kindly. She had undertaken to keep the place clean until Janine came back, though he doubted if his mother and sister would allow a stranger in his flat.

The bus journey was a nightmare, and long before he realized he was anywhere near home, he had arrived. A reluctance to go into the house came over him, and he played with the idea of going to his mother's. Visions of questions, and having to tell them, decided him against such a course, and he went slowly down the basement steps while he fumbled in his trousers pocket for the front door key.

"Do I love Janine?" came a startling question. Startling, because he had never dared think it before, and now it took him unawares. The answer unnerved him. Whatever it was he felt for her, he knew now with certainty that she didn't love him. She had wanted a husband, because she didn't want to stay unmarried, and as

19

husbands went, he had filled the bill. She
had even wanted the child, he now saw,
because most of her friends had children,
and to be childless was a sad and disgrace-
ful state in Bletchbury standards. Janine
had achieved wifehood and motherhood
with determination, but without emotion,
without love.

CHAPTER II

JANINE lay in the hard white bed, watching
the April rain sting against the frosted
glass of the windows. Speculatively she
considered the hump in the bed next to
her, and wondered if the still white form
had also been through a number of weary
months to no purpose. They had brought
her in during the night, a moaning bundle
wrapped in one of those grim red blankets.
Janine knew she would never be able to
look at a red blanket again without feeling
ill in the pit of the stomach. Red blankets
and chloroform, the rustle of starched uniforms, dimmed lights and pain . . . all
these things went together.

The hump moved, and a yellow-blonde
head, touselled and half-curled, raised
itself. Two pale eyes regarded Janine

sombrely for a minute, before a high Cockney voice said:

"'Allo! 'Nother inmate?"

"I've been here all the time," Janine told her.

The girl flopped back again, and impatiently pushed the blankets away from her face. "'Ow long?" she wanted to know.

"Four days," Janine replied. "They tell me I can get up to-morrow."

"My mum got up on 'er second day and done a day's washing—didn't arf know it later on, though. Bad legs."

There was a pause, before the little Cockney shot at her: "Baby all right?"

Janine stiffened, and met the expected question with less trouble than she had imagined. "It was stillborn," she said, collectedly. With a sense of utter relief, she knew that she would never flinch from that question again. It was easy. Just say that he was stillborn; better still, "it" was stillborn, and the whole thing became impersonal. She said it over and over again to herself, until it became a parrot-like line with no meaning. Now, if only people would dry up after being told that. . . .

There were so many who would enquire. Aunt Bee and Aunt Agnes. Stacy's gentle mother, whose deceptive air of placidity hid an inflexible will, and an all-enveloping dislike of her son's choice of a wife. Stacy's sister Merrill, whose nature was so broad and generous that she couldn't dislike anyone, and whose only fault was an overwhelming joy that became tiresome because you couldn't personally find life so good, and couldn't somehow see what Merrill found so good about it, either. Then there were the near neighbours, the landlady, the tradesmen; all the inquisitive yet kindly people who had speculated on one's enlarging figure, and had been getting ready for some time to partake of the event by way of enquiries, suggestions, unwanted but no doubt sensible advice. Janine spent five whole minutes hating the lot of them, and unaccountably felt better.

The little Cockney moaned. "I've got 'em agin," she said, obscurely. "'Ad 'em all night, I did." She had a little birdlike face, pinched and ill-looking, and irregular features that were in no way unattractive, but gave the girl a piquancy which became more likeable as the minutes went by.

Janine watched her resentfully, and felt she would be liking her soon, as no doubt the nurses and doctors would.

Janine said, politely, "Had what?" and started an odd conversation that lapsed and whipped itself up again at irregular intervals over a period of days.

"Labour, o' course! Niggling pains."

With a shock, Janine realized the girl had yet to have her baby. "Oh, I hadn't realized," she gasped, and with a sick sense of having lost a round in a fight, she was aware of the tightness across the base of her throat again. So she wasn't immune yet. She couldn't bear the knowledge that this girl might yet have a live baby. It would have been easy if she had been in the same position as herself.

"In fer a bad time, though. I know that. They told me so—just like my mum."

"How long have you been in pain?"

"On an' orf fer days. Likely to, an' all."

"I wonder they put you in here—I'm supposed to be on my own," Janine murmured.

"Nowhere else ter put me, see? Wards all full. Six a night, they said, down the end."

"Down the end" was presumably the receiving office, through which all new patients went, and were entered to the cheerful rattle of the receiving nurse's conversation. Babies, dead or alive, were her daily bread, as dictated letters are to a typist. Her cheerfulness was constant and brittle, in every way as tiresome, Janine considered, as the kindly enquiries of the people awaiting her discharge from this place.

"I hope you'll be all right," Janine offered, but the words sounded hopelessly insincere. "Really I do," she added.

"S'all right, ducks," the little Cockney said, astutely, and gripped the sheets while another spasm passed. "I know what yer feel—can't expect nothink else, seein' as yer lorst yer own! Mine'll be all right, though. Always are, when yer don't want 'em."

"*Don't* you want it, truly?" Janine was shocked.

"'Course not. Would you, if you was me? Look at me!" she invited. "Me 'usband left me soon's 'e knew I was carryin'. I lorst me job because of it— I'm a waitress, see? Can't 'ave a waitress faintin' all over the place, carryin' trays o' food! Wouldn't do, like, an' it's bad fer business, anyway. So I gets

24

another job, but I 'ad ter give that up at seven months. Well, now where am I? Can't go on gettin' relief fer ever, can I? Can't afford ter put the kid out, cos that takes money, much as I earn at most things."

"Haven't you any female relations who'd look after the child for you, while you were at work?"

"Who, me?" Scorn whipped the words from the Cockney's twisting lips. "Not much! I'd 'ave ter keep my ole mother in gin if she was ter be asked ter do anythink fer me! 'Sides, I wouldn't trust no kid to 'er, not me! I ain't that 'ard! No, I'll 'ave ter put 'im up fer adoption. It'll be a boy, o' course—everyone says so. Tell by the way I'm carryin'."

At intervals during the day they resumed the conversation. Daisy Jenks obligingly dug out details of every relative, far and near, that she had, and together, she and Janine considered the possibilities of each, for a likely foster-parent for the unborn infant. Janine hadn't believed that anyone could have such an interesting yet hopeless bunch of relations. None were in any way suitable even if willing. Sadly, at the end of the day

25

as both women finished their evening meal, balanced precariously on their knees, and thought about preparing themselves for the evening visiting hour, they decided that there was nothing else for it but official adoption.

"Shame, ain't it?" Daisy sighed. Her pains had gone again to her infinite disgust. She had prayed that the child would be born before nightfall, so that she could get some sleep.

Janine nodded.

A nurse came and took away the plates, and brought bowls of hot water for their evening wash.

"Don't give yer much peace in this place, do they?"

"No, but think how nice it'll be when we get home, and don't have to keep to a time-table," Janine retorted, then bit her lip. She had planned a time-table so carefully for her son.

"Thinkin' of 'im, ain't yer?" Daisy probed. The way she divined Janine's thoughts was often uncanny, and always embarrassing. "Yer didn't arf want 'im, didn't yer?"

Janine busily rubbed soap on to her flannel, and didn't answer. The water was

nearly cold. Last night it had been too hot, and she had had to wait until it was cool enough to use.

" 'Ere, I'll tell yer what. *You* take 'im!" Daisy burst out suddenly.

The words hung on the air, quivered, and settled. Both women were suddenly still, staring at each other. Janine startled, Daisy excited and rather over-awed at her own daring.

"Oh, I wish yer could bring yerself to," she breathed, in an urgent voice. "Yer do want a boy, an' it won't arf be rough if yer go 'ome empty-'anded, after gettin' everything ready an' all. 'Sides, I'd like ter think you was goin' to 'ave the kid, seein' as I know yer . . . not like strangers. . . ."

Her voice trailed off, and in an excess of embarrassment, she plunged into the business of washing with such gusto that she upset the bowl over the bed. Her howl brought two junior nurses and a midwife, who thought of other possibilities and were suitably annoyed on finding what had really happened. During the mopping and bed-changing process, the subject of the unborn child was temporarily dropped.

Stacy came five minutes before time,

27

flushed, and loaded with gifts. Tulips—pale lavender in colour—and delicate pale lemon daffodils; these from himself. From his mother, a bunch of black grapes, a packet of butter, and some boiled sweets. From Merrill a bundle of new and snappy magazines, a box of face-powder and a package containing "everything for the well-groomed head", from hair-grips to net, curlers and setting lotion. Stacy told Janine about each parcel in a wild jumble of words, then sat down breathlessly and said he wished the visiting hour could take place twice and not once a day.

Janine looked abstracted. She fingered the parcels and nodded, but he could see she wasn't really listening or seeing them.

"What's the matter, dear?"

"Stacy," she plunged, "could we adopt a baby?"

Afterwards, Janine looked back on that moment with a kind of wonder. Always she recalled so vividly Stacy's dazed look, a look of unbelieving mingled with joy. A look which said that although he didn't care overmuch for the idea of someone else's child, he would be happy for her to have a child to fill the gap. Although nothing had been said by nurses or medical staff, there was a general impression that another child later on was not possible: this Janine had faced, in the darkness of the hospital night, to the accompaniment of quick footsteps in empty corridors, and the intermittent squealing cries of the babies in the nursery. An unwelcome thought, this impossibility to have another child, and one which could only be buried in the adoption of a stranger.

Stacy didn't speak at once. He couldn't. He just nodded. That nod was the seal on the finishing of her childless state. At once, Janine felt that she was again awaiting her child. Not quite the same, perhaps, for the discomfort of both pre-birth and post-birth had gone, and she began to feel normal again. To-morrow she would be getting up for the first time. The next day she would be taking a short trip to toilet and bathroom. The day after would progress further, until she was allowed to wander about the wards at will. But for her, all this was no longer significant. What mattered was the hump in the next bed, the girl from the poor quarter behind the hospital, who lay looking at the ceiling, alone, because her husband had left her, and her mother was too drunk to come on a decent visit.

"It's that girl's baby," Janine ventured, in a whisper, and Stacy obligingly looked past her shoulder, to the next bed. "She isn't quite—well, our sort—but that doesn't matter, does it?" she urged. As he didn't answer, she continued, "It's environment that counts, isn't it? Not heredity?"

An old question, an older argument. Stacy didn't venture an opinion. He just said quietly, after a short pause, "If you want her baby, and she's willing, I don't mind."

She told him the whole story, as briefly as she could, for fear of taking up the whole visiting hour, but she could see he was hardly listening. Oddly, the details didn't matter to him; that could be settled between the two women. He was not bothered about that. It was something else.

"How do you know—I mean, supposing—?" he faltered, and could hardly meet her eyes.

"It's going to be a boy," she said, with confidence. "Everyone has told her so. It's

30

something to do with the way she's carrying," and Janine smiled thinly, the first smile since she had come into hospital.

Stacy thought, "An old wives' tale. I hope to God it *is* a boy!" but he said nothing. Janine prattled happily about arrangements for the child, as she would have done had her own lived, and he could only listen amazed. It seemed to him incredible that she could transfer hopes and plans to this new baby with such facile speed. He didn't know how he would tell his mother and sister, or indeed how they would break the news to the aunts. Neither family would like the idea. His only thought was to meet Janine in her whim as far as possible, and be ready to help her afterwards if (and this was likely, knowing Janine), she regretted her rash action.

"When is this child expected, Janine?"

"Oh, any time now. It's overdue."

Any time now. He panicked, and felt an unaccountable revulsion for the child of a Cockney mother, whose husband had deserted at such a time. What would it be like when it grew up? What could environment do, to iron out a poor inherited basis of character?

He took a firm grip on himself, and said, "Well, what do you intend to call it, when it does arrive, and all the arrangements are got through?"

"What arrangements?"

"Well, darling, you can't just take over another woman's baby, just like that!"

"She doesn't mind—she *wants* me to! She *said* so!"

He did his best to explain about official adoption, and the thousand and one regulations to be met, and obstacles to be overcome, so far as the hospital authorities were concerned. Unconsciously he made the thing seem more difficult than it really was, hoping that Janine would falter. But she held on, tenaciously.

"I don't care, Stacy. You fix it. Take our savings to pay for it. I'll go out to work, if you like, just to help."

"Don't be silly!" he snapped, then patted her hand to show he didn't really mean it.

"I'll call it the same names as—" she began, but he cut in, savagely:

"No! Not the same names as we chose for *our* boy!" It had been a source of great sadness to him that the child hadn't lived a few hours, so that it could have been baptized. As it was, the infant was a non-entity; it hadn't even been. . . .

"What, then? You'd better choose," Janine said, without rancour. "I thought giving him your names would make him seem more like our own."

"No," he said, again, and Janine recognized and accepted the mutinous set of his chin. "We'll call him Michael, after the hospital and its church."

"Then everyone will know he was born in St. Michael's Hospital, and I want them to think he was born at home," Janine wailed, reverting to the old dislike she had always cherished for babies born away from home.

"You're telling no lies," he told her severely. "Everyone's going to know it's not ours."

Daisy Jenks held on for two more days, and her child came at midnight the following night. She was rushed to the theatre, and wasn't brought back again.

"Is Mrs. Jenks . . . all right?" Janine kept asking, whenever she could buttonhole a nurse, but beyond the "Yes, of course," she could get no information.

"Why isn't she back in her own bed?"

she wanted to know, but everyone was too busy to say. Finally, a junior nurse came to collect Daisy's personal belongings from her locker, and came back with another nurse to strip the bed and make it up with clean bedding. Daisy wasn't returning. . . .

Janine stopped her questions, and lay with closed eyes. She had been cheated again. Daisy and the child were dead, of that she was certain. Slow tears crept down her cheeks. It was as though she had just heard that her own child hadn't lived. A re-living of the agony over again.

She refused her lunch, and had to have her temperature taken.

"What's the matter, Mrs. Conway? Don't you feel well? You've been getting about too much. Better stay in bed to-day."

Janine didn't care. Despondency clamped down on her. There was nothing left. A bitter resentment welled up, that this should happen to her. Of Stacy she thought nothing, but quite unaccountably she remembered Hugh. Hugh, with his bold eyes, and devil-may-care smile, his fine physique and tremendous capacity for enjoyment. Hugh had been in love with her, but hadn't wanted to marry her, or indeed do anything beyond taking her around and showing her off to his friends, before he got the urge to travel again. That was before she had met Stacy.

"Janine, you're an enigma," Hugh had said, on that last evening, "You tantalize but never fulfil." She could never understand half what Hugh said, but he was excitement, gaiety, life . . . while Stacy was reality, and pretty dull reality at that.

She dragged her thoughts back to the present, and found the reception nurse standing by Daisy's bed. Aggressively cheerful, as ever, she turned and nodded brightly at Janine.

"Well, we're all set for some new bods!" she said, gaily. "Observation cases, horribly swollen, and as interesting as we could wish for! Ah, life's never dull around here!"

"You're beastly," Janine said, wrinkling her nose.

"Rubbish," sang the reception nurse. "Healthy way to look at it. You're getting out of 'em in here—the worst case of the two, my girl—company for you!"

"Did Mrs. Jenks—she died, didn't she?"

"Good heavens, no! Caesar, nice a job as I ever saw! She's sitting up and taking notice all right, never fear!"

Janine gaped. "Oh, I thought perhaps...."

"Oh, yes, you're taking over her baby, aren't you?" The reception nurse came back, with renewed interest. "Oh, I wish you luck. You've got a whopper coming."

"Is he very big? What does he weigh?" Janine was wreathed in smiles now. Everything was all right, her heart sang. It's all right again. How like everyone in this place, not to let you have the good news at first! They must have known how she'd be waiting to know that it was all right.

"Eh?" The reception nurse gaped, then guffawed. "*He*?" She laughed again, savouring the joke. "You've got a nine-pounder coming, my lass: a bouncing, carroty-headed girl!"

CHAPTER III

THE ginger nurse had been off duty for some days, and when she came back, she was posted to night duty. The night staff came on at the same time as the visitors were leaving. For the first time since the day Janine's child had been born, Stacy came face to face with the girl.

36

She had just come on, white and yawning, after a sleepness day. She hated the start of the night shift, when the body was not yet attuned to the difference in waking and sleeping hours. He was just leaving, the last and most reluctant of all the visitors. Reluctant because there was still so much to say to Janine—about the adoption and about themselves—and so little opportunity in which to get it said. For although Janine was excited and talkative about what she would do when she came home with Daisy Jenks' baby, and although she had thrust aside the disappointment of its sex, her happiness was synthetic. Beneath the apparent recovery was a new hardness which Stacy was quick to notice, and whenever he ventured to discuss themselves and their future together, she skilfully evaded the question.

The little nurse blinked up at his tall figure looming suddenly in front of her, from round the screens inside the door of Janine's ward, and recognized him.

"Mr. Conway! How's your wife? I haven't seen her—"

"I know," he said, hastily, pulling the door to behind him. "Nurse, I want to talk to you? Have you a minute now?"

"Well, just a minute," she said, with a hasty glance up and down the corridor. "Sister will be round soon. . . ."

She led him to a small alcove in the corridor, which was used for parking the vases of flowers at night; the long benches were full of them, and the alcove full of their heady sweetness.

She said, "What is it, Mr. Conway?"

"I want you to talk to my wife. Find out what's worrying her. You'll be able to do that, won't you? There must be a few minutes when you could snatch a bit of conversation. . ."He broke off, conscious of the rushed air of the place, the subdued hurry of every member of the staff, the constant impression of working perpetually against the clock. "If it isn't asking too much...I can't find out, myself. She hedges. The visiting hour isn't very long, for finding out. . .Women do talk to each other pretty freely, don't they?"

His anxiety touched her. In a world of anxious husbands and emotionally unbalanced wives, he alone was able to pierce the crust of professional indifference, the casual acceptance of life in a maternity hospital, and made her acutely aware of the personal side of it all. She didn't like it. It made her uncomfortable. Guilty, somehow. And helpless.

"I'll see what I can do, Mr. Conway," she murmured, propitiatingly. "But I don't promise anything. Women are always rather difficult, at a time like this. Besides, it may turn out to be nothing at all. . . ."

There was impatience in his face. "If you don't want to bother—" he began, then realizing he had no right to ask her to do this, anyway, he said, hastily, "but if you could manage to, I'd be grateful."

As he walked away, after what was, after all, a very unpromising conversation, he felt curiously comforted. Without making a binding agreement, she had somehow conveyed to him that she would do something to help him, in some way or other. She had a warming quality about her, that little nurse. He tried to analyse it, as he boarded a bus, and climbed to the top to have a smoke. As he thoughtfully packed the short briar pipe, he tried to visualize her face, but only Janine's would come before him. Janine as she had looked to-night; pale, dark-eyed, with faint shadows beneath them and the darkness emphasized by the black hair which she was now allowing to flop untidily in great waves on her shoulders. Over all was that curious, cold remoteness, which even the bright conversation about Daisy Jenks' baby didn't dispel.

"What shall we call her, Stacy? How about Michaeline?"

He had screwed his face up in disgust. "Why ever?"

"Well, the feminine of Michael. You remember?"

He accepted the thrust, and said nothing.

"Well, if you don't care for that, Stacy, I suggest Philomina. No? Well, Petula, then we can call her 'Pet'. I read about a girl called Pet, in one of their magazines here. It's supposed to have auto-suggestion, and makes the baby grow up a pet."

"Oh, hang it all, Janine, your name's bad enough. We can't have a child with a daft name out of a magazine. What's wrong with Jane or Elizabeth?"

The old petulant expression had come back, for a fleeting second, as he made that reference to her own name. It had always been a sore point with him. As always, she rose to the bait, and told him yet again

40

how it had originated.

"It's a combination of Janet and Pauline, after my two grandmothers. You know that, Stacy!"

"Yes, I know that, but it still makes it a daft name!" He was being childish now, and knew it. There was a strained atmosphere between them again. The subject of the name dropped for the time being; he strove to get back to the superficial friendliness which existed at the start of that visit, but it was gone. He knew it. Janine knew it. That was why he had, in distraction, asked the ginger nurse to help.

Sitting on the upper deck, smoking peacefully, he asked himself what had made him consult that girl, of all people. He had only seen her the once, and at that time he was hardly in a condition to take in any details about her, or to form any opinion or liking. Odd, that. Now why, he asked himself, had he gone to her?

There was a note for him at the flat. Merrill and his mother wanted him to go round to their place for supper. Lately they had seemed to become remote to him. He had been in a world of his own, a disappointed world, in which his wife tended to drift further from him, and the son he had lived for had become nothing but a rather vague dream, a dream that began and ended with a little nurse, whose compassionate dark eyes asked a perpetual question.

Walking from the bus stop, he had decided to thrust the thought of her from him. It was becoming a little too persistent. He didn't like it.

Now, with his sister's note in his hand, and the prospect of the rest of the evening spent at his mother's house, he revolted. Not against his mother, whose gentle manner was always a source of irritation to him because he knew what lay beneath it; nor against Merrill, whose happiness always seemed to him to be as much of a cloak over the real Merrill as his mother's mask of gentleness. But rather against his whole life. He wanted to get away from it, to start afresh as he had wanted to, that sprang when his firm had sent him to Bletchbury, and he had been so full of bright hopes.

Standing there in the small sitting-room of their basement flat, he saw himself and Janine once again, standing at the altar of St. Jude's; Janine with an angelic look on her face as she held in her little white-gloved hands an ivory-covered prayer-book from which hung white ribbons and two madonna lilies, himself white and set—he had caught sight of himself in the mirror above the organist's seat—and with a look of near-panic on his face. Panic because somehow, without quite knowing how, he had slipped into marriage before he had begun to do any of those things he had wanted to, planned for, since he left school.

He put out the light, and picked up his hat again, to go the few short steps to his mother's house. Not because he wanted to. He didn't want people to make him live over the visiting hour again. He wanted to be alone, or if possible, with someone who didn't need to have everything put into words, as the members of one's family inevitably did. In the few brief seconds he had had with the little ginger nurse, whose name he didn't know, he had felt that she was the sort of person who had that understanding which didn't require everything to be explained.

"We are dying to hear all about the little girl Janine is taking," Merrill wrote, "and when she is coming home. What does she want in the way of clothes, as she's

43

prepared everything for a boy?"

Merrill and his mother were artless in their helpfulness, and could not know how he would wince at the tacit reminder of what might have been. There was nothing for it: he would have to go and visit them, or they'd be hurt. Besides, to stay here alone would be to court the landlady's appearance for a comfortable gossip, and to tell him yet again, the story of her own lengthy stay in hospital.

His mother's house was large and old-fashioned, the end house in a cul-de-sac. Long before he reached it, he knew in which room his mother and sister were, by the lighted windows, and by that means he could often divine which guests they had, if any, and what they were doing. If one of Merrill's many men-friends were there, it would be the drawing-room that would be lit, because Merrill was interested in music, and her friends all played some instrument or other. Among his mother's treasures was an old sweet-toned harp, and this appeared an item of attraction to Merrill's set. There was a violin, a grand piano with a Spanish shawl flung over the top, and Merrill's own radiogram. The room was large, and boasted a fine wood floor which could be used for dancing when the rugs were flung back. In this room had recently been entertained a young Spaniard with bright hopes for the concert stage, a man with a fine baritone voice, who had never got beyond the "Mr." stage because Stacy's mother hadn't liked him and the feeling had been reciprocated, and two crooners—one in a famous West End dance band—whose personalities had appealed to Mrs. Conway, but whose talents hadn't. Stacy smothered a grin as he thought of the chagrined gentlemen, and wondered again how Merrill could possibly let their mother rule her life in this way. Not that Merrill seemed to care over-much: as fast as one male made his bowing exit, she'd find another to replace him.

It had always been like that. Merrill with men round her for the asking, and he living an almost monastic existence, with his books and dreams. In the almost always darkened window of the attic of that house, he had spent so many hours. There was a deep window seat, where he had sat and studied foreign languages, while Merrill, two years younger, was out dancing, or at some musical party or concert. In that room was a huge, roll-type school atlas taking up one wall, and a globe on a side table. His books were in serried rows all over the other three walls, on shelves made cheaply for him by the local carpenter; books of travel, mostly, for here lay his dreams. His mother referred to the attic as Stacy's junk-room, and, he reflected, his lips twisted in a sad smile as he soberly walked up the front steps, in a way that was true. His dreams were undoubtedly on the scrap-heap now, and it was fitting that the place in which they were hatched out should be referred to by such a name.

He wished he hadn't come, and hesitated before ringing the old-fashioned bell, for it was not the drawing-room window that was alight, but that of the morning-room—the room used now when his mother's friends came. Of the two parties, he preferred Merrill's visitors, because they at least were too full of themselves to have any interest in Merrill's brother, while his mother's friends had no other interest than in the lives of other people.

"Well, Eustace Conway, I declare! Congratulations, proud father!" This from Mrs. Westlands, Dr. Westlands' sister-in-law who kept house for him since his wife had died. A large, florid woman, with three chins and sparkling little black eyes that were for ever darting about in an effort to miss nothing, Honoria Westlands invariably got the story wrong because she never stopped to listen properly before dashing off to repeat it elsewhere.

"The baby died!" her daughter whispered loudly, and everyone heard, including Stacy, standing in the doorway, his fair skin flaming with embarrassment.

"Oh, dear lord!" Mrs. Westlands exclaimed, clapping a hand to her mouth. "Well, never mind, he *was* a proud father, and he will be again, no doubt! Or won't he?" she demanded, as the implication struck her. "Come and sit down by me, Eustace, and tell me all about your wife, and how she's getting on in that *dreadful* hospital! Why not my brother-in-law's nursing home, I'd like to know?"

"Shut up, Honoria!" Dr. Westlands said, mechanically, but since it was his usual remark, neither he nor his sister-in-law were particularly interested in it. It was accepted by her as one of his many little habits.

"Because they can't afford it, mother!" her daughter whispered, again loud enough for all to hear.

"Violet, dear," came Mrs. Conway's gentle voice, as she moved forward to greet her son, "I'm sure you mean to be helpful." And to Stacy, "I'm so glad you could come, my son. I've someone here whom I'm sure you'll like to meet. A Mr. Torrington. He tells me he knew our Janine some years ago."

His mother performed the introduction, though it struck Stacy that the guest would have much preferred to continue his conversation with Merrill, in the far corner.

"My son Eustace—Mr. Hugh Torrington." His mother's gentle voice seemed to be saying, "Whatever you feel about this, I've decided I'd like to see my son sitting talking with social friendliness to his wife's former lover," though her face gave nothing away. She smiled at them both, patted Stacy's arm and drifted off.

The two men stared at each other, measuringly. Torrington got out cigarettes, and Stacy leisurely filled his pipe. As if by mutual consent, they both looked round at a couple of empty arm-chairs, a little away from the women, and wandered across to sit and smoke in a silence that prepared the way for anything that had to be said.

"I came with the Westlands," Torrington offered at last, quirking an eyebrow at Stacy, and grinning ruefully. "I'm a sort of distant cousin of theirs. It looked like being a pretty dull evening until your sister came in."

Stacy considered this. "Did you really know my wife years ago?" he asked mildly, at last.

Torrington nodded. "Didn't Janine tell you?"

"No. Perhaps she didn't think it worth mentioning."

"Perhaps she didn't," Torrington agreed cheerfully. "She had a good many friends. I was but one small fish in the sea."

Stacy flushed. He hadn't known that, either. Of the two bits of information, he thought he preferred to know that Janine had had another man-friend before he came along, rather than that she had had crowds of friends, for that raised the inevitable question: where had they gone, and why? She certainly had few men-friends in his time—her circle seemed to consist of girls, pretty frumpish ones at that, and their equally frumpish brothers.

"You lived in Bletchbury?" Stacy probed, wondering how a man of Torrington's type came to know the Stanhope women.

Torrington said, aggravatingly, "You mean how did I come to know Janine? Ask her yourself."

To Stacy's intense annoyance, and the other man's relief, Merrill came over at that moment, and perched herself on the arm of her brother's chair.

"What are you two boys talking about?" she said, gaily. "Let Mr. Torrington go, Stacy. I want him to see the drawing-room. He's musical, he tells me."

"Don't tell me you play the harp!" Stacy observed, tartly. Merrill whooped joyfully, and took Hugh Torrington's arm.

"Not yet!" Torrington said, with a grin, and allowed Merrill to walk him off.

"I don't think that was very clever of you, mother," Stacy said, getting up as she came across the room to him. "Or very kind."

Mrs. Conway smiled vaguely. "Don't be tiresome, darling. I've come to talk to you about the baby you're taking. Are you sure

50

it's *wise*? Is anything settled yet? Is there time to back out, because I've heard—"

"Mother, it's all settled," Stacy said, firmly, though he was by no means sure that it was. "Janine's happy about it, and I don't want anything said, or suggested, to upset her, or in any way spoil that happiness."

"No, dear." Mrs. Conway lowered her eyes, and fingered her long string of pearls. "Of course, so long as she will give it the attention and devotion a mother should—even a foster mother—" She broke off, and glanced towards the door, as if conjuring up a picture of her daughter and the guest, as they had stood there a minute ago. "It seems that Janine was rather—er—gay, shall we say? Of course, many years ago—" and again she trailed off, leaving many things unsaid.

"Does it?" Stacy's voice held a warning. "Janine feels you're no friend of hers, and I'm wondering if she wasn't right after all."

It might have been strained, that little patch of the evening, if Violet Westlands hadn't broken into the conversation just then.

"Uncle says when are we going to get some cards to-night, Mrs. Conway? Isn't he awful? He only comes to your house for whist, I believe."

She spoke to Mrs. Conway, but smiled at Stacy, an arch, though hesitant smile, which did nothing to help her thin sallow face look less unattractive. "Shall we go to the drawing-room, too, Stacy?"

"No, I think I'll have to be going, Violet," he said, hastily, but his mother forestalled him.

"I want you for a fourth, my son," she said, firmly. "Violet doesn't play, do you, dear?"

"Not very well," the girl admitted, reluctantly. "But I'd like to sit by Stacy and watch."

Dr. Westlands played with intensity, but the women talked between the hands, much to his annoyance. To Stacy's annoyance, too, since their talk consisted of questions, fired at him, and they were questions which required his full attention, to parry; attention which he could hardly spare, if he were to play a less poor game than usual.

"What's the little girl weigh, Stacy?"

"Who is her mother?"

"Why doesn't she want her? Is she *very* low-class? Is there disease or insanity in the family? You'll have investigations, of course?"

"Don't you think such an adoption *unwise*, Stacy?"

Mrs. Conway's questions were the less searching, apparently mild ones. Mrs. Westlands asked the questions which went deeper, and saved them from being too personal by her little shamefaced laugh at the end of them. Her daughter helped make them sound audacious rather than frankly inquisitive, by saying every so often, "Oh, mother, you are awful!" and looking shocked. Between them, Mrs. Westlands and Mrs. Conway asked enough questions to get the whole story and more, if Stacy had not kept a guard on his tongue, and if Dr. Westlands had not helped occasionally and quite unwittingly, by testily asking if they could possibly remember that they were supposed to be playing cards.

The evening wore on, and at last there was reprieve, in the form of a sandwich supper. Merrill and Torrington came back from the drawing-room, laughing, and considerably more advanced in their friendship than when they left the company an hour before. They squatted

53

side by side on a corner divan, eating sandwiches and drinking coffee together, then vanished again as the company were getting up to go.

Here Mrs. Westlands dropped another of her famous bricks. "That naughty Hugh, there he goes again! Sneaking out with pretty Merrill! Just the way he used to with Janine, that time she stayed with us!"

Again she clapped a belated hand to her mouth, and rolled startled boot-button eyes round the company, lightly evading any direct look in Stacy's direction. Again Violet hissed a warning at her, and again Stacy was the focus of all eyes in a silence that was almost unbearable.

He spoke, because they seemed to expect him to say something.

"I know, Mrs. Westlands," he said, quietly, though it was a lie. "I know about that. Janine told me."

He said good-bye briefly to his mother and the company in general, and went. Merrill, who had just come back, said in surprise: "What's bitten Stacy?"

No one answered, but Violet Westlands flashed a quick look at Hugh, and back to her mother.

Stacy didn't return to the flat until the small hours. He walked round the deserted streets, hardly knowing where he was going, thinking over the evening's innuendos, and trying to fit them into the rather scanty past he had shared with Janine. It wasn't that visit to the Westlands that worried him, nor her acquaintance with Torrington, which was, after all, before she met him. It was the more cogent reason: how was it all these people knew about Janine's life before he himself had come to know her, and why did they think it necessary to acquaint him with the details, though Janine herself seemed to think it unnecessary?

CHAPTER IV

ST. MICHAEL's turned out the maternity patients at the tenth day, unless there were complications. Cases such as Janine's, where the infant didn't live, were usually sent home earlier, from the humanitarian point of view; change of environment was better, it was argued, for the bereaved mother, than the special facilities the hospital could give to ordinary patients.

In Janine's own case, however, she was

allowed to stay, in order to go through the ordinary routine in the nursery, with the baby she was adopting. This consisted of a comprehensive course of modern baby care, covering not only bathing, dressing and nappie-changing, but the scientific method of administering nourishment to the infant, whether by bottle or breast.

Daisy Jenks, recovering from her caesarian operation, loafed about the wards and corridors, taking a cursory interest only in the babies and mothers, would come into the nursery at feeding-time to watch the "shindy" as she called it, with ill-disguised disgust.

"Gawd-elpus," she muttered to Janine one day. "If my ole girl was only sober enough to come 'ere, what she'd 'ave ter say about all this 'ere'd be nobody's business! Why, ten of us there was, and did anyone show 'er what ter do? Not much! Soon 's a kid come, she'd up an' bung its mug on the tit wiv one 'and an' be wipin' the other kids' noses wiv the other! She wouldn't arf've told 'em suthink if they'd made 'er put the kid on the piller in that fancy way!"

"Mrs. Jenks, if you've nothing better to do," the nurse in charge said tartly, "you'd

56

better go and help lay the tables for lunch—you're merely a nuisance in here."

Janine was giving Daisy's baby the bottle. It was a lumpy child, with great rolls of fat beneath its chin, and deep creases at wrist and ankle. It was easy to handle because of its size, but Janine looked enviously from time to time, at the delicate little six-pound girl on the lap of her neighbour, and wished Daisy's baby had been smaller.

The girl next to Janine was fair. There was a transparency about her that was at times a little frightening. Her baby had been grossly under-weight at birth, and there had been a struggle to keep it alive. Mother and child had tenaciously held on, and come through after a fashion, but were still a source of anxiety to the staff.

"How old is it?" Janine asked her, the day before she went home.

"Seven weeks." The girl looked up with her lovely smile, a smile that quietly blazed with happiness. "I've been in here two months, but we're both going home soon."

Between feeding times—the girl was in a ward at the far end and their only point of contact was the nursery—Janine discovered quite a lot about her. She lived in one room, in the house of a one-time neighbour of her family. Her husband had been killed in an accident at work, two months before the baby came. She had no family, and would have to rely on the pension she was to draw from her late husband's firm, with the capital from a life policy to form a nest-egg and to keep against a rainy day. "Until I can go to work again," she added.

"But you always look so happy!" Janine said, mentally comparing the quiet serenity in this girl's eyes, with the rather noisy joy which one connected with Merrill.

"Oh, but I am!" Yvonne Ashley quietly protested. "I've got my health, haven't I? And I've got Georgie—she's a nice little girl, though I would have liked a boy. But I think she's going to be like George. I hope so, anyway."

"You called her Georgina?"

Yvonne nodded. "Oh, yes, after my husband. What are you calling your little baby?"

"Little" was an idiotic term to apply to the Jenks infant, and Daisy, who was lounging in the doorway at the time, having a few minutes' peace in the absence of the presiding nurse, loudly guffawed.

"Little's right, ducks!" she chuckled. Between you an' me and the G.P., she ain't over-taken with my pore kid. Tells me she ain't even thought up a name fer 'er, yet. Might just as well call 'er Ginger an' done wiv it, I say."

Yvonne smiled as Janine flushed guiltily. It was true. She hadn't thought up a name for the child yet, and they were to go home the following day. Daisy would have liked to know what her daughter would be called, and Janine knew that was only to be expected.

"I can't think of a name that would fit her," she said, feebly, "and I just hate 'Ginger' for red-heads. I can't think why people will do it!"

"She *is* a little copper nob," Yvonne murmured with a smile.

"Coppernob! 'Ere, why don't yer call 'er that?" Daisy was enthusiastic, and oddly amused at the comic name for her baby.

"I've still got to find a proper name to have her christened," Janine protested.

"Oh, no, none o' that!" Daisy protested. "I don't 'old with it! Our mum was christened, proper posh do they 'ad, my Gran always said, an' look at our mum now! No, I want 'er ter be a little 'eathen, I do! Like me—I ain't bin done neether, an' I'm prard of it!"

Daisy marched out at that. Janine couldn't decide whether she had managed a strategic and glorious exit, or whether she had heard the nurse returning, and retreated before she got into more trouble, but her vanishing so precipitately was certainly effective.

"She can't say that, can she?" Janine asked Yvonne, bewildered. "I'm adopting the child legally. It's what *I* want, isn't it?"

"I'm not sure," Yvonne murmured, "but ₁ il talk her into it, if you like. She shouldn't be against it like that."

"You'll never do it!" Janine said, irritably. Happy people always had a curiously upsetting effect on her. It was, to her mind, rather poor taste, like lovers who made their devotion too indecently obvious to the world around them.

Yvonne said nothing further, but her serene manner must have weighed with Daisy Jenks. Next day, the day on which Stacy was to bring up her clothes, and those procured for the new baby, there was the ceremonial of good-bye. This happened with all the mothers. They made a

this brat from my whims, aren't you, Stacy?" then she was ashamed, and that made her angrier.

They wrangled for a time, and then she dealt a final blow. "All right. She shall have plain names, but not the one you're evidently thinking of. I wouldn't call her Maud, anyway, even if it weren't your mother's name!"

He hadn't had that in mind, but it was a barb that hurt badly. He retaliated.

"Well, it can hardly be Janet or Pauline, for those names can scarcely be termed 'plain'!"

Stupid, stupid wrangling. They both hated themselves for it after they had separated, though they could do nothing about it while together. It was as if both were in a fever, fever that could only be quenched by hurting each other, as spitefully as possible. The business of the names seemed to be a sure way of inflicting wounds, wounds of the tiny unhealing kind. Finally, Janine told him the child would be called Agnes Belinda, after her two aunts.

"And she *won't* be called 'Bee' for short, either!"

"Don't tell me you've thought of a cute

pet-name, Janine!" Stacy's tone was scathing.

"No, I didn't happen to think it up. Her mother found it. It's 'Coppernob'."

Now Daisy waited with ill-disguised impatience, for the name—a name she had been talked into agreeing should be bestowed on her child over a font in a church. She shuddered.

"Well, keepin' it a secret?" she demanded.

Janine brought herself back from last night's painful scene, and repeated the chosen names. "After my aunts who brought me up," she explained.

Daisy turned her nose up. "Bloomin' old-fashioned 'andles, ain't they?" she grumbled. "Why couldn't yer call 'er Pearl or Aloma? 'Ere, 'ow about Coral? Or Lana?"

The hopeful look died on her face as she read Janine's thoughts. "No, I see whatcher mean," she mourned. "My kid ain't got the mug for it, 'as she? Too fat, an' all. Oh, well, what's it matter? All be the same in an 'undred years!"

"Oh, I don't know—" Janine was moved to murmur, hating herself for her insincerity.

"Well, let's see 'er, 'fore she goes—I'd like ter see what yer make of 'er, in 'er noo clothes. Bet yore taste'll make 'er look nicer'n I would've done!"

Janine promised to bring the child along just before she went home, but it was a promise she broke. She hurried out of the hospital, flaming with anger, a few steps ahead of Stacy, who carried the child himself, in the offending outfit he himself had chosen.

He had brought it up in the cardboard box, just as he had brought it from a famous West End baby store. He had spent far more on it than he could afford, hoping by this one small personal act to propitiate Janine. It was significant that after a year of marriage, though he could have told what her own taste in clothes would be, he knew nothing of her idea of small babies'—and this after having to suffer all her excited prattling about this child when she first decided she'd like to adopt it. So it was with a sinking feeling that he took the assistant's advice on at least the colour to choose for a girl.

"She's a big child—enormous, in fact!" Stacy boasted, with a pathetic attempt at appearing the proud father.

"Oh, then you'll be needing the second size," the saleswoman said, doubtfully, thus ensuring trouble for the unfortunate Stacy, whose idea of size had sadly miscarried, in his one surprised glance at his adopted daughter. His second mistake was to choose elaborate things, when a plain outfit would have better become Daisy's very plain off-spring. But it was not these points which angered Janine so much.

"Oh, you chose these yourself?" she began, in a disappointed tone, as he thrust the boxes at her. "I hope you brought white, Stacy. I don't like babies in colours."

A bad beginning. His heart sank as she ripped open the boxes and held up the garments before the highly interested faces of the observation case in the next bed, and a couple of junior nurses who were supposed to be tidying the ward.

Janine gasped, and her face went like a thundercloud. "What were you buying for—a baby elephant? And the colour—did you forget she's carroty with white eye-lashes? My God—*pink*!"

CHAPTER V

FENELLA HELSTON sat on a seat in one of the many nooks in the public gardens, where an unfrequented path ran in front, and through the shrubs and trees a glint of the water could be seen. The early spring sunshine touched the surface, sending blinding flashes of light occasionally off the ripples, and part of a boat would shoot across the opening, and be gone before a constructive eye-picture of it could be formed. May, in the public gardens, was a time for sitting in a quiet nook and thinking; when your home was set in the beauty of the Lake District, you had to think sometimes, of the promises of a career you made yourself before you left it, or the tugging back would be overwhelming and you'd find yourself chucking the odious job of bed-making and bed-panning, and be off and away.

This was a short leave, a stretch of a few hours, between duties, and she always spent it in an open space where there wasn't a sign of the wilderness of grey stone and dingy brick that, for her, was London. Here she could remember, without the irritation of her present life intruding, the long silences that belonged to home. Here she could pretend that that glint of water through the trees was the lake she could see from her bedroom window, and with a bit of imagination, she could conjure up the mountain behind. "The Hill", it was called locally, because it was so much smaller than the other mountains and, in comparison with Skiddaw and Scafell, it wasn't really a mountain at all.

There was a warmth about the valley, the garden and the house, a warmth for Fenella that was unique. The colours of interior and exterior had been carefully chosen to suggest light and air, for Fenella's mother was a confirmed invalid, and everything had to be as beautiful as possible for her. There were stretches of velvety green turf dotted with circular flower-beds, for her special delight, and there was a balcony running round the whole of the house, on first-floor level, so that Adelaide Helston's stretcher-like couch could be wheeled to any position. From there, the frail, lovely little woman could see the whole of the grounds her husband had designed for her, in those far-off days when Kevin Helston had been young and strong and handsome and untouched by care.

Fenella dragged her thoughts sharply back. Sooner or later, on these quiet afternoons, she would find the memories of home too poignant to remember. Feverishly she opened her bag and got out cigarettes and a lighter, but before she could get the recalcitrant flame to appear, a thin sensitive hand shot forward with a lighted match.

She stared at the hand before looking up at its owner. He had quietly sat on the seat beside her, and one glance at his thin, unhappy face was enough.

"Why, it's Mr. Conway!"

There was no real reason for her to be so surprised. She had heard Janine Conway tell little Daisy Jenks that this park had been a favourite rendezvous of hers and her husband's since they had been in town. Yet it seemed strange to her to see him sitting there beside her, offering her a light.

"I didn't recognize you at first," Stacy said, in a puzzled voice. "Without that white thing on your head," he enlarged.

She laughed. "Our uniform caps aren't

very becoming, are they?" On the seat beside her was a black velour hat with a band and crest, rather like a schoolgirl's. Her red-gold head was bare, and her hair, he noticed, was cut short, in an attractive curly crop. Her lashes were not ginger, but a dark brown; infinitely attractive over her dark brown eyes, eyes that were so dark as to be almost black.

He flushed a little, conscious that he was staring, and that she had noticed and was waiting for the result of his long scrunity.

"Did you speak to my wife after all?" he asked, a little lamely, and she was disappointed and showed it. How quickly the hospital and its affairs intruded in her off-duty hours.

"No. There wasn't an opportunity, and somehow I don't think Mrs. Conway would have liked it." She spoke slowly, and carefully, and he wondered what relationship there had been between his wife and this girl, who would have so many intimate things to do for her, and yet couldn't get close enough to speak to her on so essential a subject. Stacy still felt that if anyone could have done anything to help Janine, this girl could.

"I thought you hadn't managed to," he

said.

"Your wife's been home a week now. Is she any . . better?"

"I don't know."

She stared at him, and he coloured again. It was such an odd thing to say, and a foolish thing considering he didn't want to go into details about it. How could he tell anyone about that distressing scene which he and Janine had had when they got home from the hospital that day? Janine, furious about the unfortunate outfit he had chosen for the baby, and furious with herself for her own clumsy efforts to do the required acts for the child which she had so strenuously practised in hospital but now found so difficult under his curious and penetrating gaze.

"She went away to her aunts' place the same night—they sent for her," he said, briefly, as he recalled how that journey had come about.

Strange how a quarrel can boil up when you wanted so badly to keep the peace. Janine in a temper was a difficult person to be with and not quarrel with. Especially when he himself was simmering with suppressed anger over the affair at his mother's house when the Westlands were

71

there.

"So that's it!" Janine had burst out, clutching the child to her in a strangely maternal gesture considering she had no love for it, not even liking. "You're jealous! You've heard something from those rotten Westlands about me, and you haven't even had the decency to ask me if it's true!"

"But that's just what I am doing," Stacy pointed out, striving to be patient. "I've heard it, and I want to know from you—what was between you and Hugh Torrington?"

Yet that wasn't the truth. He didn't want to know that at all. He didn't want to hear it, didn't want her to start telling him about a man he didn't know and didn't like, who had had the luck to know Janine in other circumstances, before he himself had come along. That was what he had wanted all the time—the opportunity to have a long leisurely friendship with Janine before he made up his mind to marry her. Time and opportunity to get to know her properly. Not to be pitchforked into marrying her without the satisfaction of—in good old-fashioned words—chasing her. Torrington, apparently, had chased her to his heart's content. What the result was, he had yet to find out.

What he wanted most of all was to find out why all these people knew about it, and he hadn't been told. He had been pushed out in the cold by Janine, left to the mercy of his mother to stage a party in order to acquaint him with secondhand knowledge—after all these strangers had known about it and no doubt discussed it (and him) to their hearts' content. Burning with resentment, he had striven to be fair, and to be honest with Janine, at this crucial moment. But the effort was a flop.

Janine smiled bitterly at him. "D'you think I'd tell you?"

"Is there anything to tell, Janine?" For the life of him, he couldn't stop his voice sounding stiff and unfriendly.

A devil in Janine made her smile secretly, infuriatingly. "I'm going to my aunts', and I'm going to leave you guessing. And I hope you stew!"

Fenella Helston said, "I suppose it's a natural thing, to want to get away from London after an illness. Oh, I know people say that childbirth isn't an illness, but I always think it is. Worse than an illness, in

73

fact, because people look on it as a natural thing and there's no sympathy wasted for the unfortunate mother. Unethical for a nurse, isn't it?" She pulled a face at him, and he felt better. She was making it easy for him, and he knew it.

"Her aunts brought her up. They live in a country town—Bletchbury. Nice place to be in, this weather." He sounded wistful.

"And you're on your own at home?"

"Oh, yes. I keep on the flat, but my mother lives just round the corner." He told her a bit about his mother and sister and unwittingly painted a careful picture of two delightful people with whom it was a joy to be. Fenella Helston was suspicious. She had heard too many husbands paint just such a careful picture, from an over-bump of loyalty.

"And you come here when you're fed-up with your job?" she gently teased him.

He shook his head. "I've got time off. I usually get a few hours off between jobs—just before I get sent away. I'll be going up North to-morrow. Cumberland."

Her heart leapt. Home. . . . "Oh, how I envy you! What's your work? What are you going there for? Where will you stay? Oh, don't look as if I'm suddenly crazy—I'd give the world to be in your shoes! Well, to be going to Cumberland, I mean. It's my home, you see, and . . . oh, lord, I'm homesick!"

She turned away quickly, and drew hard on the last of the cigarette. He lit another for her, from his own case, and one for himself, putting his pipe away.

"When's your next leave, then?"

"I don't go home on leave, Mr. Conway. I daren't—it's too much of a drag to get away again. I've made up my mind to stay in London till I've finished my training. Then I'll go home. I'm going to work in a nursing-home run by a friend of ours." She gulped, and fastened her thoughts determinedly on her future. "He's young, and only just got started. I've only another year to do, then I'll be free to go and join him. He wants to marry me."

"Make sure you know him well enough before you take the plunge." It was out before he realized it, and he regretted it. She looked sharply at him, surprised by the depth of bitterness in his voice.

"I've known him all my life," she murmured. "Still, I have asked myself whether what I feel for him is all that's necessary for marriage. Tell me, Mr. Conway, is it enough?"

Her earnestness embarrassed him. "What *do* you feel for him?" he asked, gruffly, forced to proceed with a turn of conversation which he himself had started, yet hating the intimacy of it.

She thought carefully before answering. "I like him very much. I'm used to him. I know he likes me, and of course, he's used to me, too. Then we've our work and mutual interests such as good music, motoring, and books. I feel secure with him. We've the same friends, the same background." She turned to Stacy, puzzled and uncertain. "But I don't ache to see him. I know he's there—he'll keep. That isn't right, is it?"

"No, that isn't right," he agreed. But there his contribution to the discussion ended. How could he tell her that although he had no time to discover whether he ached for Janine or not, because of the conventional courtship thrust upon him, yet he knew, deep within him, that she was the only woman in the world for him? How could he tell her that although he often quarrelled with Janine and now had the added distress of being hurt and humiliated by her and her friends, she still dominated his thoughts, his waking hours, his whole world? He said, instead, "You'll always know when you're in love, but until you are . . . well, there's just no way of knowing."

"Yet lots of people marry as we're going to, and they make a go of it," she argued. But she knew she was arguing, and she shouldn't have to argue if she were certain.

The afternoon grew chilly. She gathered her purse and gloves together, and put on the offending hat. It hid her bright hair, and reduced her to an ordinary nurse, off-duty. The glow had left her eyes, and there was an air of disappointment about her. Stacy felt he had failed her in some way, perhaps by not assuring her that hers was undoubtedly the "real thing". On impulse, he said, "What time d'you have to get back to your squealing brats?" He could joke about it now, so numb was the place inside him where he had buried the bright hopes of his stillborn son.

Weeks afterwards, when life became so tangled for Fenella Helston and Stacy Conway, he asked her how it had all started. She repeated the question he had put to her, and reminded him that he had merely been kind and taken her to have a bite to eat, and told her about his boyhood in an effort to assuage her bout of homesickness and take her mind off her doubts about her future marriage. "What time d'you have to get back to your squealing brats?" An idiotic question, a simple one, yet one destined to alter the course of not only their lives, but Janine's and many others.

CHAPTER VI

JANINE was tight-lipped as she got out of the station cab at her aunts' house, and struggled with her purse to pay the driver. Coppernob was heavy, and she was showing signs of being a fretful child. She was always hungry, yet the patent food in the bottle never seemed to satisfy her.

Aunt Bee came to the window, and peeped from behind the white lace curtains. A cab at the door was a rare sight. She bobbed back again almost immediately, and miraculously Ethel appeared at the door, disapproving as ever. It seemed to Janine that her aunts' maid was thinking that even if Stacy weren't there in person, his child was, and that was just as bad.

"So this is your child!" Aunt Bee began, as she pecked her niece on the cheek. It was difficult to know why she and her sister had ever adopted Janine, except perhaps from a strong bump of duty. Janine's father had been the child of their only brother, and as such, rather a pet with them, but they had never liked Janine's mother, and this dislike was constantly uppermost in the minds of both Bee and Agnes, because of Janine's strong likeness.

The girl sat down with the baby on her lap, and Agnes came fussing in. "So this is your child!" she said, in exactly the same tone as her sister had used, though she could hardly have heard, since she had been upstairs at the time.

"I'm calling her Agnes Belinda," Janine said, and for the first time realized that she had put the name of the youngest aunt first. "Well, Belinda-Agnes would sound awkward," she added, lamely, as she saw the red tide rise in Aunt Bee's face.

"What do you call her, for short?" Agnes asked, in a pleased voice, feeling she had scored over her elder sister for once.

"Coppernob," Janine said, shortly, and dumped the baby on a nearby couch. Coppernob immediately woke up, and set up her usual howl, which was at once lusty and off-key.

"Oh, dear, how distressing!" The sisters were perturbed. Ethel looked round the door, and her mouth turned down at the corners. Ethel was difficult to please, and though she had been in the service of the sisters for many years, she had always had a choice array of threats to hold over their heads. One of them was that she didn't hold with young children, and would never work in a house where they were.

"Our niece is only staying the night," Miss Bee said hurriedly.

Janine looked up angrily, hesitated, and finally said nothing. This was a new state of affairs to her. She knew Ethel's vagaries only too well. She shrugged, and rummaging in her hold-all, found a clean nappie and began changing the child.

The aunts looked on, at once fascinated and nonplussed. Somehow they hadn't been able to imagine Janine as a young mother, and had been looking forward to seeing her with the baby from a sense of curiosity, yet were delicately repelled by the thought of intimacy with so young a child and its welfare.

Ethel, preparing to leave the room in high dudgeon, cast one backward glance at Janine bending over the child on the arm-chair, and expressed horror. She came back into the room, pushed Janine to one side, and picked up the baby.

"I cannot abide children, especially *young* children," she said, again, "but then I cannot abide seeing young mothers being useless with them!" She sniffed, her special sniff which expressed the very apex of her disapproval. "Changing nappies on a *chair*—what's wrong with your lap?"

She picked Coppernob up, seated herself in the full presence of her mistresses—a thing she had never been known to do in all her years with them—and proceeded to make the child comfortable. Her thin bony hands were surprisingly deft, and Coppernob stopped yelling. At the same time, she made a curious clucking noise for the baby's benefit, and Daisy Jenks' child responded with a wide toothless grin.

"She's smiling!" Janine gasped, rather cross to think that Ethel could produce any sort of pleasantness in the baby where

Janine herself failed so miserably.

"Nonsense!" Ethel snapped. "It's wind!" She sat the child up, balanced its chest over her right arm, and rubbed its back vigorously. Coppernob burped loudly and satisfactorily. Ethel picked up the baby and dumped it on Janine's lap, and marched out before the others had realized she was going. The baby promptly yawned widely, and prepared to go to sleep.

"Well!" the aunts said. "Where did Ethel get it from—such experience, in a respectable spinster!"

"Perhaps she isn't respectable!" Janine said crossly.

It was late before she got to her old room, to go to bed. A compromise had been effected, as she had known all the time would happen. They had had a "long talk", she and the aunts, and old Ethel had been called in towards the end, and consented (in view of her experience with her sister's children), to stay on, because poor Janine would no doubt be needing her valuable advice. Janine had writhed under all this, but knew better than to interfere. It was true. She probably would need Ethel—not for her advice, but to take over the care of Coppernob whilst Janine stayed in her aunts' house.

Curiously enough, Ethel was swayed by the thought that this wasn't the offspring of the odious Stacy Conway. That it was someone else's child, away from its own mother, produced in the gaunt elderly servant a compassion deep enough to overcome her dislike of babies. She looked at the child with new (though perhaps unconscious) tenderness.

The story of the adoption went badly, however, with the aunts, before they had acquainted Ethel with it. As with Stacy's mother, they had expressed prompt surprise, and asked Janine if she thought it was wise. They asked the most searching questions as to its parentage, and the arrangements made, and shook their heads.

"What did you expect me to do, then? Sit and cry over the death of my own child?" Janine's bitter tone rang harshly through the over-furnished sitting room, and both the aunts bridled. It was, they felt, extremely bad taste, and said so. They said a number of other things, including the obvious references to its baptism and Janine's churching. They hoped she would attend to both without delay, and suggested themselves for the godmothers. The doctor, they felt, would make a nice godfather, or their old friend, the professor. Janine made no reply, and knew that there was none to make. For the sake of peace, and for further favours, she must comply with their wishes over these things.

Janine slowly undressed, and wondered why things had turned out as they had since she had last slept in this room. Why had she, for instance, not kept her vow to Daisy Jenks, and pretended that Coppernob was her own child? She had meant it, when she had told Daisy that she was not to visit the child unless she were prepared to take a hand in the deception. Now, unasked, she had blurted out the truth to her aunts. Perhaps it was the goading of past years and all the bitterness of being an orphan herself, that had made her tell them what she had done. Their instant anxious question, "Was it wise?" had sent her ready anger flaming sky-high.

"What's the difference? You adopted me!" she retorted.

Both the aunts had bridled at once. "But you were our own relative," they had protested, with righteous indignation. "Of our own blood," they had added, in the tone which implied that in such a case nothing could possibly go wrong.

I'll see Coppernob doesn't have to remember, every minute of the day, what it means to be adopted, Janine vowed, as she slipped into bed. I'll see she doesn't have to be grateful all the time.

Slow tears coursed down her cheeks. Reluctantly she foresaw that Coppernob would come to mean a great deal to her, principally for this reason. Without realizing it before, there was that bond between them; Coppernob had been pitched into someone else's household to be brought up without the comfort of her own mother, and Janine herself had had no parents either. From the age of two she had been with the aunts. Before that, she had been in the care of a nursemaid, until her father had died.

I'll have to give Coppernob something, Janine told herself. I can't love her as I would have done my own baby—at least, I don't think so, yet—but I'll give her things that I missed.

The darkness closed round her suffocatingly, and she got out of bed and switched the light on. That was just one little thing that had got under her skin so much before her marriage. No bedside lamps were allowed, because of the temptation of reading in bed. No comforts at all (unless they were the kind the aunts had and approved of) were allowed Janine. The aunts were convinced that it was their duty to bring her up firmly, and firmness had been the watchword.

Stacy had no idea of this. He had seen so little of Janine in her own background. To his mind, she had been the pampered niece, with two old aunts cooing over her all the time. That was the impression the aunts had intended he should have. They believed that men still liked a girl with a sheltered background, and to this end they put up a very good show. Only Janine—boiling with inward fury, and appearing cold and unemotional in her efforts to hide her true feelings—had seen this. Perhaps old Ethel saw, too, but she was so dyed-in-the-wool an old servant, that her loyalty to her mistresses took on fantastic proportions. She was, Janine considered, hopelessly prejudiced in the aunts' favour.

Janine's own feelings towards Stacy had

been regulated by all this from the first evening he had spent in their house. In church, he had looked nice. Rather fun, Janine considered. She had been astonished at the way the aunts had cultivated him. Ever since that row over Hugh Torrington, they had kept her even tighter on the rein. That they should encourage a young man to the house again, had for the moment floored her. From then on, it had been easy for them. For Janine it had appeared to be escape. Life with this nice young man who let her have her own way, could hardly be worse than life in the aunts' house, under their perpetual supervision. She had been a prisoner, in effect, since Hugh. . . .

Resolutely she had tried to make a go of her marriage, but there had been one all-insurmountable difficulty. Stacy was in love with her and wanted to show it, all the time. With a less affectionate man, she would have succeeded; succeeded in making a good wife in all but the (for him) essential thing. He wanted her to show she loved him, and for her, that was impossible. When she flinched away from his caresses, he retired, hurt. It never occurred to him to ask her why, and if, it had, it was doubtful if she could put her thoughts and feelings into words. How could she tell a new husband that all her capacity for loving had been spent on (and rejected by) one man. She had nothing to offer anyone else, and to do her justice, she had not realized that Stacy would want anything else but a good and efficient wife. In his old-fashioned desire not to press his attentions on his fiancée before marriage, he had given her this wrong impression. After marriage, they had both felt cheated, for different reasons, but she on her side had blundered along, trying to make a go of it, and he had got more hurt and frustrated as the months went by. With the coming of the child, both had believed in a different outlook for the future, and again it had come to nothing.

Janine roamed restlessly round the room, and stopped at the dressing-table to finger her travelling brush and comb set, yet another gift from Stacy. Dumbly he had offered her things, hoping for the return he desired, hurt because it wasn't forthcoming. Never realizing that his gifts embarrassed her because they left her helpless and frustrated.

There were so many scenes in that basement flat, scenes that had left tiny scars. Scenes which had been started mostly by Janine, in her misguided attempts to show Stacy that if only he would leave her alone, they might get along well enough together. That time, for instance, when they had just returned from their honeymoon. Stacy had come behind her, and kissed the nape of her neck, just as Hugh had done. Caught unawares, she had spun round, happy and aglow. She had felt her face fall with disappointment, the minute she saw it was Stacy. All the joy went out of her, and his own face went dead as he watched her. He said nothing. It would have helped then, if he had . . . .

Sometimes she made a terrific effort to put things right, such as the making of a long trip, just to get something out of season which she knew he liked, or the cooking of a special dish which she had heard his mother say was a favourite of his. But as time went on, these efforts merely aroused a suspicious look in his eyes, and a hesitation which she knew would culminate in an attempt to caress her. The pleasure would leave her own face, and distrust take its place, and Stacy, quick as always, would notice, and the pleasure of her offering would fade.

The day she came home from hospital had been particularly disastrous, because she had known he had reverted to her own tactics and was doing things to propitiate her. The child's clothes, for instance. She had felt specially bad about that, for a purely feminine reason. Stacy could hardly be expected to know that she had wanted to take Coppernob round, proudly, to show her off to everyone in her new clothes. She had relied on Stacy's mother getting them, knowing that her choice would be impeccable. Janine felt like crying with disappointment when the pink outfit was uncovered, for it made Coppernob look more like Daisy Jenks' child than anything else could.

Going home, back to the poky little basement flat, in that mood, was an invitation for trouble. Even the flowers which Stacy had thoughtfully bought, and bundled into a most unsuitable vase, in the middle of the sitting-room table, could do nothing to put her in a happy frame of mind. Whatever she or he tried to do, it seemed, was destined to produce further misunderstandings, further unhappiness.

On the side table was a letter, addressed

to her, in Aunt Bee's flowing hand-writing. She picked it up, and fingered it, but made no attempt to open it. Aunt Bee, Bletchbury, all the old repressions and misery rose and threatened to choke her. Suddenly she knew that whatever happened, she could never bear to leave Stacy, or to lose him. He stood for the things she had never had; security, a home of her own, a right to be there with him, instead of being on sufferance, adopted... Whatever lack of visible affection there was there, Janine knew that they should be able to overcome it all, if they knew the way to cope, for on her side at least, was the desire, the need, for the more important things, the things that lasted. If only she could put it into words, let Stacy know, she felt he was fine enough to understand.

She went into the bedroom and stared. He said, from behind her, "I've bought a cot. I'm afraid it's pink again." His voice was tired, dispirited.

She wanted to say, "Oh, it's lovely, Stacy!" but the words stuck in her throat and choked her. He had tried so hard—too hard, as always—and the results of his trying were everywhere. He had stuck one or two nursery rhyme medallions on the distempered wall above the cot—the kind of cot that can be carried about, and infinitely more suitable for Coppernob than the frilly muslin type—and there was a low wicker nursing chair beside it. A pale pink bath was tilted against the wall, and a pale pink baby basked, filled (no doubt by the shop people) with things for a baby's needs. He had spent too much, she knew. It came to her, too, in that blinding moment of perception, that it must have meant a great deal more to him to have to dip into his precious savings to spend on someone else's child, instead of on his own son. It was for her, and her alone, that he had done all this.

From behind her, his voice came again, this time with hesitation, almost timorous, apologetic. "Mother's having sent a chest of drawers—cream, I think, with pictures on. For the baby's clothes." Then, as she didn't answer, he ventured, "And Merrill's sent a set of mugs and things—a spoon and pusher, I think."

Janine, her back still to him, felt a tear run down her face, and saw it splash on to Coppernob's cheek. The baby stirred restlessly, but didn't wake. "Oh, how nice," she managed to say.

"It's pink," Stacy added. It seemed to be an obsession with him now.

She didn't know how long she stood there, staring at the things he had bought, taking in the fact that someone (probably Stacy himself) had freshly cleaned the bedroom, and put fresh runners on the dressing-table and chest, and dusted the nooks and corners. He knew how she got irritable when there was dust about, and how she liked clean runners and covers everywhere. She battled with the rising tears, and won, and then she turned determinedly to him, to say what she had in mind while the mood was on her. But he had gone. Silently left the room.

She put Coppernob down in the new cot, and noticed that Stacy had remembered to buy appropriate bedding for it, but had not had the sheets washed, nor had he remembered to take off the price tags. She removed the pins and scraps of paper, and for a brief second a tender little smile hovered round her mouth. How like Stacy to leave the prices on.

Some day, she told herself as she left the

bedroom and quietly closed the door on the sleeping baby, some day I'll tell him about Hugh, and what happened, but to-day I'll just tell him how I feel about himself.

Stacy was pretending to read a news-paper. There was something akin to hostility in his attitude which puzzled her. Surely Stacy hadn't got angry because she hadn't answered him? He of all people would be the first to realize how a woman felt in the first overwhelming minutes of being home again.

She said, "I'll get the tea," and began, in a tired way, to put a cloth on the table. The vase of flowers took up a lot of room among the tea-things, so she put it on the side table.

Stacy said, in an offended tone, "Yes, that's right, put them out of sight. They're only what I bought for you. If Torrington had bought them, they'd be in the fore-front, I s'pose."

She stared at him. "What do you mean?" she whispered.

"I was at my mother's one night, when some people were connecting your name with his." He paused, to let that sink in. Then added, with tremendous effect,

"Torrington was there too."

That was cruel, Janine reflected, as she paced her old room at her aunts', in far-off Bletchbury. Cruel, because her face inevitably flushed and whitened, at the knowledge of Hugh's being in the vicinity, after all these years. She had thought he was still abroad.

She said, without thinking, "The Westlands, of course!"

Stacy flung his head up at that, surprised that she should fall into his trap so easily.

"I'm happy to know you're not denying it, Janine," he said, stiffly.

All the softer thoughts left her, and the ready anger of the past few weeks flamed up again. She accused him of being jealous, and he flared at her with all the bottled resentments of months. In a matter of minutes they said enough spiteful things to each other to last a lifetime, things too spiteful to be meant, but uttered in the heat of the moment. At the end, when both were spent, and Coppernob had awakened at the sound of their voices and joined in with her lusty howl, Janine snatched up her aunt's letter and tore it open.

"That's right, read your corres-
pondence, don't listen to me!" Stacy
shouted. "For heaven's sake, shut that kid
up! Couldn't you select a quieter one while
you were about it?"

Aunt Bee was demanding that she take
the baby up to Bletchbury right away.
London, she said, was no place for a new
baby, nor for a recuperating mother. The
country air was what Janine needed, and
she, Bee Stanhope, insisted that mother
and child made the journey right away. No
hesitation, she said, could be tolerated.
Pack an overnight bag and come. Janine
needed no further pressing. If they had not
quarrelled, she and Stacy, Janine would
have ignored such a letter. Having got
away from her aunts' house, she was not
likely to want to go back in a hurry. But as
things were, she plunged hot-headed into
the chance of walking out on him, and did
so with even greater effect than she knew.

"All right, I'll shut Coppernob up—I'll
remove her offending presence from this
flat altogether! We're going to my aunts,
where they don't mind children crying!"

That wasn't true, but Stacy wasn't likely
to know it. He kept up his indignant air
until she had gone, then he slumped into a

chair, defeated. For her, the one pungent thing was that he had let her go and hail a cab herself and put herself and her bags into it, without attempting to come to the door and see her off. Nor had he bothered about what train she would catch. All very unlike Stacy, and in that mood it had merely heightened her fury.

Now she saw Stacy as he had been then; hurt, bewildered, rushed off his feet by her sudden decision to go, and the hurry in which she went. It was only after the cab had left the street, that he realized he should have gone with her, put her and the child into the train, too, and made some effort to find out when she'd be coming back.

A far-off howl brought her back with a jerk to the fact that her adopted child was splitting the peace and quiet of the Bletchbury night by yelling for food. The aunts had insisted that a spare bedroom should be equipped as a nursery. So far, they had not dared to put in nursery furniture, however temporary, because of offending Ethel. Now, however, Ethel seemed to have been propitiated, they talked of having a room specially set up with baby furniture.

"But I'm not going to stay here long enough for such an expense," Janine had protested.

"Oh, but you'll be coming here quite a lot. I insist," Aunt Bee had said, and when Aunt Bee insisted, the things usually happened. "You must have at least two long holidays with us each year—we *can't* allow that poor child to grow up in a *basement*!" and somehow Bee Stanhope made the term "basement" sound like a doubtful slum dwelling.

The room selected was next but one to Janine's. Ethel had already emerged from the room between, and was hovering uncertainly. Obviously, she didn't want to appear to be interfering, although at the same time she was not at all certain of anyone else's powers of soothing a howling infant in the night. On seeing Janine, she backed into her room, and shut the door.

Janine went down to the kitchen first, to mix the food. When she returned, Coppernob had thrust all the coverings off her, and was lying flat on her back, yelling. Her face was purple, and her fat fists clenched with rage. Her back was stiff. She obviously objected to being allowed to remain hungry for more than a minute.

"All right, all right, the larder's arrived," Janine said, with a shade of irritation. Coppernob in a rage was very like Daisy Jenks—unrestrained, rather earthy. But Coppernob feeding was rather like a Murillo cherub: a cherub who sucked noisily and made effectual clutches at the fingers which held the bottle.

"You little devil," Janine murmured, as she settled herself more comfortably in the low-seated arm-chair provided for the purpose; "if I'm not careful I'll be getting soppy over you before long!"

Feeding an infant, she found, tended to make her pleasantly sleepy, and liable to dream. Dreams over Coppernob's red head were all of a pattern, an unacknowledged pattern. Now, following on her miserable thoughts in her own room, Janine allowed the daydreams to take shape. It would be nice, her thoughts clamoured, if this were happening in the bedroom of the flat, with Stacy lying in bed looking on; a Stacy who was content to accept her as she was, without immediately wanting to pet her and receive returning caresses. She built a picture of Stacy as the father of an infant, a Stacy who held the baby easily and confidently, and smiled occasionally. The smile, her dreams insisted, would be a slow, pleasant smile, with no timorous quality, no hesitation. Stacy's smile as she knew it, had a heartbreak quality, like the expression on the face of a dog who had been kicked too much.

Twenty minutes of daydreaming saw Coppernob near-doped, and Janine almost asleep. As she put the child back, and gathered up the empty bottle, and the bowl which had contained the hot water, she wondered how it would be if she went back to London and had yet another try to explain to Stacy. She owed it to Coppernob to give her a father, and if she and Stacy went on like this, the baby would be no better off than if her own mother had kept her.

Besides, she knew she would be less happy in this house than back there with Stacy. She was missing him already, despite their constant hit-and-miss association. She missed his long thin body lying beside her, and found she hated sleeping alone just as much as she had in hospital. She found, too, that she had been yearning for a long time, to be back over her own stove, cooking for Stacy. There was an endearing intimacy in just being in the flat with him, even though she was inclined to shrink when he came near her.

The kitchen in her aunts' house was large and clean and bare. The scrubbed cream surface of woodwork was unfriendly, because Ethel worked for work's sake, and never let a speck or crumb lay for more than a second. It made Janine's own poky little kitchen a nostalgic memory. So much so that she did a thing she had never done before: she let herself imagine what it would be like if she allowed Stacy to make love to her—what it would be like if she allowed herself to reciprocate.

Puzzled, she faced the fact that such a thought was not repulsive. All she had been fighting against was one man's caresses being unwelcome because she pined for those of another. And, because she found Stacy to be tiresome rather than repulsive, she decided to go back. Go back and try again, because of the dread fear that she was throwing away the one thing she had had of any value in her whole life.

After that decision had been made, sleep came easily, and in the morning, she hastily gathered together her few things she had brought, and prepared to pack.

There was no time to do much before breakfast, and when she arrived downstairs, she found Aunt Agnes in a flutter, with red-rimmed eyes, and Ethel flying around looking grim.

"What on earth's the matter?" she gasped.

"It's one of your aunt's attacks!" Ethel retorted, and hustled to the door to answer the bell.

"That'll be the doctor," Aunt Agnes said, and burst into tears again. "Oh, dear, oh, dear, I know one of these days it'll be the last—the doctor has warned us, and I know it will come soon!"

Janine could get nothing coherent from her, and found out from Ethel eventually that Aunt Bee's heart was shaky. It had been so for some time now, but neither of the sisters would let Janine be told.

Janine decided she would have to stay until her aunt was about again, before she went back to London. There was little enough she could do there, but it seemed somehow all wrong to go away suddenly when there was illness in the house, although the girl could not honestly say she had much feeling for either of the older women. They had just been an accepted part of her existence, but there had been no affection on either side.

It was a full week before Aunt Bee was allowed to get up—seven days of hesitation over writing to Stacy and deciding not to—and even then Janine didn't get so far with her plans for returning home, as to tell her aunts. She was once more forestalled, this time by a letter from Stacy. He said he hoped she was well, and that the baby was progressing. He also said he had been asked by his mother and sister to send their love and best wishes. It was all very formal and Stacy-ish. Not until the end of the short missive did Stacy drop his bolt, however, but he did it beautifully briefly and casually. It was as well, he said, that the aunts wanted Janine there with the baby, and he hoped it was an indefinite period they thought of having her there, for it would not be pleasant for her, alone in the basement flat, while he was away. Indeed, he had decided to relinquish the flat for the time being and put their furniture in store, on the grounds that it would be a needless expense to keep on for so long. His firm, he added, were sending him up North for six months.

CHAPTER VII

STACY'S letter was an unpleasant shock to Janine, but a pleasant surprise to her aunts. It was, to them, one thing to move heaven and earth to marry off an orphan niece and so shelve their own responsibilities for ever, but quite another thing to be thrust into the background by that niece's husband. Stacy had, they felt, been instrumental in keeping Janine from writing regularly to them, and also from visiting them during the first year of her married life. Now it seemed that Stacy was relinquishing his tight hold on the girl, and they would now be able to have her company, and introduce a vital new flow of conversation into their narrow circle, without necessarily having to be responsible for her.

To Janine, their line of reasoning was preposterous, and tiresome. She didn't want to stay in Bletchbury. She wished she wasn't tied by Coppernob, so that she could dash back to London and see what was happening about the flat. She wanted the opportunity of suggesting to Stacy that she keep it on herself and stay there. There were many reasons why she would rather be in London than in the Midlands. For one thing, there was the hospital to be attended, and later the clinic, for both herself and the baby. There was, too, the question of discouraging her aunts from expecting to see too much of her, and also the drugging effect that their house and life had on her; Janine found that already she was slipping back into the old existence, as if there was a drag-net round her feet, sucking her down. . . .

It was, curiously enough, to Ethel that she finally turned. There was no one else to whom she could take her problems, and since Ethel had taken over the bathing and to some extent the feeding of Coppernob in the week they had been in Bletchbury, the old woman seemed to have become more human. Her rusty black gown and billowing white apron, out-dated yet comfortable, made an ideal lap for the hefty infant, who seemed utterly content to be there, and had to some extent abandoned her habitual yelling. On Ethel's face, too, was a new look, a rested look, an almost contented look that made her yellowish face look less pinched and bony.

105

"If only I could get up to Town before Stacy does anything definite," Janine exploded. "Fancy deciding to give up the flat before he found out if I agreed!"

Ethel grunted. It was no more than she would have expected of the despised Eustace Conway. She said as much, and was surprised that Janine said nothing in his defence.

"What would you do with yourself, living there all alone, miss?" Ethel said, at last.

Janine stared down at Coppernob, doped with patent food, but still hanging on to the teat of the bottle, loathe to let it go. Ethel expertly removed it from the child's mouth, and stood the empty bottle on the table, and sat the child up over her arm with the terse command: "Let's have some wind!" Coppernob obliged in a manner which could hardly have disappointed Daisy Jenks herself.

Janine chuckled. "She likes you seeing to her. You know Ethel, if it weren't for the fact that you hate babies so—"

"Who says I hate babies?" Ethel demanded, bridling.

"Well, don't care for them overmuch—I'd be tempted to ask you to look after her for a day or two, just while I slipped up to Town to see Stacy."

"None of yer wheedling, miss. I'm not taking on any such thing at my time of life. Besides, what'd yer aunts have to say about that, I'd like to know?"

"Oh, they wouldn't mind, if I promised to come back again."

"Yes, I know, miss, but would yer? Would yer come back on yer honour?"

"Well, you don't think I'd leave Coppernob on your hands do you? Besides, I might persuade Stacy to come back with me on the way up North."

Janine's voice sounded more wistful than she had intended, and the old woman looked up sharply.

"Look here, miss, you and me, we both know yer aunts wouldn't mind yer going off for a day or two, and you know as well as I do, that the baby'd be all right here with me. I would do it, too, if I was to be sure you really want to see that good-fer-nothing husband of yours. But if you're just playing about, miss, angling fer a day or two to get away from caring for this mite, well, I just wouldn't do it. I wouldn't want to encourage you, see what I mean? You've taken her on, as yer own, and you've got to stick to the job now, for always. For this mite's sake. That's only right."

Janine flushed angrily. "You've no right to talk to me like that, Ethel!"

"Oh, yes I have, miss, and you know it! Don't put on any of yer airs and graces with me, my dear. Who looked after you when you was a mite like this, eh? Well, not so small as this maybe, but when you was young enough to want someone to turn to, and not know or care who it was, so long as they was kind! Not yer aunts—oh, no, they wanted nothing to do with yer while you was in the nuisance stage. It was to old Ethel you come. Don't remember that, do yer? And when yer aunts see how attached I was getting to yer, and you to me, then what did they do? Packed you off to one of these here fancy toddlers' day-schools. 'You was too noisy,' said they. But I know better—and so do you!"

Janine was sceptical, but later when she approached Aunt Bee with her proposed flying visit up to Town, she was forced to admit that there might be something in what Ethel had said.

"It's all right, Aunt Bee. You don't have

to worry about the baby—Ethel'll look after her for me. She said she would."

Aunt Bee frowned. "Take care, my dear. The woman is an excellent housekeeper, but inclined to be possessive with children. I know too well, do I not, sister?"

Agnes twittered around the arm-chair, and arranged the rug over her sister's legs. "Indeed, yes, we know too well how it was with Janine here, when she was small!"

"For heaven's sake, Aunt Bee, I'm only going for a couple of days. Even Ethel can't do much harm in that space of time!"

"Why are you making such a long journey, dear?" Aunt Agnes asked, in her deceptively mild tone, when she wanted information badly. "Surely it would be better for Stacy to come here to see you on his way up North?"

"And to see us, too!" Aunt Bee added with asperity; she didn't like Stacy, but it was a sore point with her that he never came to see them.

"You wouldn't be wanting to persuade him to keep the flat on, would you, dear?" Aunt Agnes probed. "Not after promising us to stay here the six months, as he wished you to?"

"I didn't promise!" Janine said. But they

insisted that she had, and it was difficult to get away for the precious two days, in time to catch Stacy before he went away himself.

On the long train journey back to London, Janine found herself huddling in her corner seat imagining the meeting with Stacy, and what she would say to him, and he to her. But all the conversations went the way she wanted them to go, and she knew by experience that the actual conversation would be far different.

In turn, she was cold and indifferent, and pleased to see him; she was gay and amusing; she was adopting the "wait-and-see" attitude. But the Stacy of her imagination was obstinately unlike the Stacy she knew, and hoped to see again, and persisted in being the exact reverse of her own mood. It was with relief that she reached the terminus and took a cab to the flat.

London was at its greyest and most depressing level. The people wore their dingiest rain-wear, against the threat of the leaden skies, and there was a sharp contrast in the temperature to that of the last few days, when Stacy had enjoyed his loneliness in the park, and finally met the ginger nurse. Janine slackened her pace as she went down the area steps, and something in the atmosphere of the place made her feel rather conscious of the week-end case she carried. The flat already seemed to be empty, although curtains were still at the windows.

She inserted her key in the lock, but the door wouldn't move. She wrestled with it impatiently, until a strident voice called from the top of the main steps, "Don't break it down—can't yer see it's bolted?"

Janine looked up into the face of her landlady, leaning over the railings and scowling down at her. As she recognized the girl, Mrs. Petts' face cleared, and broad, toothy grin spread over her dough-like face.

"Why, it's you, dearie! Didn't expect yer, that I didn't, not seein' as yer 'usband'd gorn off in such an 'urry. Come on up, and 'ave a cuppa tea with me, an' we'll 'ave a nice ole chin-wag, just like we useter!"

Mrs. Petts' sitting-room was at the back, overlooking a dingy yard with a solitary lilac tree in the far corner, a tree whose meagre blossoms always seemed rather grubby.

111

Mrs. Petts seated herself at the round table, whose burgundy plush cloth had several bobbles missing from the border, and leaned her chin on her arms invitingly. "Tea'll be in, in just two ticks," she extravagantly promised. "Now just you open yer 'eart ter me, dearie. Left yer, did 'e? Thought as much the minute 'e come ter me and said 'e was closing the flat. I said to meself, 'Ah,' I said, 'leavin' 'er, is 'e!' The scoundrel!"

"No, no, Mrs. Petts, you don't understand. My husband just had to go up North—" Janine began wildly, when Mrs. Petts broke in sagely.

"Ah, yes, my dear, that's what they *all* say. It's always 'up North'. I don't know why, and never did. They don't seem to go South at all. Funny, don't yer think?"

"—and he wrote and told me to stay on at my aunts', as it was no use keeping on a flat, empty, and paying the rent for six months."

"Six months, eh? Coverin' 'imself nicely, I must say!" Mrs. Petts was scathing.

"Oh, no, you don't understand. I just seem to have missed him, that's all. I'd have been up last week, the day after I went, in fact, but I couldn't get away. My aunt was ill. Did he leave any message for me?"

"Message!" Mrs. Petts was cynically amused. "Message she asks! Lor, no, dearie. He just sez to me, 'Mrs. Petts', 'e sez, 'I won't be wantin' this flat any more. I'm havin' the things sent round to my mother's to-morrow. Will you take a month's rent in lieu of notice?' Would I not! 'Evelina Petts,' I sez to meself, 'just you take four weeks cash an' arst no questions,' that's what I sez. But what I thought was an 'orse of a different colour!"

Janine was exasperated, and very anxious. Something had gone wrong, and she couldn't understand what it was. Surely Stacy hadn't heard any more stories from those Westlands people, about herself and Hugh? Surely he would have given her the benefit of the doubt, come and asked her for her version? Not just closed up their flat and gone away?

Little by little she got from her landlady information that led her to believe that Stacy had been very moody this last week, and had been home a lot, with presumably no work. Mrs. Petts was of the opinion

113

that he had got the sack, and had cleared off to get something else in another district.

"'Sides, there was that woman! Ginger, she was, and a real bad lot, if you arst me!"

"What woman?" Janine gasped.

Mrs. Petts had, it appeared, seen Stacy walking with Fenella Helston, the night he had taken her to dinner. The landlady's description was unflattering, and incorrect. Janine had no idea whom the girl could be, and was half inclined to put the story down as a piece of Mrs. Petts' malicious imagination. Yet there was a nagging certainty that there was a grain of truth in it.

She flung up her head angrily. "I won't wait for the tea, Mrs. Petts. I'm going to see my mother-in-lw."

That, of course, was the obvious thing to do, and Janine had every intention of doing it, as she left the dingy house and the garrulous Mrs. Petts behind her. But a backward glance down at the windows of what had been their home, made her pause a second, then abruptly alter her mind. It was the curtains.

Mrs. Petts had not said why they had been left up at the windows, though the

114

rest of the furniture had been cleared out. Janine hazarded a guess. If their home had been stored for the moment at his mother's it was quite likely that Mrs. Conway told Stacy not to bother with the curtains. Janine, herself had made them, by hand since she had no sewing machine. She had been especially proud of them. Stacy's mother, and even Merrill had been extremely critical. Not by word of mouth, but by those expressions of theirs, which said so much more than chosen words could say. Stacy's mother had fingered the material, examined the hems, frowned, and said nothing very significantly. Merrill had expressed surprise and swiftly composed her face after a second's amused glance at her brother. True, those curtains didn't compare with the heavy lined velvet and rep window hangings in Stacy's mother's house, but Stacy need not have left them up at the windows for someone else's use.

Janine turned away, blinking savagely at the tears which rose quickly in her eyes. Stacy, kind as he was, could be surprisingly hurtful in strange little ways, such as this.

She decided to go to a teashop and get

some food, but only when she came face to face with boarded windows and "Closed" notices on the doors of several did she remember that this was Sunday. Sunday, and no flat to go to. No food, and hotel restaurants were out of the question, since she hadn't much money on her. Going to see Stacy had been her only intention, and beyond her fare and a little odd change, she hadn't thought it necessary to bring any more. Since her marriage she had had less ready money than when she had been a ward of two tight-fisted old maids.

It would have to be Stacy's mother's, then, she decided distastefully, despite the rankling left by the curtain episode. She was turning back when a sharp Cockney voice hailed her.

"'Allo, 'allo, 'allo, look 'oo's 'ere! Well, I never! Wonders'll never cease! 'Ow are yer, Mrs. C?"

Janine spun round, trying to place the voice, and found the peaky face of Daisy Jenks thrust close to hers.

"I bin tryin' all week ter find yer, ter tell yer I've changed me address. Got a live-in job, bit o' jam an' no mistake. 'Ow's the little nipper, eh? Ain't got 'er wiv yer, I see."

"She's at my aunts' house, in the Midlands, where I've been staying. I'm only in London for a day or two. It's rather altered our arrangement, I'm afraid, Daisy. You won't be able to see Coppernob after all. At least, not for several months. Shall you mind very much?"

"'Ere, 'ere, 'ere, wot's all this?" Daisy was immediately suspicious. "Never said nuthink about it ter me before, did yer? What's goin' on?"

Daisy was at once belligerent and frightened. In her Sunday best—a cheap suit cut in the very latest fashion and a trifle too short in the skirt, preposterous shoes, more strap and pin-heel than anything else, and her too-gay handbag which nearly matched the bright blue of the scarf she had twisted round her head turbanwise—she was the typical working girl showing herself to the world on her one day off in the week. Janine was more sorry for her than angry with her.

"You haven't the right to talk to me like that, Daisy. It was your idea that I took the child off your hands. I've done it legally. In the eyes of the law, she's mine. But I'll let you see her, when and where

117

possible." She paused, and studied the bewilderment her words had conjured up in Daisy's face. "Oh, look here, where can we go and talk? It seems ages since I saw you last!"

Daisy said, "What's the matter wiv your flat—or ain't I good enough fer yer 'usband's eyesight?"

Janine bit her lip. "Well, to tell you the truth, my husband's gone away and shut up the flat. I had hoped to catch him before he had to go, to ask him to leave the flat open for me, but he'd gone. His firm's sent him up North."

Daisy's face creased into an incredulous stare, and then into a knowing look infinitely worse than the avid expression of the landlady. "Oh, up North, eh? Gawd, fancy you joining the ranks of grass widders. 'Ere, ducks, fergit what I said at first, see? We'll git tergether an' 'ave a nice old talk. Now I can't arst yer ter my place 'cos I ain't got one. At my job we don't get allowed visitors, see? But I know where we could go—t'ain't fer from 'ere. Remember Mrs. Ashley? Go'n, yer do. In the 'ospital, 'er wot 'ad that white-faced little kid wot was always screaming!"

"Yvonne Ashley! Yes, I remember. Why,

what's that got to do with it?"

"Well, lives near 'ere, she do!" Daisy was triumphant. "Said I'd go an' look 'er up, 'fore I left the 'ospital. Now's the time. We'll both go. Come on!"

Janine demurred. Yvonne Ashley might have other visitors—it might not be convenient for them to go on account of food, or the baby. But Daisy Jenks was determined.

"We c'n take some in wiv us, can't we? Orf a barrer!"

Daisy bought fruit and nuts, and dived down a side street to a sweet-shop she said she knew, and got chocolate. The woman in the shop, a large old woman with a wart on the side of her nose, greeted Daisy with exclamations of joy, and "obliged" her with a pint of milk and a rather burnt white loaf, when they told her of their visit. As a parting shot, she pressed a grimy newspaper package into Daisy's handbag.

"Two o' me noo-laid," she whispered, triumphantly, and said she kept all her eggs for those just emerging from lying-in. Janine left the shop bewildered, with a picture of countless new mothers rising from childbed to be presented with two eggs from Daisy's friend.

Yvonne's room was what had once been two attics, knocked into one, and hidden behind a stone balustrade on the top of an old decaying house in a faded tree-lined street. Daisy led the way up the steps, and looking all about her and up and down the front of the house, expressed an opinion for both of them.

"Dreary, ain't it?"

Dreary was the word. There had been no paint on the woodwork for years, and even the stone steps were crumbling a little at the edges. The door was opened by a thin, deaf old woman, who turned out to be an ancient distant relation of the family, and who finally called to someone in a back room for confirmation of the fact that a Mrs. Ashley was living in their house before she would allow Janine and Daisy to enter.

"Yes, Aunt Liz, you know she lives in the attic!" a voice screamed from the back regions.

"Eh?" Aunt Liz put her hand in cup-shape round her ear, and bent her head in the direction of the voice, which obligingly screamed the information again.

Then the whole performance had to be repeated to obtain permission to go up and see Yvonne, and at last, very reluctantly, the old woman stood aside and watched them very suspiciously as they went up the stairs.

"You know, Daisy, I still think we shouldn't have come. How d'you know she'll want to see both of us? Friendships made in hospital are like those made on board ship—you can't expect them to last."

"Well, seein' as I ain't never bin on board ship, I don't see wot that 'as ter do wiv me seein' Yvonne!" Daisy said briskly, then guffawed noisily at her own wit.

At the third floor, both girls stopped, winded. "What a place to live in!" Janine gasped. "Does she *have* to keep on this room? Surely there are other places...."

"It's the cash wot counts," Daisy said, sagely, and equally out of breath. Her feet, in their preposterous shoes, were also bothering her, and she eased them by standing first on one foot, then on the other. Finally, she took them off and carried them, padding up the rest of the stairs barefoot. "Don't charge 'er much, 'ere, seein' as they wos friends of 'er fam'ly, so to speak."

At last they reached the attic. The door

had a cheap knocker fixed to it, and Yvonne had put up a neatly printed card, with her name on it. Daisy laughed, and thought it was a good job. "Cute idea, eh?"

"Necessary, I should think," Janine said, recalling the kind of people who lived in the rest of the house. Aunt Liz might have no scruples whatever about walking into a room that had no lock or knocker. Neither did Daisy, after knocking twice and getting no answer.

"Oh, don't try the door," Janine protested. "She can't be in—look, there's the milk left there. Looks like two days' supply."

Daisy experimented with the handle, and found the door opened. "Who sez she's not in?" she demanded, triumphantly.

Janine followed her, helplessly. The attic was still virtually two tiny rooms, with a hole knocked into archway shape where the middle door had once been. The outer room was a sort of kitchen sitting-room, the inner one obviously a bed-room. Daisy marched through, with Janine protesting at her heels.

The room was in wild confusion. The bed was unmade, and a heap of ashes in the grate. The greyness of the day and the height of the windows made the room look even more dreary than it would have otherwise been. Silence was everywhere.

"She *must* be away," Janine murmured, then gasped. "Look, there she is!"

She pointed to a huddled figure in the depths of a great shabby arm-chair in front of the fireplace. A figure with tousled hair and an old check dressing-gown. There was no food to be seen, and the room was cold. Of the baby there was no sign.

CHAPTER VIII

STACYS train left London soon after Janine's steamed out of Bletchbury. He had no thought of her dashing up to Town to see him, neither did he think that she would experience anything other than relief that their existence in the basement flat was finished. He had, after much thought, decided it was the best and only thing for them both. For to him, it was obvious that what she wanted most to do, whatever she might say in letters to the contrary, was to stay with her aunts, or at least, to be comfortably away from him.

He went over the turmoil of this week again. A week that had been stranger than those in which Janine had been in hospital, because then she had been within easy distance of him. The unreality could be tempered a little by that one hour each day when he could go and see her, even though it usually meant a quarrel or at least a difference of opinion and a certain coldness between them. But now, it was as if he had no wife at all. He might have been a bachelor again, because he had no idea when he would see her again, since his own job had fatefully intervened.

Dispassionately he reviewed his future. There was nothing now. Nothing but a job which was good enough, but had no prospect of advancement, but infinite variety if you liked being sent all over the country, and never knowing for how long you could expect to stay in any one place. And under and above it all was the certainty of living with Janine under your skin.

He had no photograph of her. That, he remembered with surprise, was a thing she would never have. Most girls, he knew from Merrill, were vain enough to want their man to have at least one good picture of them. Janine had shied from such a thing. He had one or two snaps of her on their honeymoon, but these had caught her frowning with the sun in her eyes, or frowning from sheer displeasure. Somehow he had never seemed to catch her with the camera when she was happy or pleased. Yet she could be both. Sometimes he had caught snatches when she was with him. Many times he had seen an enchanting smile on her face when talking to other people. Once he had surprised a heartbreakingly lovely expression on her face when she had thought he was someone else. . . .

After two hours, he fell asleep. He dreamed; a curious dream of Janine on a sort of sliding way which took her backward slowly, out of sight, and she had her arms outstretched to him, with a sorrowful expression on her face. Then the sliding way changed its direction and came back, but the girl on it was not Janine, but Fenella Helston, in her nurse's uniform, as he had first seen her in the park. There was, on her face, a look of complete bewilderment, somehow mixed with eagerness, and she was coming closer and closer.

He struggled, and forced himself awake,

125

but she was still before him, though not in her nurse's uniform. He shut his eyes, and fought with the nausea the dream had conjured up. There was a tight, sinking feeling in the pit of his stomach as he thought again of Janine going from him, and he himself unable to reach her or to stop her. The helplessness that is experienced in dreams was still with him. He opened his eyes again, and looked at the corner seat facing him, and found Fenella was still there.

"How do you do, Stacy," she said, smiling a little. "You don't look very pleased to see me."

He jumped. "Good God, you're really on this train! I thought. . . Just what *are* you doing here?"

"Were you dreaming? You cried out," she told him, "but I couldn't understand what it was you were saying."

He repeated his question, nettled.

"Why shouldn't I be on a train going to the place that's my destination?" she asked, still smiling. "Remember? I told you I lived in Cumberland. Well, that's where my journey's going to end."

"You didn't tell me last night that you were going home to-day!" he said, and he couldn't keep the accusing or suspicious note out of his voice.

"Unbelieving male!" she teased. "You don't believe in coincidence. Confess it!"

"I don't believe in coincidence," he affirmed, waiting.

She sighed. "All right, I'll own up. It wasn't coincidence. You told me you were going on this train, so I went to the powers-that-be last night when I got in, and asked if I could have my overdue leave. It's not usual to get it so quickly, but as it happened, it fitted in with matron's plans. She's got too many of us about at the moment, and we're slack this week, too. I couldn't believe my ears when she said I could go, but it was worth trying for, anyway. So—here I am. Satisfied?"

He didn't answer, and she flushed.

"Really, Stacy, you don't think I'm chasing you, do you, after your kindness in taking me out for a meal last night?"

Again he didn't answer.

She shifted uneasily. "I suppose it does look rather like it. Especially as you said we could dispense with formalities and use our christian names. But believe me, it isn't that at all. I'm engaged to Richard, and I'm going to marry him. I'm not the

127

type to want anything else as a sideline. But—it's difficult to explain, but I wanted to be with you to-day. At least for a travelling companion. I hate long journeys. But more than that, I wanted to talk to you again, about me, Richard, you perhaps and your own problems, and about life. I never met anyone quite like you before." She paused, and looked uncertainly at him. "Quite a speech, isn't it?"

"Don't mind me," Stacy said. "I'm a bit prickly. I had hoped that my wife would come with me on this job, but I suppose you can't expect a woman to travel with a young child, especially when the alternative is living comfortably in her old home."

"She travelled as far as the Midlands," Fenella murmured, but Stacy was looking out of the window, chasing the last ghost-like shreds of the dream. He didn't hear what Fenella said.

They lunched together, and had tea at the same table. Inevitably, as the end of the journey drew near, Fenella's thoughts turned to her home, and she tried to describe it to him.

"Whitestone House is the name of it,"

she said dreamily. "It isn't white. It's mellow and beautiful. It gets its name from the loch. Whitestone Water. Compared with Ullswater and the other big ones, it's only a puddle. But a lovely puddle. Then there's 'The Hill'."

As he listened to her description, he noticed how first her clothes, then the atmosphere of the train and the journey, and now her nearness to home, had changed her. She wore beautifully cut tweeds, and instead of being a nurse, just one of many who wore the rather ugly uniform of St. Michael's, she was now a young woman of means, and a very attractive one at that. He gathered from what she said, that her father was not in the medical profession, but was some sort of professor, now retired. Kevin Helston, it appeared, was some sort of hero to his daughter.

Adelaide Helston, however, predominated. Her frail beauty stretched out to touch them from far-off Whitestone House making the end of the train journey rather unreal, the beginning of the journey extremely prosaic and fraught with anxieties and unhappiness. Stacy listened to it all in a trance, a trance because

Fenella Helston belonged to a different world from his own, and was beckoning him into it. Unresisting, he was following.

Impulsively, Fenella said, "Stacy, I know you'll have to stay at commercial hotels while you're up here—during the week, that is. But the week-ends, what will you do then? You'll have nowhere to go, will you? Surely you won't keep going back to London to your mother's?"

He opened his mouth to say he would probably spend the week-ends going down as far as the Midlands to see his wife, but the truth of that was doubtful. Fenella noticed his hesitation, and because she was so close to him mentally, she divined this. Without waiting for his answer, she said, casually,

"I merely mentioned it because our house is open to as many week-end guests as we like, my sister and I. It would be nice if you could come over. I'd like you to meet my mother, too. She's a tremendous character, and a lovely person."

"I didn't know you had a sister," he said.

"Yes," she said, briefly.

The rest of the journey was spent in silence. A little of the warmth seemed to have dropped out of everything. Both sat

130

looking rather gloomily out of the windows, as if each knew that, if neither did something about it quickly, this was to be a parting, and a definite one.

"Stacy," Fenella said, suddenly. "Come to our house for next week-end. Let's make it a definite date. To please me." She smiled winningly at him.

He shifted uneasily. She was difficult to refuse, in this mood, and there was the feeling, too, that he wanted to be with her. It had been the same feeling that first day when he met her in hospital. He wrestled with himself. What was wrong with him? Was he falling in love with her? Swiftly he put the idea away. It wasn't possible, feeling as he did about Janine. But could a man love two women at the same time? Or was it a natural attraction that Fenella had for him, an attraction that was as inevitable as the dawn, and as difficult to resist as the smiling face of the country-side on a summer's day when there was work to be done in the city. Fenella was the ideal, the woman all sick men dream of finding in a nurse's uniform by the bedside. What was it the poet said? The perfect woman. . . .

"I feel I ought to keep myself free this

first week," he stammered. "One never knows what might happen with a new job. My wife might write to ask me to.. ."He broke off, and deliberately left the sentence unfinished, simply because he couldn't imagine Janine writing to ask him to do anything. But the wish was there, not that she should write to ask him to go down to Bletchbury for a week-end, but that she might come up to Cumberland and live near his job for the six months.

"I understand," Fenella nodded. "Well, here's my card. Telephone if you feel you'd like to come after all. Or the week-end after. When you like. Whitestone is open house, you know. My parents love young visitors."

Janine's aunts were not on the telephone, but the house next door had one, and it was a long-standing arrangement that the sisters' few calls could be taken and received there. The Monday Stacy started his new job, in the Northern head office of his firm, was too hectic a day to have any thoughts outside the small room in which he worked with two other men. But on the Tuesday he was again transferred to a small branch of his firm, in an old-fashioned town which unaccountably turned out to be on the doorstep of Whitestone Water.

He chafed at the way he was being pushed against his will to do something he felt he shouldn't. Fenella's was a friendship that would do him no good, in the sense that it would render him less able to make a contact point with Janine. The idea of telephoning Janine at her aunts', took shape and grew, and on the Wednesday he made up his mind, and put the call through as soon as he left the office.

The neighbour of the Stanhopes brought Miss Agnes to the telephone. She was too surprised to be frigid.

"Eustace? But isn't Janine with you?"

"What?" he shouted.

"Janine went to London to see you, before you were to go up North," she explained, obviously bewildered.

"I'm speaking from Cumberland," he yelled, as Miss Agnes' voice got fainter. "When did Janine go to Town?"

She told him all she knew about it, and both grew more worried as the minutes sped by. The pips came before either had been satisfied.

After he put the telephone down, Stacy reasoned with himself. He couldn't imagine why Janine should leave it to the last minute before going to London. Miss Agnes had omitted to mention her sister's illness as the reason for Janine's delay. Her old dislike of Stacy crept back into her voice after the first startled seconds, and she made little attempt to co-operate, beyond her anxiety for Janine's whereabouts.

Stacy did allay his own fears, however, with the thought that when Janine found the flat closed, she would no doubt go straight round to his mother's. After some hesitation, Stacy telephoned his home. Hesitation because he knew instinctively that Janine wouldn't be in a very receptive mood after finding that her journey had been fruitless, since she had been too late to contact him after all.

There was no reply from his mother's house, and only after ringing off for the second time did he remember that she and Merrill had booked seats for a play for that night. They must have taken Janine with them, he reasoned, and went to bed in a less anxious frame of mind.

When he rang the next morning, however, his mother tartly told him she hadn't seen Janine. In her voice was the same dislike for his wife that his wife's aunt had shown for himself. After a short conversation with his mother, he sat down to tackle his morning's work, but the thought of Janine kept intruding. He pictured her in London with the added burden of the baby, because Miss Agnes had not told him Janine had left Coppernob behind. She hadn't mentioned it because it was a point which Ethel was already fuming over; Janine had promised to stay away two days only. The mention of the baby's name was thoughtfully suppressed; Miss Agnes was not going to have Stacy think her niece would go off in such a manner, neither was she giving away such information to the hovering neighbour. Janine already had the name of being flighty, in Bletchbury, a name which had only been stifled because of the local prestige of the Stanhope family.

Finally Stacy rang Miss Agnes again. It was nearing lunchtime, and he could wait no longer. The telephone call yielded only Ethel, who said the sisters were entertaining and couldn't come. She had Coppernob on her arm, and quenched the child's wailing with difficulty. Tersely she gave Stacy the whole story, and

135

mentioned also that they had had a letter from Janine that morning, saying she was staying with a Mrs. Ashley.

The name meant nothing to Ethel, or to the aunts. Did Stacy know such a person? Off-hand, he couldn't connect the name and it was only when Fenella herself mentioned Yvonne Ashley at a later date, that he recalled Janine's mentioning to him while he was still visiting her in hospital. For the moment, however, the name "Ashley" had a somehow sinister sound, because it was strange. Oddly, he connected it with Hugh Torrington, and wondered if she were a friend of his. His old jealousy flamed again, and replacing the receiver, he resolved to leave Janine to her own devices. It looked to him at that stage, that the reason for her visit to London had not been a true one.

He telephoned Fenella, and arranged to spend the week-end at Whitestone House, and went out to fix up new lodgings in the only hotel in the place. He had given no forwarding address because when he left his first digs he had no idea where he would be staying until he reached the town, so he had no means of receiving Janine's letter, giving him her new address, an address she had not yet given her aunts, since she had not known it when she wrote to them. An address which she, Yvonne and Daisy had stumbled on, indirectly, through one of Daisy's innumerable friends; a converted attic at the top of an outside iron spiral staircase, known picturesquely as 13b, St. Botolph's Mews.

CHAPTER IX

JANINE wrote to Stacy and told him of the situation, adding, in a propitiating tone utterly unlike her usual one:

"We, Daisy Jenks and I, found Yvonne Ashley alone in her attic room, looking very ill. The baby wasn't there and we were scared. You remember I told you about her in hospital. They were both very delicate. It seemed that they had kept the baby in hospital and sent her home, and she was fretting. She wasn't even bothering to get herself any food, and she had 'flu coming on. It was a good thing we got there in time."

Janine went on to explain that she hardly felt like leaving Yvonne in that state, and Daisy had to get back to her quarters that night, or run the risk of losing her job—that of a waitress in some sort of club. So she wrote to her aunts to say she would be staying in London the rest of the week. The baby, she felt, would be in excellent hands, left to the care of Ethel.

The letter to her aunts was carefully worded. It painted a picture of a sick young mother who couldn't be left, and of Janine herself, worried and uncertain, feeling all the time that to go back to Bletchbury right away would be the last thing her aunts would wish her to do in the circumstances.

That letter was posted first. It was necessary that the aunts should know in good time.

To Stacy, Janine confided the new address, and how they came across it. But it was not in her limited vocabulary to paint a true picture to him, and when at last the letter did reach him, he had already become acquainted with that address via his bank, whom he had instructed to pay Janine's house-keeping money each month. From habit, Janine went there that first Friday in London, and because her purse was nearly empty.

She and Yvonne had been in the Mews since the Wednesday. A Wednesday of sudden brilliant sunshine, after the grey and wet of the past few days. The attic which Yvonne had shared with her husband for those first few precious months of their life together, suddenly repelled her. The sharp bout of 'flu, checked by the strenuous efforts of Janine and Daisy, had left her depressed. The absence of the baby, and the doubtful reports from the hospital, all had a bad effect on her. She sat about on the verge of tears, and left everything to Janine.

"I don't know why you came," she said, that morning. "I don't know why you should stay here now and look after me! I'm a complete stranger to you. I'll never repay you, I'll never be able to!"

Janine looked at her in amazement. Gone was the quietly happy face that had had such an effect on her in hospital. Yvonne was just like anyone else now, and oddly enough, Janine—who had been so irritated at first by her radiance—was now deeply disappointed. There was an urge in her to bring back that sunshine. She was shocked at the change in Yvonne's appearance, and suddenly decided to try and do

139

something about it.

"We're going out!" she said, briskly, pulling Yvonne up out of the old arm-chair. "Come on, my girl, on with some clothes and make-up, and let's see what we can do with this hair. Doesn't it look dull? What d'you usually do with it to make it shine as it used to?"

Yvonne reluctantly made the required effort, and between them they brushed her long blonde hair, and wound it in a double twist, coronet-fashion, round her small head. Janine chivvied her until at last she said she was ready, but would really rather stay at home.

"Nonsense! A walk in the open air will do you good. Besides, I'm fed up with this place. What made you stay here so long, Yvonne?"

"Oh, I don't know. Memories of George, I suppose. But mostly because I never felt well enough to make the effort to look for something else. I wish you could stay with me all the time. But of course, you can't," she added hurriedly. "There's your husband, and little Coppernob. . ."

Janine was silent. The idea was attractive. She didn't want to go back to her aunts' house, though she wanted the baby with her. If she had good enough reason for wanting to come back to London, she felt sure they wouldn't try to keep her in Bletchbury, but at the same time, she hardly felt like exchanging the big house in the clean country town, for this poky double attic at the top of all those stairs. The place wasn't very clean, and from the lower regions was the perpetual smell of stale cooking, stale tobacco, and something undefined which might have been damp. Janine shuddered.

"If you could get somewhere else," she began, half-heartedly, and Yvonne interpreted it that she didn't want to share a place with another woman, although her husband was away so much.

The sunshine outside hit them in the eyes with its brightness, as they emerged from the gloom of the entrance hall, and for the moment they didn't see Daisy Jenks coming up the dirty white steps.

"'Ere," she began, "where are you two off to?"

"Daisy!" Janine gasped. "Wednesday morning? What's the idea? Why aren't you at work?"

"Got the sack!" Daisy said, triumphantly. "'Ad a row with the old cat, and

walked out on 'er! I'll teach 'er ter tell me
not ter waste 'er time. On'y 'avin' a smoke,
I was! As if a girl can't 'ave a fag between
jobs. . . ."

She trailed off, and the gloom on the
other two faces reflected itself in her own.

"But you've no job now," Yvonne
murmured.

"And nowhere to go, have you?" Janine
hazarded.

"S'right," Daisy agreed, glumly.
"Unless I go back ter my old woman, but
I'll 'ave ter keep 'er in gin if I show me face
there. Where yer goin', you two? I'll walk
with yer. No odds, now. Time's me own."

They walked towards the park, slowly,
and with the air of having nothing to do
and a lot of time in which to do it. They
walked in silence, too, each preoccupied
with her own thoughts. Daisy looked back
on the hot, steaming kitchen, and the cold
bare living quarters, and forward to a bare
future, a future in which she had not even
the slender wage she had just given up.
Yvonne remembered George's parting
injunction that day he had been killed; an
injunction to go out and buy herself a new
hat, as a tonic. She had never bought that
hat. Neither would she now, because his

pension was so small, and the policy money must be invested for Georgina. Janine puzzled over Stacy and the odd way he was acting.

"Funny thing," Daisy said suddenly, pausing by the park pond to stare at the ducks. " 'Ere we are, all three of us. Women without a man, yer might say."

"Women with very little money," Yvonne added, grimly.

"And with nowhere to go," Janine added.

"Well, that's what I mean," Daisy expanded. "Why don't we all find a place an' live in it tergether? Eh? What d'yer say, girls?"

"How can we?" Janine said, impatiently. "Unless we find somewhere mean or shabby, there's nothing we can take on our slender means."

"Oh, I don't know so much!" Daisy was indignant and purposeful. "Take me, fer instance. I chuck jobs, but then I find others quick, like. It's a gift, with me. I'd find a job fer Mrs. Ashley 'ere, if she wanted one!"

"Washing dishes?" Janine said, scathingly. "Don't be silly! Besides, she isn't fit to work. There's the baby, too. It'll soon be out of hospital, won't it, Yvonne?"

"I hope so," Yvonne whispered. "But the idea of working isn't so silly. I mean, if we could get somewhere where we could all live, you and I ... but there's your husband."

"'Ee's gorn orf up North!" Daisy said, shouting, with laughter. "Sorry, ducks, but you must admit it's got its funny side, if yer see what I mean."

"I don't," Janine said, icily. "My husband was sent away by his firm. That's all."

"Then you *are* free, Janine?"

Janine stared. "Yes, I suppose I am. He closed the flat without asking me what I was going to do. But then he thought I'd stay with my aunts. I don't want to go back there. It's dull, among other things."

"We could put the babies in one room, we three in another, and a kitchen-sittingroom ... quite a place. We can't afford it," Yvonne mused.

"I'd pay my share, if I was working," Daisy averred.

"Even if we could scrape up the rent between us, that wouldn't be enough," Yvonne said. "Babies are expensive luxuries, then there's our food, lighting,

144

heating, clothes . . . and furniture. The furniture in the attic isn't my own. We said, George and I, that we'd wait till we saw something we really liked. That day didn't come."

They walked on. Alternative ways lay open to Daisy; a job with a man she didn't like, in a factory, and a job as barmaid in the pub on the corner, near the job she had just thrown up. After a brief struggle, the factory job won. It held the promise of more money, though her man-friend would be a nuisance.

Janine said, "There's the furniture of our flat, at my mother-in-law's place. I paid for half of it. I could get that back . . . I think. It came out of a legacy from my parents. The rest of the money went on my trousseau. Wish I hadn't spent so much of it now."

"We haven't found a place yet," Yvonne reminded her.

They left the park by the far gate, and turned into wide residential streets where large houses had been converted into expensive flats. Commissionaires stood at hall doorways in their bright uniforms and looked superciliously at passers-by, or imperiously beckoned taxis. Nursemaids pushed stream-lined baby carriages towards a small private park marked "For Residents Only". Long-nosed cars purred along the roads.

"I smell money," Daisy remarked, sniffing noisily.

"Makes you feel poor," Yvonne said wistfully.

"'Ere, we could live 'ere!" Daisy said, excitably. "I just remembered. There's a girl wot worked in our place, wot I've just left, an' her aunt cleaned fer a fella wot 'ad a studio, see, an' 'e noo a fella with a posh flat in a mews who wanted someone ter live in it rent-free but ter keep it goin' till 'e come back an' take telephone calls." She paused for breath. The other two stared at her in a pitying way.

"Oh, don't look at me like that, soppy things!" Daisy exploded. "Straight, I mean it! We could live 'ere!"

"Whose flat is it?"

"The fella wot...oh, you got me all in a muddle. I know a girl wot's got an aunt—"

"Yes, you told us all that before. What we want to know is, what's the name of the wolf who wants three nice girls to take over his flat for an unspecified length of time?"

"Eh?"

"I think she means it, Janine," Yvonne said. "I wonder if there's anything in it? Who do we have to see about it, Daisy?"

"Dunno. I could ask Sybil for her aunt's address, though. She'd know."

Sybil smartly gave Daisy the address of her aunt over the telephone, then rang off without saying good-bye.

"The ole cat caught 'er, I expect," Daisy said. " 'Ope she won't get in a row."

They tracked the aunt down, a thin respectable woman who obviously cleaned because she could do nothing else, and was very anxious to help. But she couldn't give the address of the studio because she didn't know it. She could, she said, point it out to them if she came with them. It was a funny place, she said, over the next-door house to the one you went in to get to it. By this time Yvonne was tired, and said she'd go home. She had to go to the hospital that evening, to see the baby.

Daisy and Janine went on with Sybil's aunt. They took a tram, then walked through a mews where posts separated it from the back of a cobbled yard, and through an archway to a wide street of hotels and residential clubs. Then through another archway and down two more narrow streets. Suddenly Sybil's aunt said, "This is it!" in her sad little voice, and dived down some shallow stone basement steps. After countless flights of stairs, they reached the top, and went along a passage lit by little panes of glass in the ceiling, through which the sun blazed in regular shafts before them. The studio was at the end.

The others paused outside. "Is it very posh? What's 'e like, the fella, I mean?" Daisy whispered hoarsely, eyeing the name-plate which read "H. CALLAHAN".

"Oh, 'e's very posh," said Sybil's aunt, sadly.

"Then you go in an' settle it, Mrs. Conway. 'E won't think much-a me, but you talk to 'im—you'll do the trick!"

Sybil's aunt nodded, and took Janine in. "This young lady, sir," she began, with a series of small coughs to excuse her interruption.

A young man at an easel turned and grinned at them.

"Come in, Mrs. M. You're early tonight."

"I 'aven't come to work, sir, not yet that is. I brought this young lady, about the flat
148

in St. Botolph's Mews, that is."

Having made the introduction, she backed out. Janine was left with the artist.

He was a pleasant young man, and chatted easily with her. His friend, he confided, was crazy.

"I don't know why he wants the wretched flat, but there it is, he won't give it up. It's pretty big, you know, for one person to rattle around in. Got someone to clean up for you?"

"There are three of us," Janine murmured, wondering if it would be wise to mention the babies yet, and feeling she'd rather see the place first.

"The Egg and I were at school together," he went on. "He's filthy rich. Never stays five minutes in one place. I daresay you'd do, but you'd better go over and have a look at it. You'll find his mother there. She'll give you the once-over. The Hon. Mrs. Lusty."

Janine was suspicious. It was too good an offer to be true, but he assured her there were no strings. "You'd have to make good any damage you did, of course," he grinned, "and the bill might be pretty high, with the Egg's idea of interior decoration, so go easy."

149

Daisy was waiting outside the house, but Sybil's mother had gone. "She 'ad ter git a bit o' fish, an' a loaf," Daisy explained, "before the shops shut."

"I don't like this flat idea," Janine said, worriedly. "How do we know what we're letting ourselves in for?" She told Daisy what he had said.

"Well, if yer seein' the fella's mother, it *must* be all right. 'Sides, Sybil's aunt wouldn't let us do nothing fishy, she's that straight. She said the bloke she cleans for wouldn't touch nothing what 'ad funny business behind it. Straight, she sez 'e is."

"You're funny, Daisy," Janine mused. "I should have thought you'd be the first to be suspicious of such an offer. But you're going into it nose first!"

Daisy grinned. "I follers me nose. It tells me when there's funny business, an' it tells me when we're on to a good thing, an' that's wot it's sayin' we're on to now!"

"I hope you're right!"

Janine went on to the flat by herself. Daisy said she'd go back and get some tea for Yvonne (whom she persisted in punctiliously calling "Mrs. Ashley" despite the other's begging her to use her Christian name) and possibly go to the

150

hospital with her.

The directions had been given to her, but she took a taxi to make sure of finding the place without loss of time. The West End closed upon her, and as the cab drew up to the entrance to St. Botolph's Mews, Janine told herself with a sinking heart that though they might be able to live there themselves, they couldn't hope to bring the babies.

The Mews was splashed with late sunshine. The outside staircases to upper flats were of gaily painted wood, and scarlet rambler roses growing from tubs had been trained up the balustrades. Latticed windows with expensively simple curtains, winked with their thousand diamond-shaped panes, and silence was over everything. Her shoes rang on the cobbled stones as she disturbed the exclusive air of the place to find the flat she wanted. There was something of the Continental about it all, too; too much colour and old-world charm and quaintness to be part of the West End of London.

There was an iron spiral staircase at the end of the Mews, leading to the top of a small house, whose front faced on to a crescent behind. The back of the house was buff-washed, and beautiful, and at the foot of the spiral staircase, which was painted blue, was a small board, bearing the numbers "13b".

Janine went up and knocked at the blue door at the top. A fashionably dressed woman in her late forties opened the door and said, "Come in, darling, I've been waiting. You're late."

Janine said, "I beg your pardon, I've come about taking the flat over. Mr. Callahan sent me."

The woman smiled vaguely. "That's right. You're Hugh's little friend. Come along in. I'm waiting to go."

Janine followed her in, wondering what the young artist would say to her being described as his little friend.

"Mrs. Lusty, I believe?" she ventured.

"Of course! Now, you're staying the night, aren't you? Here are the keys. Thank heavens I can get away. The dear boy insisted on *someone* being here each night, and really—"

Janine cut in with difficulty, protesting that there must be some mistake and that she had only come to view the place.

Mrs. Lusty stared. "Oh, but my dear, I *know*! But you'll *love* it! It's *marvellous*!

*Nat*urally, since it's my boy's place!"

It was impossible to make her understand. Even when Janine got her to keep quiet while she told her story over again, she could see that Mrs. Lusty wasn't really listening. Her thoughts were all over the place.

"Well, darling, it's a very *funny* story, I'm sure, but then it's bound to be all *right*, or Hugh wouldn't have *sent* you! Now I really *must* go, as I'm late for the party already, then we're travelling all *night*, and I'm not absolutely *packed* yet! Here are the keys, and don't *leave* the place at *night*! 'Bye, now and tell Hugh I think you're *sweet*!"

She was gone in a flurry, and almost before the door had slammed behind her, she was back again, to snatch up her gloves and week-end case which she had forgotten. Then Mrs. Lusty had really gone, and Janine was standing bewildered, with the keys of the flat in her hand, and a sense of being tossed on the wildest of oceans.

The flat was large. There was ample room for the three of them, and beautifully furnished. Janine had misgivings when she thought of the attic where Yvonne was living, and wondered how nappies could be hung out to dry in this luxury place.

There was a ring at the blue door. A girl stood outside holding a milk-bottle. "Mrs. Lusty sent me with it. She forgot—as usual!" She wore an artist's smock, and said she hung out in the flat below. "All alone?"

Janine smiled, a slow smile which committed them all. "No, thanks a lot; there are three of us. The other consignment comes to-night!"

CHAPTER X

ADELAIDE HELSTON regarded Fenella's new friend with undisguised interest, and curiously enough, Stacy didn't resent that interest.

She was a small woman, frail with a long-standing illness, beautiful in features as well as with that ethereal beauty that comes to some women with the pain and suffering of a hopeless ailment. With her beauty, Stacy felt, was intellect, patience, and a rare understanding of her fellow men.

It was from Adelaide Helston that

Fenella got her rich red hair, though her mother's was long, and beautifully dressed in coils round her small head. Her eyes were dark, too, as dark as Fenella's, but there was a different expression in them. Stacy couldn't put his finger on the word he wanted to describe that expression, but it made him feel that though his friendship with Fenella was innocent, what he was seeking from that friendship should have come from someone else; an older person, perhaps? Restlessly, he wondered if Fenella's mother were not the person he was seeking, rather than Fenella herself.

He suddenly wanted to tell Adelaide Helston all about himself and Janine, and to ask her opinion and advice. There were so many people in the room, and the conversation remained general, though the party was split up into small groups. Stacy himself sat by Fenella at her mother's couch-side; Kevin Helston, tall, loose-limbed and slightly stooping, with iron-grey hair, and tired grey eyes, was talking to a dark-faced young man who had been introduced to Stacy as Dr. Mayo. This, then, was Fenella's Richard, and Stacy had to admit to himself that while he himself had instinctively liked the fellow at first sight, he must have been pretty dull to a woman, especially a young, lively woman. Still, both Fenella and he were in the medical profession, and, according to her, had many other tastes in common, so why the fuss? He noticed that Fenella wasn't wearing any sort of engagement ring, and racked his brains to recall if she had worn one the first time he had seen her in hospital. As far as he could remember, she never had. Yet she had said definitely that she was engaged to Dr. Richard Mayo.

There were Dr. Mayo's parents, an aesthetic old man of seventy with silver-white hair, and short-sighted eyes behind thick lenses, and a thin angular woman whose homeliness was belied by a natural charm of manner. And there was Louise.

Stacy was puzzled about Louise Helston. Puzzled because Fenella had only mentioned her the once, and then only briefly, almost as if she disliked her. Yet it didn't seem in keeping with Fenella to dislike anyone.

Louise was fair, ash-blonde. She had wide grey eyes and her father's colouring, and was chocolate-box pretty. She had in addition a flair for colour, and for dress, and had a whole box of tricks such as crinkling her nose when she smiled, biting her bottom lip to reveal tiny even white teeth, hunching a shoulder in a provocative manner, playing with a handkerchief to show off her lovely plump little hands, and peeping up suddenly under her preposterously long dark lashes. Dark lashes that were rather too long and beautiful to have been the unaided work of Nature. Yet with all this, Stacy found himself unable to keep his eyes from the girl. There was a piquancy about her, a juvenile sense of mischief infinitely attractive, and, he considered, rather endearing when you got to know her.

Adelaide Helston watched him. She, too, would have liked an uninterrupted conversation with him, and it was to this end that she manoeuvred.

"Fenella, dear, Kevin has surely had enough of your Richard, and I know he wants to put in some work on his index. Do take Richard into the garden, dear. Your friend, Mr. Conway, will keep me amused, won't you, Mr. Conway?"

Stacy would have liked nothing better, and said so. Fenella raised her brows, but looked pleased. As she complied, Mrs.

Helston nodded to her husband, and with a fleeting smile, he made his excuses.

To Richard's parents, Mrs. Helston said, "Thomas, take Blanche to see the new vines. They're a picture, and I want to make her jealous, so she'll pester you for some."

The old man rose with a twinkle. "Are you ejecting us, Adelaide?" he chuckled. And to Stacy, "Young man, I haven't yet placed you, but I warn you, you're going to be subjected to what the United States police system has labelled a 'grilling'. I trust your conscience is clear!"

Stacy, standing, grinned. He looked much younger than he was, and very much as if he needed taking in hand by such a person as Fenella's mother.

Mrs. Helston smiled at Professor Mayo.

"Of course I'm ejecting you!" she told him. "Only, Thomas, I would call it throwing you out! As to this young man, he can take care of himself, so don't waste your sympathy on him! Off with you, old friend. And don't let him come back too soon, Blanche!"

Used to their hostess, after a lifetime's friendship, and in addition, liable to pander to her every whim, no matter what it was, the old man and his wife went from the room with a smile. Only Louise remained.

"Now, darling," her mother said, with a slight frown, "don't let me have to ask you to go!"

"I'm not going, Mummy," the girl said, with a saucy grin. "I want to hear what you're going to say to Mr. Conway, but more than that, what he's going to say to you! That *is* important!"

"Well, it looks as if you're going to be carried off anyway," Adelaide said, blandly. "Here come the Chatsworths, bless them!"

"Damn!" exploded Louise, momentarily abandoning her naïve air, and scowling, very much as a young baby scowls when feed-time is late but not late enough to produce a howl. Stacy smiled. The girl was really such a baby.

The Chatsworths were five young people round Louise's age, and obviously her close friends and neighbours. Rather noisy but likeable, they trooped in, the two girls bending to kiss Mrs. Helston, the three lads cheerily waving and greeting her, and in the same breath shouting for

159

Louise to go and join them. All in such a
hurry, they were at the door again, bearing
Louise between them, before Stacy had
had time to look at them closely. He had a
confused impression of five young people
amazingly alike, clean-limbed in their
tennis kit, healthily tanned, and as unlike
the kittenish and made-up Louise as could
be imagined.

After they had gone, Adelaide Helston
turned to him with a slight smile of
triumph. He noticed that nothing about
her was very pronounced; all her
expressions, her voice itself, were only half
those of other people, possibly because she
hadn't strength enough to make the full
effort. Yet she probably achieved far more
in the way of results.

"Now, young man," she began. "My
daughter introduced you as a friend from
London. Now that is very vague. Tell me
something about yourself."

Stacy returned her look unwaveringly;
then dropped his eyes to study his inter-
locked hands. Much as he wanted to talk
to her, it was difficult to know how to
begin.

"I think," he said at last, "that our
friendship developed because we were two

people with a problem, a problem that didn't exactly make us unhappy, but, shall we say, robbed us of the capacity to *be* happy."

"My daughter? Fenella?" She raised delicate eyebrows and waited.

He nodded. "It would be betraying a confidence to tell you what her problem is. From my point of view, it's irrelevant, anyway. I merely mentioned it to show you the basis of our friendship. It will never be anything but a friendship on that basis: she's engaged, I'm married."

"I thought so, Mr. Conway. Where is your wife?"

"She *was* at her aunts', down in the Midlands. Now she is in London, living, I understand, with a girl-friend."

"Oh?"

"Don't misunderstand. We're not separated. It's all my stupid fault. I was angry and high-handed, and shut up our London flat without consulting her. When she went back there, it was too late to do anything, so she went elsewhere."

"You have no people in London?"

He shifted uncomfortably. "Yes, my mother, my home is there. But my wife and my mother don't exactly get on together. I don't know why, but there it is."

"And what are you going to do about all this, Mr. Conway?" Adelaide Helston asked gently, her eyes delicately searching his face.

"I don't know." He hardly noticed himself framing the words. His mind was active on the problem of why Fenella hadn't told her mother that she had met him in hospital, when his wife lost her baby. Surely that would be the logical thing? She had had time to say that much, surely, in the week he had been in Cumberland? Now it was for him to say so, yet the subject was too close to mention. Even now, he seldom let himself think of the boy who had never really lived. So he let the opportunity slide by, and was sorry for it later.

"You know, perhaps, Mr. Conway, that my daughter is a nurse in a maternity hospital?"

"I know she is a nurse," he said, and wondered why he had phrased it like that. He didn't want to talk about the hospital, or about Fenella. He wanted to tell this kind, understanding woman all about himself and Janine, and to ask her advice.

They were alone, now, in a quiet, restful room, with presumably unlimited time at their disposal. But he was at a loss to know how to put his thoughts into words, fairly, with no suspicion whatever of bias. In himself, he knew that he couldn't. Essentially, he believed he was right, and it came to him that nothing Adelaide Helston could say to him would be of use, because she'd never be able to get the true picture since only he was in a position to give it, and couldn't.

"My daughter always says that a child is the only solution to a marriage that is tottering. I mention it because I know so many young people shrink from starting a family in these uncertain times, and it is refreshing to find anyone as young as my daughter, believing in the family life."

"Yes," he said, but offered no information. Now is the time, his brain clamoured. Take the opportunity, you fool, or it will look peculiar if she finds out about the boy, and Coppernob! But his tongue was silent. He couldn't make it act.

"Does your wife want children?"

"Honestly, I don't know what she wants," he heard himself say, and in a way, that, too, was true, but didn't by any

163

means present a true and fair picture. He was dealing in slants of the truth, rather than half-truths.

"But you'll try and find out, won't you?" Fenella's mother probed with infinite gentleness, but telling determination. He felt he was being pushed with far greater momentum than he had ever experienced before, and by a woman at that.

He looked at her, enquiringly. He wasn't enjoying the conversation a bit now, and he had thought he would. Yet he was honest enough to admit that it was his own fault. He could have poured out his story, if he'd liked. Now, like a mettlesome horse, Mrs. Helston had taken the bit between her teeth; the conversation was hers, now, to direct as she would, and he found himself wondering if perhaps it wouldn't have been like this anyway, whatever he had said.

"I ask, Mr. Conway, because I am anxious for my daughter's sake. I know that in the ordinary way, Fenella can take care of herself quite adequately. But I am a little alarmed at the way she has reacted to this friendship you offer her; in fact, I am more than a little alarmed at the way she reacts to you! I have watched her since she

164

returned from London. I do not say she is in love with you, but I think that unless you repair your marriage, and soon, she may well be."

He flushed painfully. It wasn't what he wanted, and somehow that made him feel treacherous. If he was arousing such feelings in Fenella, he should at least be aware of them and in a position to reciprocate or at any rate appreciate them. As it was, he had no feelings in the matter, beyond that infinitely satisfying bond their friendship had welded. He had thought that was all that Fenella had wanted from him; now it seemed that against her will, it was not so.

"You see, Richard is almost like a son to me. Since they were children, Richard and Fenella have been closer then most people ever get. It was almost preordained, perfect, this friendship of theirs, that led to courtship, and will, I hope, lead to marriage. Until she met you, Fenella wanted nothing else." Fenella's mother smiled a little. "If she had wanted something else, believe me, I would have been the first to help her, so don't think—as I see you are thinking—that I am a possessive mother, designing my daughter's future and hand-picking the son-in-law of my choice."

He was shocked at the ease with which she read his thoughts; shocked and uncomfortable. Was this what illness did for you, or had she always been an astute and understanding woman? He thought, with schoolboy truculence, that it must be very uncomfortable to have to live with someone like this. Yet he liked her.

"I don't want anyone but Janine," he said irrelevantly, yet with a startling intensity. He was thinking savagely how unfair everything was. If he had had time and opportunity to get around and see life before he had been coerced into marriage with Janine, how different would everything be? Would he have still wanted her? She didn't want him, that he knew. But perhaps if he had had some experience with handling young women, as other men of his age seemed to have had, he might have made a better contact with Janine, probably offered a better substitute for the man she had evidently wanted and not been able to marry. He didn't know. But he was convinced that in Fenella's case the same applied. She should have had other men-friends before allowing herself to be engaged to Richard Mayo.

They were in an ugly position, the pair of them; two young people whom their elders considered were in a hurry to be married, and then discovering they weren't satisfied, whereas it was marriage and ultimate marriage that was showing them that somehow they had both made the wrong first choice. Even now, Fenella was about to make a wrong second choice; if she fell in love with him, Stacy knew he'd never be able to reciprocate, and again she would be frustrated, hurt.

"You don't want anyone but your wife," Mrs. Helston mused, softly. "Aren't you afraid that while you stay so far away from her she may find someone else, or in turn imagine that you are doing the same? Such an absence, with such distance between, has one significance only, you know."

"I can't go back until my firm send me," he said, defensively.

"Not even for a week-end?" She smiled. "Your wife could come up here to see you, surely? If you asked her to?"

"To stay with me in a pub?" He was derisive, to bolster up his own argument.

"No, that wouldn't do, that wouldn't do at all," Mrs. Helston admitted. "But she could come here. I'd love to meet her. I'm sure she'd like to stay with you here for a week-end. How would it be if I invited her to stay?"

He stared. Janine would remember Fenella as the hospital nurse, and heaven knew what construction she would put on the whole thing, and who could blame her?

"Your wife needn't know that Fenella is your friend, and there's no deceit in that! We could be people you had met, who took pity on your loneliness. I think it would be a very good thing, Mr. Conway. What do you say?"

Stacy laughed shortly. "I don't think it would answer," he said, capitulating, and producing another of his near-truths. "You see, my wife knows Fenella, and I don't think she likes her much. You know what women are, how they sometimes don't take to each other."

"I see," Mrs. Helston said, and a little of the friendliness left her face.

CHAPTER XI

THERE was a little delicatessen round the corner of the block which contained St. Botolph's Mews, a quaint little shop kept by an old Belgian known as Papa Omalique. He was quite bald, large and fat, with rolls of flesh billowing out from beneath his chin, and more forming a vast heaving ocean of obesity where his stomach used to be. Over this he wore a very greasy white apron, with one very large patch of grey over the mountain, where it caught against every jutting box, case and jar in his over-crowded shop, and collected yet another layer of dirt. This patch of grey always interested Janine, and she found it hard to keep her eyes from it.

Papa Omalique loved the girls. From the first night they had wandered into his little place, amazed to find it still open, he had become their friend. He liked the acid East End twang of Daisy, the soft blur of Yvonne's tones and the clipped, precise, yet pleasant way Janine had of speaking. He thought them a rollicking, un-English trio, and joyously believed every tall story they pitched for his benefit, and discounted the truth.

They had climbed on to three stools, that first evening, and sat up to his counter nibbling bits of this and that, and counting themselves very lucky to have found any food at all. For the sake of keeping an eye on the flat that wild woman, Mrs. Lusty, had thrust upon them, they had left Yvonne's attic as soon as she and Daisy returned from the hospital visit, and took with them a bottle of milk only, and a few oddments of dry stores. It was when they arrived at the Mews and had wasted a lot of time examining and chortling over the luxury of the place that they realized they had nothing for supper.

"'Ere, t'ain't arf lucky we found this place!" Daisy commented, eating a sandwich which contained for her a beautiful mystery, and which the old Belgian assured her was "his special".

"You have then no home?" he enquired.

Janine looked doubtfully at Yvonne. "Shall we tell him? What do you think?"

Yvonne shrugged. "Why not? What have we to lose?"

Papa Omalique watched the by-play and started to laugh, and when Janine told him briefly and pithily what had happened, he slapped his great belly, and yelled, "Ha-ha, you mad English, I know you! You make de joke, yes?"

His laughter was infectious. They all joined in.

"You are friends, no? Live together, no man, no?"

"How dare you!" Janine said, with mock indignation. "We're respectable married women!" She thrust out her ring finger for his inspection, and the others did the same.

The result was as before. He held his sides and laughed till the tears rolled down his face.

"Ah-ha, you naughty ones, you make pretend, heh? You get those from the sixpenny store, I know you!"

He flashed them a saucy wink from one bulging eye, and laughed some more. It was useless. They joined in the laughter helplessly, and as the days wore on, and they made his shop their rendezvous for food (since they were all rather afraid of doing more than make tea in the streamlined kitchen of the flat, and indeed, none of them knew how the electrical gadgets worked and were afraid to try) it became a rule to tell Papa Omalique a tall story and set him laughing.

Just for fun, they told him their husbands were triplet brothers. This he believed implicitly, and when he asked Yvonne her name and mastered the pronunciation of "Ashley", he called them all that, and sorted them out by referring to them respectively as the brunette, blonde and *blanche* Mrs. Ashleys.

His buxom wife was let into the game, about the middle of that first week. It was, perhaps, unfortunate that she should have heard the rest of the story from Daisy Jenks, whose terse though limited Cockney gave a quite erroneous picture for the woman, who was already primed by her husband to discount everything.

"We all 'ad a baby, see?" Daisy enlarged, as she gathered into her skinny arms two large loaves and a quart bottle of milk. It wasn't possible to impress on Daisy that in this district, if one had to carry stores, it was advisable to decently hide them in some sort of bag or basket. "My pal, the blonde one, 'er's is away. The dark one lorst 'ers, so she took mine, see, an' left it at 'er auntie's."

Mama Omalique nodded at her husband, and laughed until the tears ran down her face. He was right. These three were indeed the droll ones. Daisy's descriptive powers and misplaced words were not helpful. "Away" was not a word to be construed by the fat Belgian woman to mean a frail, ailing baby detained in hospital under observation, neither did the words "took" and "lorst" conjure up the picture of adoption because of straightened means, to replace a stillborn infant. And so she laughed, and her husband laughed, and they looked after the three girls so well that the first week in the flat was not unduly difficult.

Daisy walked through back streets each morning to the nearest point on the tram route, and rode to her new job at the factory. Janine applied her housekeeping money to their food, and Yvonne set aside her pension for what must be a staggering laundry bill, since there was obviously no facilities for even washing and drying their "smalls". Between them, they faithfully dusted the place, and shelved the question of the great rugs. They had taken it on themselves to dismiss the daily cleaner the first day, since her charges were too staggering for their limited resources.

"Besides, we don't want the likes of 'er pokin' 'er nose in 'ere, do we?" Daisy reminded them.

"I'm worried," Yvonne said. "We ought not to have got rid of her. Suppose the owner wants her when he comes back?"

Janine shrugged. "He (or his silly mother) should have made better arrangements. We can't keep any cleaner—we can't afford one, so that's that!"

Daisy whooped with laughter. "Still ain't settled what yore both goin' ter do about the babies, 'ave yer?"

That question stared the other two in the face all the time, but so far they had shelved it. Yvonne was certainly covered, so long as the hospital kept her baby there. Meantime she had had to give up the attic, though the people in the house had let her keep her trunk and boxes there in the cupboard on the landing, till she had a permanent place and could remove them.

Janine nibbled her fingertips worriedly. "I've got till the end of the week. I must go back to my aunts' then, and see what can be arranged. Wonder if they'll keep Coppernob there for a bit? Honestly, we *can't* have her here, can we?"

They stared at each other, helplessly.

Daisy said, "'Ere, I'll lose me noo job if I don't scarper—ta-ta, girls! Be good!"

"Yes, and I'll have to go out and get some more food," Janine said.

But she didn't go at once. This was

174

Friday, and the journey to the
was to be discussed. Someon
arrange to stay in the flat, and l
(for the sake of keeping in
foreman, who had got her the new job)
reluctantly decided to accept his invitation
to spend a day at the sea. So all day
Sunday Yvonne would have to be alone.

"I shan't like it," she said, with a shiver.
"I hate being alone here. It's different from
the attic. There were people in the house,
popping up and down now and again. I
didn't feel so isolated somehow."

"Well, there's Zena underneath us,"
Janine said, with a frown. She was
sometimes uneasy about Yvonne. The girl
looked so frail, and was obviously fretting
about her baby, and her dead husband,
though she said nothing about it.

"Zena's inquisitive," Yvonne said,
briefly. The sunshine Janine had
wondered at, in the hospital, seemed to
have gone for ever, from the girl's face.
Daisy, in her rough way, hazarded a guess
that Yvonne had been building her life on
that baby, and was riding a tide of
happiness when it arrived. That it was
hanging on by such a slender thread to life,
was an almost unbearable anxiety, and the

of being left alone, especially with nothing of her dead husband, forever haunted her.

So it was nearer mid-day before Janine got up to go to the delicatessen.

"Come with me, Yvonne. We might as well get a snack lunch now, while we're about it."

"No, I won't come, Janine. I don't feel like Papa Omalique's nonsense to-day. There's some corned beef left. You go and get some potato salad and tomatoes. And some of his little messy cakes. I'll make some coffee while you're out."

Papa Omalique was disappointed to find only one of them visiting him, and that one in a great hurry. He scowled at the large lady hovering in the doorway, staring so inquisitively. If she was going to buy something, he wished she would come in and get it over, so that he could have a bit of fun with his favourite customer.

"You do not stay so long to-day," he mourned. "Getting tired of old Papa Omalique, no?"

Janine grinned. "Of course not, silly. I'm just in a hurry, that's all. Come on, Papa, look sharp with those things, now!"

He didn't ask where the other girl was,

because the large lady outside was fretting him with her staring, now through the plate glass of his window. Janine glanced up to see what he was staring at, and caught a back view of the woman as she moved away. Because she wasn't expecting to see anyone she knew, Janine didn't recognize Honoria Westlands, who was waiting for her daughter Violet, who had been left by her mother at the smart West End dentist's, and would be picked up later from there by her mother, and carried off on a shopping trip. Violet's wardrobe was still hand-picked for her, and the girl made no attempt to protest.

Honoria Westlands had recognized Janine, however, not because she had expected to see the girl in this district, but because she had an overwhelming interest in everyone, and made a point of staring at people in case she missed anything. Janine was also, at this stage, uppermost in Honoria Westlands' mind, because of her curious disappearance last Sunday. Stacy's mother had talked the whole thing over with her best friend, and both ladies were in a wild fret about it.

Having stumbled on the girl, Honoria Westlands couldn't decide whether to wait outside and confront her, risking failure because Janine would undoubtedly be freezing and give her no information whatever, or to keep out of sight and follow her or make discreet enquiries in the shop.

Papa Omalique, whose voice was as big and imposing as his frame, said, "You vill not disappoint poor Papa Omalique to-night?"

"All right, to-night, then," Janine said, and left the shop with a cheery grin.

Being Honoria Westlands, she mis-contrued. She firmly believed that Janine would do anything that her Violet wouldn't, even to being nice to a tradesman for food. She swept back to the shop, and sailed in before the old Belgian realized she was there, and for effect, started selecting one or two tins of fish.

As she opened her purse, she said, casually, "I think I know the young lady who just went out. Where does she live?"

Papa Omalique frowned. What did this gross, hard-faced woman want with his gay young friend?"

Honoria tried a little guile. "If she is the one I think she is, then I haven't seen her since she was so high," and demonstrated.

"Ah, the image of her mother, she's growing!"

The simple old Belgian beamed. This was different. "Ah, you must mean my Mrs. Ashley, my good friend Mrs. Ashley! I see her often—often she comes to visit old Papa Omalique. I do not know the—what you call it?—address, but it is over there!"

He waved vaguely towards the passage that led through to the Mews, but his action was too vague to be of use to Honoria, and Janine was already out of sight.

"Ah, she is the gay one!" Because this woman was the declared friend of Janine, he treated her to his best saucy wink. "How she deceives old Papa Omalique! Many are the tales she tells him, and how does he know which is true? She has friends—I tell you, they are the gay ones! And I think she has a lover—how else is she so happy? And she lives in the flat of a man, that she has told me!"

He was enjoying himself, acquainting another friend of a joyous bunch of people who brought sunshine into his life. In this grey city, it was like being in his own land to see that trio come gaily into his place, and he wanted this dull-faced creature to see how he felt. It was disappointing for him when she hurriedly paid for her goods and swept out of the shop.

His wife came through. "Ca vache! Who was that?" she spat, staring at the unwieldy back of Mrs. Westlands vanishing round the corner.

Papa Omalique spread his hands in an elaborate shrug. "A friend of our Mrs. Ashley!" he gasped, surprise and dismay struggling for expression over his fat countenance.

Mrs. Westlands went back and picked up Violet, who had a lot to say about her fillings and possible extraction.

"It looks as if I shall have to come up West again, Mother," Violet ventured.

"We shall both be coming up West again," her mother said grimly. "We won't be stopping for shopping to-day. I have to see Mrs. Conway about something, something more important than shopping!"

Honoria Westlands went straight to Stacy's mother, just as she was preparing afternoon tea.

"Well, Honoria, this is a surprise! How do you do, Violet." Stacy's mother was polite, but none too pleased. The Vicar was expected. She liked to entertain the Vicar in the peace of her drawing-room, without the disturbing influence of any of her women friends, particularly Honoria Westlands.

"I have some news for you, Maud. I've found Stacy's wife! Near Violet's dentist. She's living in some man's flat, under an assumed name. Mrs. Ashley! And she's hobnobbing with foreigners to get food for nothing! And what's more, she's going around with a gay crowd—she's already getting talked about!"

She sat down suddenly breathless. Violet stared. She had heard nothing of this. Her mother had made the journey by her side in grim and foreboding silence.

Mrs. Conway received the news quietly. She never betrayed surprise. Honoria Westlands should have known this, and not been so disappointed.

"How did you come by this information, Honoria?"

Mrs. Westlands told the story, with a certain amount of garnishing which didn't help Janine. Violet listened with wide popping eyes. Mrs. Conway listened with composure.

At last, she said, "Well, it's an incredible story, but I can't say I'm surprised. I had no great opinion of the girl when my son first presented her to me. You must go now, Honoria. I've things to do."

"Go?" her friend squeaked. "What on earth for?"

Mrs. Conway tightened her lips. Honoria could be very tiresome at times.

"I've the Vicar coming," Mrs. Conway said, bluntly. "After that, I must consider what to do about Stacy and his wife."

"Well, I thought we could talk it over, Maud. After all, I got the news for you—you'd have known nothing, but for my gift for being observant!"

Mrs. Conway smiled at her friend's way of describing an unfortunate streak of inquisitiveness. "Nevertheless, Honoria, I must ask you to go. We'll have a talk about it some other time. Good-bye, Violet."

"Come along, Mother," Violet said, uncomfortably. She had hated the whole thing. A bit of harmless tattle about Janine, she didn't mind. She didn't like Janine. She never had, since she had been in love with Stacy since her schoolgirl days. But somehow this was going too far. Something would be done about this. It was much more serious than the silly story about Janine and Hugh Torrington, a story which she personally had never believed, but which seemed to go over very well with her elders.

Honoria Westlands swept out, with Violet in tow. She and her mother were literally being thrown out, but, Violet reflected, it had happened before.

The Vicar was ambling along the road. A tubby little man, with a perpetually wondering look, as though his parishioners were always surprising him.

Honoria sailed up to him. "Well, Vicar, I've just missed you, but I couldn't stay. I said to Maud Conway, 'I've just popped in to tell you I've seen that naughty Janine, and you'll never guess where!'"

"Mother!" Violet warned, urgently plucking her mother's sleeve. The Vicar, kindly as he was, would spread the news without even realizing he had said a word.

Mrs. Westlands ignored her daughter. "I've found out she's living in a West End flat, and it isn't *hers*! O-o-oh! What *have* I said? Really, Vicar, I didn't mean that at all—I mean, I'm sure there must be some reasonable explanation, but—well, that's what I *heard*!"

"Oh, there *must* be some other explanation," the Vicar murmured vaguely, racking his brains to recall what it was he had last heard about Janine Conway, and wondering why such a nice girl should be so disliked by her elders.

"Really, mother!" Violet protested, as soon as they were alone again.

Honoria Westlands looked at her daughter sharply. It was nothing new for Violet to say, "Really, Mother!" In fact it was one of the girl's stock phrases. But somehow, this time, it was uttered in a different tone, almost a tone of contempt. And contempt from Violet was something new.

CHAPTER XII

STACY made up his mind not to go to Whitestone House again. Mrs. Helston had said no more to him after that one conversation, and purposely left him in the air. He felt, as she had intended him to feel, that it was up to him to make the next move, and if he meant to stay in her good books, that next move was to contact his wife. She also conveyed to him without putting the thoughts into words, that she intended her daughter to be left alone, free to continue her engagement to Richard Mayo. Any interference from Stacy, however indirectly or unintentional, would not be tolerated by her.

That left him with the coming week-end on his hands. Twice during the week, Fenella had telephoned him. The first time he had answered her himself.

"Don't 'phone me, my dear," he had pleaded. "I'm very busy, and the firm doesn't like personal calls by employees."

"I'm sorry," she had said, humbly almost. "I can't get you at any other time and I did so want to speak to you."

He hadn't answered.

"Can you hear me, Stacy?"

"Yes. Go on."

"I want to talk to you, somewhere private. Where can we meet?"

After a pause, he had said, "I'm too busy in the evenings now, Fenella."

"Well, the week-end, then. Let's go on a ramble or something."

"What will Dr. Mayo think?"

"What he likes." There was a pause. Then, "I've broken my engagement with him. That's what I wanted to talk to you about."

Stacy shifted uneasily. "We can't discuss it over the 'phone. All right, then, to-night."

He arranged to meet her and take her into the big town to dinner. There was a small hotel that they both knew, which she said did nice evening meals, and there was dancing there.

Still at the back of his mind was the thought of the week-end. There was an unformed decision to go to London and have it out with Janine, breaking his journey in the Midlands for a flying visit to her aunts' to collect any address they might have got from her meantime, and any other information about this London visit of hers.

Later that afternoon, Fenella's young sister Louise, rang him. This took him completely by surprise.

"I expect you'll be surprised to hear from me, Stacy Conway," she said. Her laughing voice was earnest now. "I want to see you, about my sister. It's very important really. I'm not going to ask you to meet me this evening. That would be too crude. Instead, I'm going to ask you to see me at your office. Will you?"

"Certainly not, Louise. You know I

can't do that!"

"Oh, yes, you can. If you don't, I'll see your boss, instead. I can, you know. He's a friend of ours. Everyone in this county knows us."

"You wouldn't dare!" Stacy's voice was low and furious.

"Wouldn't I! I happen to know your firm is old-fashioned. The sort of people who don't care to employ a coming accountant who philanders."

Stacy thought quickly. The girl was exaggerating, of course. But he didn't disbelieve her statement that she knew his boss, although he could well believe that his boss merely looked on her as one of the bright kids of county society, and would hardly see her as she threatened. Still, she might make a nuisance of herself if he didn't see her.

"All right, Louise. I get a tea break. I can go out if I like. I'll see you at the little café on the corner, The Blue Bird. Do you know it?"

She did. "Your boss goes to tea soon after you, so you can give me half an hour without his knowing."

He scowled into the telephone. She was right. She knew quite a lot about his boss.

She also knew that his boss didn't patronize The Blue Bird café.

She was there the minute he arrived, and they walked in together. She looked cool and lovely in white piqué, with open chunky sandals and provocative shaped handbag in white suede. Men stared at her and she liked it. She walked well, he noticed, and although she made a great show of her lovely hands, she didn't make the mistake of decorating them with rings and bracelets. Nor did she use nail varnish.

"Now, Louise," he began, with determination, as she poured him a cup of tea, "what is it you wanted me about?"

"Sugar?" She smiled prettily at him.

"No, no. I don't take sugar. And if you haven't said all you want to by the time my tea-time's up, I'm afraid I shall walk out on you. I'm warning you!"

"You're rude." She stared wide-eyed at him. "Rude and definitely working-class, yet my sister's crazy over you. I wonder what it is about you . . . yet there is something. Yes, I'll hand her that. You've got something. . . . "

He flushed angrily. "Now look here—" he began, but she cut him short.

"My sister's broken her engagement for

you. I told her she's a damned fool. Poor old Richard's dull as can be, but he's our kind. He's got money. What's more, Stacy Conway, he's got his freedom. You haven't. Are you going to get it for my sister?"

"Heavens above, child, does your sister *know* you're seeing me? Has she any idea of what you intended to say to me? I'll bet she'd tan your seat if she knew!"

"Adult blustering," Louise said, calmly, and smiled at him, a lingering soft smile. "Of course she doesn't know. Of course she'd pitch into me if she did. But you're not going to tell her. Neither am I. We're going to be much more canny. Besides, what good would it do? It's too late for anything now. Know why? She's chucked up her hospital job, too. All for you! Now what d'you say?"

He stared. "I don't believe it!" he said at last. That first conversation with Fenella, the day he met her in the park, came back to him. She didn't seem to want to give up her career then, and that was the last day she spent at the hospital. Her two weeks' leave were nearly up. She should soon be going back. Why this sudden change?

"Mummy's furious. She upset herself

and the doctor had to come and give her a sedative. She says it's your fault. It is, too, you know."

"And your father? Is he going to get out his horse-whip?" Stacy asked, tartly, well aware that Louise was enjoying herself very much, but he was unable to see what was behind her move in telling him all this.

"Kevin isn't in this world, poor man," Louise said sadly. "Give him a book or another professor to talk to, and he forgets he's got any daughters, let alone the fact that their honour happens to be at stake."

"Well, it's nice to think that only one of your parents is after your blood. From what I saw of your mother, I formed the opinion that she was too astute to attribute such wickedness to an ordinary fellow like me." He studied her. "What would you say if I were to tell you I'd made up my mind not to see your sister again?"

"What about your meeting with her to-night?"

"Oh, you know about that, do you? What did you do? Tap the telephone?"

"No, Fenella told me herself. She also told me what she wanted to see you about. That's something you don't know. But I do, and that's why I came to ask you not to see her again."

After a short, and rather puzzled silence, Stacy said. "You know, Louise, I can't make you out. I should have thought you'd have better sense than to act like a schoolgirl and come to plead for your sister. Fenella can take care of herself. Besides, though you won't believe it, what there was between us was just a rather nice friendship. It arose out of a bereavement, my bereavement. Did she tell you that?"

Louise shook her head.

"Well, Louise, I can't think why she didn't. It's no use my telling you now—as you say, it's too late. Your sister seems to have done one or two rather wild things, such as chucking her job and her fiancé, who seemed to me to be a decent fellow. As for me, I'd made up my mind to see my wife this week-end. I told your mother I would, if I remember rightly, or at least, I gave her to understand I had it in mind. You take in what I'm saying, young woman, because I'm not saying it for fun. There's no reason why I should explain things to you. The fact is, you're a little firebrand who'll do quite a lot of damage if I don't."

"I think you're marvellous, too," Louise

said, dreamily. "I think I'm going to pinch you from my sister Fenella."

At that point, Stacy's patience gave out. He felt if he stayed a minute longer, he'd take her over his knee and spank her. He got up, paid the bill hurriedly and stalked out.

Louise smiled a soft little kitten smile of satisfaction. "Yes," she told herself, "I think I'm going to pinch him, for myself."

Stacy irritably resumed work, and kept at it hard to get done before he left for his meeting with Fenella. He was irritated particularly because she had told her sister (or had she?) what the subject of the meeting was, and hadn't told him. He was irritated too, by Louise's own intervention. He wanted to wipe out the memory of that frustrating half hour with the child. Furthermore he was irritated because he could feel he was fascinated over Louise. He supposed that most men were. You couldn't help being fascinated by her.

His irritation rose to boiling point when he saw that it was not Fenella who waited in the lobby of the hotel, but Louise again. Louise in yet another outfit; a soft deep blue suit, with a little skull cap of blue

192

sequins.

She was sweetly contrite. "Stacy, I *had* to come, to tell you not to wait for Fenella. She decided not keep the date at the last minute, and I did happen to be coming into town, so I thought . . . well, you're too nice to be let down like that, despite what I said this afternoon!"

He stared. "How do you know Fenella altered her mind?"

She shrugged. "I saw her going off with some of her friends, with tennis rackets. She called to them that she wouldn't be going out for the evening after all, and pelted after them, so . . it rather looks like it, doesn't it?"

He was annoyed. He hadn't wanted to see Fenella that evening, but having put himself out to keep the date because she had made it difficult for him to refuse, he wasn't pleased at her running out on him. Who did she think she was, he asked himself, angrily. But the old bond he had felt between them still tugged, and he found himself feeling rather hurt that she could do this to him.

"Oh, well, now you're here, and seem to be got up for the evening—" he began, ungraciously.

"Oh, I was only going to drop in on the gang, only Mother likes me to dress decently, even for a casual evening out. I needn't go and join the others—we just move about in a crowd. Nice arrangement," she laughed.

"Right. Well, this is where we were going to eat, so in you go."

Louise turned to go in with him, when he stopped and looked back across the road with a frown. Fenella was stepping off the curb to cross over. She saw him with Louise, and her face was suddenly flooded with colour, which as swiftly drained away, leaving her pale and furious. After a second's hesitation, she turned and walked back towards the garage, where she had left her small two-seater.

Stacy swung round on Louise. She, too, was staring prettily perplexed. "Well, so she thought better of it. What's she playing at?" She sought his eyes with as innocent a pair of wide blue ones as he had ever seen. "Aren't you going after her, Stacy?"

"No," he said, savagely. "I'll be damned if I am!"

Spending an evening with Louise was a rather different matter from spending one with Fenella. Louise, young as she was, had more skill than her sister for making an evening go by too quickly. She didn't make the mistake of talking about Fenella, nor about her family or friends. Instead, she told him about the county, the things one could do, the history and traditions, and the places where one could have fun. Fun, he decided, savagely, was the ruling word in her life. Yet he was envious of the young people she mixed with, because gaiety and goodwill were also keynotes of their existence.

With infinite care, Louise worked round to what she personally liked, and then what he personally liked. She got him talking, against his will, of the things he had done before he met Janine. Staggeringly, she proved herself to be no mean linguist, and captivated him with stories of their holidays abroad. Stacy, who had always wanted to travel, was caught unawares, and found himself completely unbent, and laughing at the things she was saying.

Suddenly, with a rapier thrust, she sprung a question about Janine, catching him completely off his guard.

"What's your wife like, Stacy?"

"Well, I'm not very good at describing, to tell you the truth . . ." he began, before he realized that he need not have answered the question at all.

"Have you got a picture of her?"

"No," he said, rather shortly, and averted his eyes.

"Oh, it doesn't matter," Louise said, airily, getting out a cigarette. "I just wondered what she looked like. I can form a pretty good judgement of other women by their photographs. Anyway, she must be a bit of an ass to risk losing you by keeping you working at your dull job when you want to be off and away all the time. If I were married to a man with an itch to travel, I'd say, 'Let's clear out together, and have *fun*!' I wouldn't care if it were on foot, or in an old army lorry, or a broken-down tub — I'd enjoy it, whatever it was!"

Stacy was startled. That was what was different about Louise and Fenella. They had that something that wasn't unbending, as was Janine's nature. They had both been educated abroad, and had been widened, almost made cosmopolitan in experience if not necessarily in outlook. Janine was a country-town girl, as narrowly brought up as they came. To travel, even by regulated tour, would have shocked and worried her beyond belief. That much Janine herself had given him to understand in the days of their courtship, when he had suggested a honeymoon in Paris.

He wondered what Janine would have said to their living abroad, or at least his taking a job out of England. But his wondering got him nowhere, for he recalled with sadness that that was half the trouble; Janine didn't even know that he wanted to work abroad. She had never asked him, and he had never brought himself to tell her of his ambitions and restless longing.

He didn't know what Louise hoped to get out of that evening. All it did for him was to cement the half-formed decision to go and see Janine that week-end.

Fenella telephoned the next day, but he wouldn't answer it, and told the tele-phonist to say he had been sent away on another job.

She wrote to him, and he received the letter the next morning: "I'm going away. Evidently your friendship isn't as valuable as I thought it was. I should have known that any woman would do, to take your mind off your wife. But why pick on a baby like my sister?"

It was a little letter of bitterness, hurt. She said she had broken off her engagement, not for Stacy's sake, but because she was honest enough to admit that she couldn't go on with it. She had thrown up her nursing career because she was tired of helping to bring other people's babies into the world, and she didn't think she was a very good nurse, anyway.

Stacy felt oddly guilty. He thought of Adelaide Helston and the vague Kevin; nice people, both of them, but what an awful pity that they should think he was the cause of their daughter's actions. They had imagined her settled for a not-too-distant wedding, and a successful nursing career. Odd, the way he seemed to upset people's lives, the minute he appeared.

He ·hurried through his work on the Friday, to dash back to the inn to pack. As he strode through to the little stair-case, the landlord called to him: "There's two ladies in the parlour for you, sir."

Stacy went to the little best room of the inn, and without being conscious of the thought, knew that one of the ladies was assuredly his mother. Afterwards, he

198

wondered why he hadn't thought of Janine's two aunts, but he hadn't. He knew one of the ladies would be his mother.

She sat in one of the straight-backed chairs, disapproving the inn, the county, the firm who had sent her son there, and the wife who should have been with him and wasn't. Stacy read all this in her face, before he turned to his sister.

"This is an unexpected pleasure," he heard himself saying stiffly. They would make him late for his train. They would wring from him the information he didn't want them to have: what he was going to do with his week-end. He perceived his week-end contacting Janine was becoming less definite with every minute.

"We've got something to tell you!" Merrill said, her face no longer one big smile, but straining with eagerness.

"Be quiet, Merrill. I'll do the talking," her mother said. "Stacy, if I weren't such a good mother, I wouldn't have made this journey," she began.

"Why *did* you make this journey?" he asked patiently. She waved him to silence. She would, as he well knew, take her time, and tell the story in her own way. He sat down, and was too nettled to light his pipe. After an unsuccessful attempt, he put it away again, and sat with tense whitened face to hear what his mother had found to bring her all the way up North.

CHAPTER XIII

" 'ERE," Daisy said breathlessly, bursting into the Mews flat on the Friday evening. "My chap's takin' me ter Ramsgate Sunday. 'E wants me ter go termorrer an' stay the night—would you?"

She broke off sharply and looked from Janine to Yvonne and back again. Yvonne stared blankly but Janine snorted.

"Please yourself, but I wouldn't!"

"No, 'tis a bit of a risk," Daisy admitted, without much regret in her voice.

"You don't like him much, do you?" Yvonne asked gently. "You're not afraid of him, are you?"

"Lor-luv-yer, no, gel! Not of 'im, that is, though I don't like 'im much, see? No, it's me own old man I'm scared of. If 'e was ever ter see me with this new bloke, well, there's no tellin' what 'e'd do, 'e's such a—well, you know what I mean. (I nearly swore!) But 'e'd knife Charlie, straight, 'e

200

would, an' Charlie's bin a good chap ter me, gettin' me the factory job an' all. Got me a rise ternight, 'e did! 'Ere, now I can give a bit more into the 'ousekeepin', from now on! 'Ow's that?"

Janine said, "Oh, it's all right. We're managing. But about that husband of yours, why don't you get your freedom? He deserted you, didn't he?"

"'Ave ter wait three years, ducks, fer that, an' anyway, I don't know as I want ter be free, not all that much. See, if I was free, I'd 'ave ter marry Charlie. I wouldn't 'ave no more excuses, would I?"

"Don't you want to marry Charlie?" Yvonne asked with a smile, as she thoughtfully hung fresh washed stockings over a towel on the heated chromium rail.

"No, can't say as I do," Daisy said, thoughtfully. "'E's all right ter go ter Ramsgate with, but marry—well, I dunno!"

"So you'll be home all day to-morrow?" Janine hazarded, wondering whether she ought to go and get her ticket for Bletchbury or wait till she got to the station.

"Oh, no, I never said that," Daisy protested. "We're goin' ter the Zoo

201

termorrer, if we don't go ter Ramsgate before Sunday. Don't often get a Sat'dy orf, so I've gotta make the best of it, 'aven't I?"

"Well, will you mind being all alone tomorrow, Yvonne? I must do a bit of shopping," Janine said, "and I suppose I'd better fix up for the train. I always manage to get late at the last minute and catch it by the skin of my teeth. Better take no chances or I may decide not to go at all!"

"Yerse, don't let anyone think you're dyin' ter git yer mitts on my kid again, will yer?" Daisy jeered, with a not unfriendly grin. "Fer two pins I'd rather that ole girl o' yourn brought 'er up than you! Fine mother you'd make!"

It didn't hurt any more, to be tormented like that, Janine reflected. Or was it because it was Daisy who was teasing her, old Daisy who had been in bed beside her, in strong labour, so soon after she had borne her own child? Curious, the strength of a friendship made under such circumstances.

"Well, I must go, much as I'd rather not," Janine said, ruefully. "I can't impose on Ethel any longer, though I expect she's getting attached to Coppernob. That child of yours has a way with her, Daisy Jenks!"

Yvonne watched them go; first Daisy, got up in her gayest finery, for a sweltering day among the animals, with her Charlie in close (and rather domineering) attendance. Then Janine, neat in her old and much-pressed navy suit, and much-polished leather court shoes, off to buy a railway ticket for a journey she would have given a lot not to have to make.

Yvonne shut the blue door with a sigh. Little Georgina made no progress at all, and the hospital authorities had cut the visits down to every other day. An inner voice told her that the child wouldn't thrive. She blinked back the scalding tears, and went round the flat, touching things, straightening velvet cushions, dusting expensive ornaments—anything, anything to take her mind off her own affairs. Least of all the insecurity of her life was worrying her beyond measure. The child, all she had left of George, was slipping quietly away, despite the hospital's assurances that once the little one had "turned the corner", it would be all right.

It was because of the turmoil of her thoughts, and the fierce battle she was having to keep tearing herself back from the pit of anxiety that eternally yawned ahead of her, that Yvonne felt no fear when she found she wasn't alone. In a dazed way she stared up at the big young man standing by her, and she waited for the next development rather than tried to remember who he was. In silence they stared at each other, and he was the first to speak.

"My mother said you were a lovely little thing. She was right," he said, quietly, and there was an unbelieving look in his eyes. He stared as a man stares who cannot drink in enough of what he is looking at.

Yvonne flushed. He realized he was embarrassing her, and turned away, embarrassed himself. "Yes, young woman, I didn't really come to say that. I came, instead, to ask what you meant by taking possession of my flat. Suppose you do some talking?"

She watched him put his hat and stick on the hall table, and come back and sit down in one of the deep arm-chairs with every appearance of a man thoroughly at home. Undoubtedly this was his place.

"Oh, dear, I wish the others were here," Yvonne said, worriedly. "I knew it couldn't be right—we all did, but what could we do? Your mother wouldn't listen, and she said we weren't to leave the place at night, so we had to stay. We didn't know where to get hold of her—she said she was going away that night, so—"

"Wait a minute," Mrs. Lusty's son interrupted. "Let's get this clear." He fastened on what was for him an essential point. "What do you mean by 'the others'? How many of you are there, for heaven's sake?"

"Three of us. Oh, we're being terribly careful. Hugh sent us, so it's all right."

"Hugh?"

Yvonne wondered if she'd done the wrong thing in mentioning the young artist, and wondered too if she shouldn't have started a cycle which would undoubtedly drag in Daisy's friend and the old cleaner aunt. She hoped they wouldn't get into trouble, but little by little (being Yvonne, and deadly honest) the story trickled out.

"Well, 'H. Callahan', but your mother called him 'Hugh'," she explained carefully.

"Oh. I see." His face cleared, and he started to laugh. "Well, let's see what damage you've done to my property."

"Oh, we haven't done any damage. I keep everything clean while the others are out shopping and at work."

The big young man strode around, and after a thoroughly intensive search, he appeared to be satisfied, and came back to the arm-chair.

"Tell me about yourself," he directed, noting Yvonne's wedding ring and little work-worn hands.

"There isn't much to tell," she said, but because in some odd way she felt it was owing to him, she gave him the briefest of details of her husband's accident, and the baby.

"So you see, there's nowhere else for us to go, unless I go back to that awful attic, though I don't think I can go back there now."

"And the other two young women?"

"They're both living apart from their husbands, and both had a baby. One lost hers and adopted the other's. It's funny we're all in the same boat, isn't it?"

"Except that you're free," he murmured. "Well," he continued, briskly, "you can't stay here, that's obvious. Besides, I want to come back here myself. I expected," he said, heavily, "to find a girl-friend of mine holding the fort. She seems to have let me down pretty badly. I'll catch up on her later. Meantime, you three will have to have somewhere to go. By the way, where's the other baby? Don't say you've had it up here?"

She smiled his alarm away. "Oh, no, it's with my friend's aunts, being looked after while she was looking for a flat in London."

Relief swept over his face. "Thank heavens for that! I suppose there isn't any food in the place?"

"No," she said, regretfully. "We usually eat out, at Papa Omalique's."

"*Who*?"

"The delicatessen round the corner."

"Oh, that old busybody! You be careful of him, he gossips like an old woman," the young man warned her. "Are you hungry?"

She nodded.

"Then come and have a bite with me. I know a decent place. Put on your hat, while I start up the car."

She protested, but he bore her off. Evidently he was a young man used to having his own way with his women friends, she reflected, and used the same tactics with everyone. He took her to a small Hungarian restaurant where the head waiter obviously knew him and gave him a great deal of attention.

"Now look here," he said, after he had given the order, and wine had been brought. "I'm going to find somewhere for you three girls to go. I owe it to you for the appalling mess my mother made of things. She *will* keep on talking, and never stops to think. She's always getting into trouble for it. Still, most people are like that, aren't they?" he grinned.

"Yes, but you don't have to—" Yvonne began, wondering what on earth this mad young man was going to propose.

"What's your name?"

"Ashley," she told him.

"What else?"

"Yvonne," she said, with reluctance.

"All right, Yvonne, how'd you like a big flat where the infants could be accommodated as well as your two friends?"

He laughed aloud at her hesitation.

"Oh, come on, it's all above board! I'm not a wolf, even if I look like one! Better take my offer, because you're all going out of my place to-night, so that I can move in!"

"No, thank you," Yvonne said, with tightened lips.

"You'd better talk it over with your friends first," he warned, attacking his meal with appreciation, as though the settling of three young women in another flat was to him an everyday affair. "They may not be so squeamish."

"They're quite respectable!" Yvonne said, stiffly, her delicate skin flushing with anger.

"Now look," he said, suddenly serious. "I'm not doing this with ulterior motive. It's simply that I've suddenly remembered a friend of mine who deals in flats. He's got a big one on his hands in the suburbs. It's too big for the average family, but for sharing it would be ideal. You could all contribute. He says it's a white elephant, and he'd be glad to have it taken off his hands. You'd all be glad to get a place of your own. Now, what about it?"

He had, he said, little to do with the rest of the day, so he spent the afternoon persuading her, via a walk round the park, tea in a Chinese restaurant, and, if she hadn't protested, dinner.

"No, really I can't. I must get back.

The others will be wondering where I am!"
Then she remembered that Daisy wouldn't
be back. Janine would be there alone, and
there was nothing to eat.

"Well, go back and tell your friend, then
come with me and see the flat. I'll collect
my car."

Yvonne broke away thankfully,
yet—honest as always—she had to admit
that it hadn't been unpleasant at all. "How
funny," she mused, "this must have been
what I've been needing all the time. I feel
almost well again. A little fun, with a man
who likes you. (I know he likes me though
he only met me to-day.) I ought to be
worried about my baby, but I feel now it's
going to be all right. That's what a bit of
fun does for you."

She wondered what Janine would say,
and reflected that she might come in for
some teasing, at least from Daisy. But
Janine wasn't there. A hastily scrawled
note said she had had to go out again, to
collect her things from the cleaners as they
hadn't been ready when she had called.

Yvonne experienced disappointment.
She had wanted to tell Janine. She found a
pad and pencil, and wrote: "Back later.
Lots to tell you. You'll never credit what's

happened. Sorry about the food," and forgot to sign it.

"Like the flat?" the young man asked, as he drove her back to the Mews that night. They had dined at seven, gone out to the suburb and looked the place over, in company with his friend the surveyor, who had the key. They reckoned they had done well to get back to the Mews by eight-thirty.

"It's a dream," Yvonne said. "I wonder what Janine and Daisy will say?"

"Janine?" he frowned.

"Yes, Janine Conway. That's the one who lost her baby and adopted the other one," she explained. She was happy to-night, happy with the old quiet joy that Janine had not seen in her face since the hospital days. It almost seemed a possibility to Yvonne that one day, not too far distant, the hospital authorities would tell her that she could take little Georgina home, and that there was a reasonable chance of the child growing fat and strong like other babies.

She chatted happily, and only when he braked sharply outside the Mews entrance did she realize that something was wrong. His face was set, and the friendliness of all day had gone.

"D'you mind waiting in the car while I go up to the flat? I'll see if your friend's back, and if not, we'll go for a spin."

"Oh, but I'd rather come up now," Yvonne protested.

"Please. I'd like you to wait here, if you don't mind," he insisted, and turned sharply away.

She watched him, puzzled, as he strode through the Mews to the spiral staircase at the end. He opened the blue door and closed it behind him with a final snap. Yvonne stared, and quite unaccountably felt shut out. What had happened? She traced back to the time when she had last seen him smile. "Just before I mentioned Janine," she told herself, wonderingly.

Janine had just got in and was reading Yvonne's note. She had had a snack at Papa Omalique's, and had been irritated more than usual by the old Belgian's friendliness, which sometimes amounted to frank curiosity, and sometimes descended to mere fatuous remarks that were no longer funny.

To-night, he had made her rather anxious. "You see your ole friend, the fat woman, yes? I send her to you—she say

212

she like you so much! He gave a fair imitation of Honoria, but Janine missed the connection, and had no idea whom it could be, but was worried, nevertheless. She knew of no one who thought as highly of her in London as Papa Omalique made out the fat woman did.

In the letter-box behind the blue door had been a letter from Aunt Bee. Janine had stopped to read it before going into the lounge and discovering Yvonne's rather obscure note. Aunt Bee said that Stacy had telephoned, but on being told of Janine's London trip, he had not asked for any more details on the telephone, nor communicated with them again.

She was more disappointed than she thought she could have been. Stacy was looming larger in her thoughts as the days wore on, and this artificial existence began to pall. She had, all day, been playing with the idea of getting his address from his firm and going to see him. The only thing that stopped her from this course was that his employers would then know that he was not living with her; one of the things they insisted on was that their employees had a happily married background, or that they were at least living happily at home. "A happy employee is a good employee" was their pet slogan.

Could she be happy again with Stacy? Could they patch it up? Worriedly she faced the fact that sooner or later she would have to try, even if he weren't willing. Then the cause of the quarrel loomed up again before her, and she knew she wouldn't be able to endure a jealous Stacy. If only he had asked her what that old story was all about! If only she hadn't been so furious and walked out on him, she would have told him, but it was doubtful if he'd have listened, in the mood he was in. Misunderstandings . . . could they ever be wiped out, in marriage?

She grappled with Yvonne's note, but scarcely took in what it said. Sooner or later she would have to take Coppernob over again, and deep as her feelings were for that poor, unwanted lump of a child, she was convinced that a father was even more necessary to her than a mother. She had her own mother, anyway, and the three women in the Stanhope house, but it was Stacy who should be there with her, from the beginning, or the home background which Janine had wanted for her would be lacking from the first, as it had been with Janine herself. Brought up by women .... Janine shuddered.

The door opened, and she said, without turning, "A fine sort of note to write me, Yvonne? What on earth does it mean? Call this being explicit?"

"Janine!"

She stiffened, and stood for a minute unbelieving, before spinning round to face him.

"Janine Stanhope! No, it's Conway now, isn't it?"

She whispered his name, and didn't move. He walked slowly over to her, reflecting how marriage and motherhood had altered her. She was plumper now, older a little, yet in an attractive way. What was it he had said to her, in those far-off days? All promise but no fulfilment. Well, this was the fulfilment. She was no longer, as he had once known her, a sweet lost child, but a woman who knew what she wanted.

He said slowly, as though hardly noticing what he was saying, "Your friend said 'Janine', and I knew there couldn't be two of you. I had to come and see for myself."

She didn't answer, but looked up at him

as a drowning man fastens his eyes on the rescue ship. She said to herself, "This is why I can't go back to Stacy. This is why I can't ever love Stacy."

"It's funny, Janine. Not long ago I protested to your husband, at his mother's house, that I wasn't the wolf in his camp. Now, by the damndest, silliest coincidence, here you are, right square in my path again. What am I going to do with you?"

"What do you want to do with me?" she whispered.

"Spank your seat and send you back to your husband, but you're too grown-up for that now. Didn't you *know* whose flat this was?"

She said, without anger, without any feelings at all, but still in that dazed voice, "Mrs. Lusty said—"

"Didn't you know she was my mother? I thought everyone knew she'd married again. She *will* be disappointed!"

"I didn't know," she whispered.

"No. Of course you didn't. I remember now—you never met my mother before. Well, now look here. I'm not going to risk upsetting the Conway camp—that'd be too tiresome for words. I'm going to get you out of here, quick! I've got a place for all three of you, I'll tell you about it later. But what I need most is a drink. It'd do us both good. Hold hard, I'll get some glasses."

He walked through to the gleaming kitchen, and over the chink of bottles and glass, she heard his voice come cheerily back: "I don't like the past rearing its familiar head at me without warning, do you?"

She didn't answer. There was a short silence, while he wrestled with the cork in a fresh bottle, and rummaged for a syphon in the deep cold cupboard which so far the girls had only peeped into but not dared to touch. Into the silence came Mrs. Conway, with Merrill and Stacy.

Janine watched, fascinated, as they charged in without knocking. How like them, to find the door open and use it! Stacy hung back. He obviously didn't like this at all. But his mother was too furious to consider the delicate point of good manners.

"There she is! I told you you'd find her here!" she said triumphantly to Stacy. To Janine, she said, "How can you have the nerve to stand there with that innocent expression on your face?"

Stacy said unexpectedly, and in a tired voice, "This isn't my idea, Janine. When my mother's finished, I'd like to speak to you, alone."

Janine still stood, hands flat down on the table, where she had been leaning reading Yvonne's note. She felt that if she stood up and relinquished the support of the table, her legs wouldn't hold her. For her, there were no women in the room. Just Stacy, looking more tired, lifeless, and rather older than before; and in the kitchen that other man, who was even more bursting with life than when she had known him years ago. One of them wanted her, but it was the wrong one.

Tears were near the surface, not for herself nor for Stacy, but for the curious twisted way in which Life spun itself out for them. She supposed that somewhere at some time there was some woman eating her heart out for Stacy, as she herself had always done for Hugh. It was so wrong that she herself was thinking of ways and means to go back to Stacy for any other reason than because she loved him. How could she go back to Stacy at all, now, while there was Hugh?

Stacy's mother never stopped talking, but what she said was extremely to the point. She evidently was certain that Janine was living there with Hugh. Merrill was of that opinion as well, but her feelings were mixed because she had fancied she had made a conquest where Hugh was concerned.

Janine said suddenly, "Yvonne, don't stand in the doorway; come on in!"

Yvonne advanced with hesitation. "I hope I'm not intruding," she said, nervously. "Mr. Lusty said I was to wait in the car for him, but there was something I wanted to get from my other handbag. I left it in the bedroom. Excuse me," and she hurried past Stacy's mother, who was frankly staring.

"His name isn't Lusty!" she said, suddenly, recovering herself, and raising her voice for Yvonne's benefit. "It's Torrington!"

"But she didn't know that," Hugh said blandly, from the kitchen doorway. "Which just shows how innocent the whole thing is."

CHAPTER XIV

LOOKING back on that scene afterwards, from the security of the flat which Hugh had found for them, Janine found it difficult to believe that it had all really happened.

For the first time, she realized how little she had told Yvonne and Daisy about her affairs. The few brief words she had used to describe the situation must have grossly misrepresented the position to Yvonne at least.

"I wish you had told me before," she said to Janine that night while they were alone together. "But, of course, it was your own business."

"Oh, it's not that. I just didn't think you'd be interested," Janine said, but it wasn't entirely true. If she and Yvonne had been living together, without the added and rather disturbing presence of Daisy, it might have been different. Yvonne was understanding, and had a nice sense of what was fitting. Daisy, on the other hand, had an extremely crude sense of humour, which often jarred horribly. She was a good sort, but not the one to entrust with one's unfortunate personal story.

Now, however, it was necessary to tell Yvonne what was behind it all, although she didn't ask. She had looked puzzled, distressed, and hurried out again after getting what she had wanted.

"Don't go, Yvonne," Hugh said. "You're in this too. I want you to tell Mrs. Conway who's been living in this flat lately. You see, she is Janine's mother-in-law, and the gentleman behind her is Janine's husband."

"I don't understand," Yvonne said, looking distressed. "I knew you'd be wild when you found out, but I didn't think it concerned anyone else, us three being here, I mean. We had nowhere else to go."

"Three?" Stacy came forward, and looked interested.

His mother snapped: "Poppycock! She's been put up to it, primed with a story, and made a nice entrance just at that minute."

"You're disappointed, aren't you?" Janine asked her mother-in-law softly. "Three girls living together doesn't make such a good story as the one you wanted to hear."

"Janine!" Stacy shot angrily at her.

"Let's keep the personal out of this. Torrington, if that's true, then we owe an apology. But I must say the whole thing sounds very peculiar to me, and I had to come and find out, my mother having told me what she'd heard."

The two men faced each other; Stacy stiff and furious, Hugh grinning easily, but obviously none too pleased. The women talked. Stacy's mother reiterated that she didn't believe it; Merrill kept saying that as soon as Stacy mentioned that Janine's present address was 13b, St. Botolph's Mews, she knew at once that it was Hugh's place; Yvonne tried her best to explain, but the other women talked her down.

Janine only was silent. She was watching Stacy and Hugh. Stacy was agitatedly filling his pipe, and Hugh was lighting a cigarette. Hugh started to explain, in an easy, matter-of-fact voice, how his mother had added to the muddle, and gave the story of the artist and the cleaner as he had had it that evening from Yvonne. Little by little the others quietened down and listened, also, but Janine still stood, an unreal figure, listening and looking, but contributing nothing further beyond that one bitter comment to her

222

mother-in-law.

Hugh made some stiff drinks and passed them round. Stacy's mother refused, and further refused the tea which Yvonne offered to make. After that, Stacy with determination put an end to that unreal and embarrassing scene, by requesting his mother and sister to go, as he wanted to talk to his wife.

"I won't go, until I know for certain why she didn't come to me in the first instance, Stacy!"

"Mother, now is not the time. You can talk to Janine about that later. Janine, where can we go for a quiet talk? There are things we have to settle."

Hugh said, "Stay here. I'll run your mother and sister down to the station. Yvonne was coming with me anyway. I'll be back later to see what you've decided."

Yvonne set the example by getting out quickly. She thought Stacy looked a very nice young man, and hoped sincerely that he and Janine would make it up and go a long way away from his nasty mother and sister. She was genuinely sorry that somehow they hadn't managed to patch it up at all, and that Janine had decided to come and share the flat with her and

Daisy. That was all right if you had no husband or home of your own, but apparently Janine had both.

"What happened, Janine?" she asked, lying tiredly back on the shabby settee. The flat was large and fairly comfortable, but the furniture was necessarily of that type found so often in furnished apartments. It had the air of having been used by many other people at different times. It smelt a trifle musty, too, having been covered with dust sheets and unoccupied for several weeks.

"Oh, nothing much. It would have been all right, I suppose—but for my dear mother-in-law! It was what she said just before she went, that caused all the trouble! It's always what she says, or infers, that breaks us up."

A pair of curtains. A small thing on which to hinge a marriage, Janine thought bitterly, as she recalled every word, every look, of Stacy's, after the others had gone, and left them alone.

"Janine, it *is* true, isn't it? It was all a misunderstanding, wasn't it? As Torrington said?"

She had nodded.

"Why didn't you write and tell me about

it then?"

She looked genuinely surprised. "But I did! I thought you didn't want any more to do with me when I didn't get an answer from you!"

"Where did you send that letter?"

"To the address you gave me when you wrote to Bletchbury and said you were closing our basement flat."

He flushed. There was resentment in her tone. So she was still smarting over that!

"Oh, well, it wasn't your fault that I didn't get the letter," he said, shifting uneasily.

"Stacy, why did you shut up our home, without asking me if I wanted to keep it on?" she appealed. It was the hinge on which their old quarrel was based—that, and his jealousy and disbelief over her one-time relations with Hugh Torrington. "How did you know I wouldn't want to live there while you were up North?"

"I couldn't afford to keep two homes going, even if I had cared to have my wife living alone with a young baby!"

"Then why didn't you come to see me and ask me to go up North with you? I would have!"

"Would you, Janine? Would you? I

225

wonder!" He smiled sadly, rather bitterly. He had seen the way she had looked at Torrington a matter of minutes ago.

They had talked for half an hour, like polite people meeting on a train, or sitting chatting over tea in a restaurant. Stacy, with little-boy belligerence and obstinacy, hid his aching longing for her; Janine, with exhausting effort, kept under the aching for Hugh that had all been reawakened on seeing him that day, and tried to concentrate on her dreams for a home background for Coppernob.

"Stacy," she said, at last, in a desperate voice, "Stacy could we try again? Could I bring Coppernob up North with me, and live in digs? It would be better for you, and—well, we could try again to make a go of it, couldn't we?"

She was puzzled at the look in his eyes, and because he noticed she had seen, he turned away and was deliberately casual. She didn't know he cared so much, and miscontrued the hungry longing for a triumphant gleam because she had made the gesture first. She was at once on her guard, and sorry she had said it.

"It won't be very nice for you up there, Janine. But we could try." It sounded flat, and he hadn't meant it to. He wanted to take her in his arms, hold her close and tell her what it would mean to him to have her up there. He wanted to tell her about Fenella, Louise, Adelaide Helston and what she had said. He wanted, too, to tell her of the dead, aching place somehere inside him, and all the loss of his baby son meant to him. But no words would come.

Janine decided that he was being dutiful, and thrust the thought from her. Coppernob should have a father, if it was the last thing she did. There was, too, and had been during this last week, a nagging fear that the baby would be taken away from her if her separation from Stacy became an established fact. It was on the strength of their marriage that they had been permitted to take her at all.

"Then that's settled," she said, with bright determination, and began planning and preparing for the removal of the baby from her aunts', and the shifting of her own few possessions, to their new digs.

It was when she came inevitably to mention their goods stored from the flat, that the question of his mother's last remark came up.

"Why didn't you go to my mother's,

Janine?"

It was a question she had been dreading, but it had to be answered.

"Because of the curtains."

Stacy had stared, and when she started to explain, her own resentment and hurt rose to the surface, and she heard herself saying, "Why did you leave them behind, Stacy? Why? I worked so hard on them, and I hadn't got a sewing machine!"

"Good heavens above!" he ejaculated. "You women are the limit! Fancy making such an issue of a pair of curtains! If you must know, Janine, I hadn't time to take them down, and to be frank, they didn't strike me as being up to much. We could have had new ones in the next place—properly made ones!"

She flushed. "There you go again! It's not enough for your mother to make slighting remarks about my poor efforts—you think they were pretty poor, too!" She swallowed hard on the lump in her throat, and before she realized what was happening, they were quarelling again. They brought up all the old bitterness, and flung them at each other, until at last Stacy got up to go.

"It's no use, Janine. It won't work. A

228

few minutes together alone, and we're at each other's throats. D'you want your freedom?"

She didn't answer, but sat staring. At that point, she didn't know herself whether it was her freedom she wanted for Hugh, more than to keep Stacy for Coppernob. As ever, there was that something about Stacy which pulled her to him, but she couldn't find a word for it. She thought it must be the familiarity of their relationship, after having been married for a year.

"You want Torrington, don't you?"

"You still believe what people tell you about Hugh and myself, don't you?" she asked slowly, in a low voice.

"That you were alone together in a house miles from anywhere? Well, everyone tells the same story, with devastating consistency!" he said, bitterly.

"You wouldn't like to hear my version, would you? You wouldn't believe it, anyway, would you, Stacy?"

He ran a hand over his forehead, tiredly. "I don't want to hear any more about it. It's all over. Finished and done with. Don't let's rake over the past. It can't help anyone now."

He went, after a few brief words about arranging for her maintenance to come through his bank, and that they could forward any letters, if she had need of correspondence with him. She hardly took in what he was saying. It was all so very unreal. She sat there watching the door through which he had gone, and a voice within her said, "He's gone for good. Stacy's left you."

She was still sitting there, staring blankly ahead, when Daisy came in a few minutes later.

"Cor, I ain't arf 'ad a time terday. Fair dead beat, I am! And wadyer think? Charlie wants me ter git meself dolled up an' meet 'im at midnight! Got a car, 'im an' another fella, with 'is gel, an' we're all goin' down ter Ramsgit by road, travel all night so's we don't lose no time termorrer. 'Ow's that?"

Janine made an effort, and said, "Sounds very nice. I do hope you enjoy yourself, Daisy!"

"So do I!" Daisy said, with a wrinkled brow. Obviously she still had doubts about her Charlie. "'Ere, oo was that good-lookin' fella comin' darn the steps—I see 'im as I come in the Mews! 'Ad 'e bin ter see you?"

"He had!" Janine said, grimly, getting up with an effort. "That, Daisy, was my husband. You'll now have the satisfaction of being right about me—he's certainly left me now!"

Daisy's mouth dropped open. "Oh, you pore devil!" she said, with genuine feeling, and came and slung a rough arm round Janine's shoulders.

The action was more telling than a similar one from the gentle Yvonne, and oddly it touched Janine deeply. Tears stung her eyes, and her throat burned. With a sudden swift gesture, she flung Daisy's arm away and got up. "Don't!" she said, in a choked voice.

"Oh, all right! Keep yer 'air on!" Daisy was offended.

"No, no, I didn't mean that," Janine said, hastily mopping her eyes. "It's not that at all! The fact is, I don't want sympathy just now—I shall break down and make a fool of myself, and I don't want to do that before the others come back. Oh, yes, they're all coming—you don't know the half of what's been happening. The owner of the flat's been and flung us all out!"

231

"Eh!"

"Oh, it's all right, he's found us another place. We're to take possession to-night, so we'd better get our things together."

"Where's Mrs. Ashley? Yvonne, I mean. I s'pose, I'd better try an' call 'er that. Don't seem nat'r'l, do it, not ter be matey with yer both, but you know 'ow it is!"

"Yes, Daisy," Janine said, with unusual gentleness. "Still, I think Yvonne would like it. So would I," she added, without quite knowing why. Daisy was growing on them both. It was a pity she was so uncouth, for she was a staunch friend.

By the time Hugh came back, Daisy and Janine had got most of their few things packed and ready, and had been to the delicatessen for some things for a meal in their new place.

"Papa Omalique, that woman who came in asking about me," Janine said, as she paid for the goods. "What did you tell her?"

The old Belgian spread his hands. "I only tell her what I know!" he mourned, conscious that something had gone wrong by the expression on Janine's face.

"Well, *what* did you tell her?"

He obligingly repeated the conversation, and appealed to them to tell him what he had done that didn't please them.

"You bloomin' ole fool!" Daisy burst out. "You've gone an' mucked everything up, you have! That's what! Nar they all think she's up to funny business, wiv anuvver name an' I don't know what all! Didn't yer know we was on'y kiddin' when we said we wos all Mrs. Ashleys?"

"Oh, don't, Daisy," Janine said, wearily. "It's our fault for carrying a joke too far. Never mind, Papa Omalique. It's all a mistake, and anyway, if my so-called friends weren't so spiteful, they needn't have believed what you told them."

They said good-bye to him, and left him with his fat wife, weeping at the departure of his favourite customers.

"You goin' up ter fetch Coppernob ter-morrer?" Daisy asked, as they left the delicatessen.

"Yes. I'll have to see what can be done, but I'd like to see this new flat first before I decide. I hope we can manage with a baby there."

" 'Course we can," Daisy said.

Janine looked at her with misgivings. It was only natural that the girl should

233

applaud the arrangements, since she would now have her own baby under the same roof with her all the time, and at the same time Janine would be responsible for the child, and her upbringing and upkeep. Very nice, Janine told herself resentfully, but how is that going to work out for Coppernob, or for me?

That, too, was a point grasped and raised by Yvonne, that night, when they were in bed together. Until they had had time to settle in properly, the two girls decided to share the biggest room, especially as Daisy had gone out soon after ten o'clock, to travel all night with Charlie and his friends.

"I'd be careful, if I were you, Janine," Yvonne warned. "You'll never have any real authority over the baby while Daisy is here. You know what she's like—she'll undo everything you do for the child, especially as it gets older."

"What can I do?" Janine asked helplessly. "I can't afford to stay in a flat of my own, even if I cared to live by myself."

"I don't want to lose you, but it would really be better if you stayed at your aunts' with the baby, at least for the time being," Yvonne said, slowly. "Couldn't you take advantage of your husband's arrangement with the bank, to get into touch with him, and get back on the old footing? Perhaps when he sees Coppernob again, he'll want you both back."

Janine shook her head. "No, Stacy isn't like that. Besides, I'm not sure that I want to go back to him now. He doesn't say such things lightly, and I know he doesn't want me any more."

Yvonne studied the other girl. "You said you knew Hugh Torrington before. It isn't because of that, as well as your not being able to get on with your husband, is it?"

Janine shrugged. She hadn't told Yvonne about the gossip that had got to Stacy's ears, and Yvonne had not pressed for any details. She said, instead, "His mother doesn't like me and never has. Her daughter Merrill is sweet on Hugh, so you can bet she isn't pleased at what Hugh's doing for us now."

"Does Hugh—like Merrill?" Yvonne asked, hesitantly.

"Oh, she likes any man. She usually has several in tow," Janine said, carelessly.

"And you like Hugh . . . very much, don't you?" Yvonne pressed.

Janine flushed. "He's an old friend.

Why not?"

Janine was up early next morning, and had very little breakfast. This trip to Bletchbury was not going to be very pleasant. Her aunts would not like to hear that she was going to bring the baby back to share a home with two other women, one of which was the baby's own mother. Looked at in that light, it didn't seem very sensible.

The journey was a dreary one. Not many people travelled by that early train to the Midlands, and she had forgotten to bring any magazines or food. She was hungry and rather cross when she changed trains, and when she reached Bletchbury it was raining.

Ethel let her in, without any great show of enthusiasm. "We got your letter, and I must say, Miss Janine, it's about time you came back!" she sniffed.

"Where are my aunts?" Janine wanted to know.

"I should have thought you'd want to know about the baby, first, miss," Ethel observed.

"She's all right, isn't she?" Janine asked, swiftly.

"Yes—no thanks to some people I could

name!"

Coppernob had changed in just that one week. Under the care and capable hands of old Ethel, the child had a more contented look, and didn't cry so much.

"She's gained eight ounces," Ethel observed, as she wheeled the pram out to the covered terrace overlooking the garden.

"Where did that come from?" Janine asked sharply, eyeing the pram with suspicion. It was obviously new, and a very smart model in dove grey, with a grey lambskin rug and a pale grey fringed canopy.

"It's your aunts' gift to the baby," Ethel said, sourly, adding, "I knitted the child a couple of vests. It was all I could afford!"

"Oh, Ethel, that was sweet of you!" Janine said, warmly, inwardly amused at the old woman's jealousy of her employers and their ostentatious present. "I think she looks bonny! You have been a pet, looking after her like that!"

The aunts were grim. Miss Bee said, "Well, Janine?" in what the girl had always known as her "special" tone. Miss Agnes twittered and fidgeted, and Janine knew she was in for an unpleasant time.

She forestalled them. "I've got a flat, which I'm sharing with two friends. One has a baby of her own. I'm taking Coppernob back with me, Aunt Bee!"

They didn't like it. They considered she should live with them while her husband was away, and had no hesitation in saying so. They said, also, that they considered she had treated them badly in not letting them know at once what she was doing, and they also considered it very bad of her to refrain from keeping her husband *au fait*; whatever they had against Eustace Conway, they still allowed that he was Janine's husband, and should not have been put to the indignity of having to telephone them for information about her.

Wearily, Janine let them talk. She stayed there long enough to gather together the baby's things, and to arrange for the bigger luggage and the pram to be sent by rail. She was back in London by early evening, with a tired and fractious baby and a lot of small bags. She took a cab back to the flat—a necessary extravagance, since Coppernob was heavy enough without the baggage.

The furnished flat was the ground floor of an old-fashioned house. Their sitting-

238

room was a large room which ran through the depth of the house, and had a large bay window at each end overlooking back as well as front. Silhouetted against the daylight in the far window, was a man's figure. Janine frowned as she went through the open door into the now public entrance hall, and fitted her key into the door of their little lobby. There was only one person that that could possibly be, but surely he wouldn't be here now?

She stood still for a second, listening. Suddenly, above Hugh Torrington's voice, came another significant sound. The thin wail of a very young baby.

She went into the sitting-room. Yvonne, her face aglow with the old happiness, was nursing little Georgina on her lap. Hugh Torrington stood looking down at them both.

Janine flushed. There was something about it which made her feel thrust aside. She told herself unreasonably that she had known Hugh first. Then it occurred to her that he must have called expecting to see her, and had waited until she came.

Her face cleared, as Yvonne looked up and smiled happily. "Janine! Isn't it wonderful? They told me at the hospital this afternoon, that I could bring her home with me!"

Coppernob, tired out with travelling, and badly needing her feed, started to yell lustily, drowning little Georgina's fretful pipe. The women laughed, and Hugh joined in. It was at once a family party.

He watched them mixing bottle feeds, with fascination. The beautiful mystery of undressing and changing a young baby was unfolded before him, and instead of being revolted or amused, he was genuinely intrigued. Janine's heart was wildly banging. The fatigue of the journey, and the tiresome interview she had had with her aunts, was all thrust to the background. Here was going to be happiness. What did it matter if Stacy had gone off in anger? If he wanted to leave her, well, let him. She could provide an adequate background for Coppernob, so long as her separation could be hidden from the eye of authority. Anyway, perhaps there would be someone else to act as a father to the infant, given a little time.

"I say!" Hugh said, after the babies had been put in their improvised cots—two deep drawers from the big chest. "I had no idea that babies were such fun! Can I come again?"

Janine opened her lips to frame an eager answer, when she noticed that it was not Coppernob's fat hand he moved to hold in his great paw, but little Georgina's; and it was not at her that he was looking—the question he was putting with such eagerness was to Yvonne.

CHAPTER XV

STACY did three things when he got back to Cumberland. The first was to write to his bank with instructions for Janine's weekly maintenance, and the forwarding of any correspondence either way. The second was to write and tell his mother that he was likely to remain up North for a long time, and that he wished Janine to have the baby's things which she was storing—the bath, cot, chest of drawers, etc., and anything else she might want, for the new place she had gone to. The third was a letter to his firm, reminding them of an old offer of a "floating" job—better-paid, but which he had turned down at the time because he wanted to stay in London after his marriage to Janine. He would need more money now that he had two establishments to keep up, and anyway, it no longer mattered where he was sent.

The days set in fine and warm, and the evenings were long and much too close to stay in his room at the inn. He started rambling the countryside, and followed guide-books to that end. Exploring the county became a feverish past-time with him, and a month went by without his seeing a soul he knew apart from the people with whom he worked and lodged. He studiously avoided the Whitestone Water district, and anywhere else likely to be frequented by the Helston family; he wrote no personal letters and received none.

July was hotter than the June, a dry close heat that was enervating in the extreme, and made work unnecessarily hard and the collection of lonely evening and week-end hours a thing to be dreaded. Even Stacy had to slow up in his furious killing of spare time, and the shelving of his annual holiday could no longer go on.

"Are you going home for your two weeks, Conway?" his immediate chief asked, with some curiosity.

He evaded the question as long as he could, and at last admitted that he was spending the time alone in the Lake District. Since some explanation was necessary to allay his chief's suspicions of a possible troublous domestic background, Stacy explained that his wife was staying with some friends who also had young babies, and that she preferred this to a holiday up North or elsewhere.

"I see," his chief said, with a frown, and Stacy wondered how long he could keep his separation from Janine a secret. He wished heartily that his firm hadn't such a deep interest in the condition of employees' backgrounds.

For his two weeks, Stacy finally decided to go to the point beyond which he had been unable to explore in the week-ends, and discovered an ancient stone inn which seemed to have been made for people who needed isolation. It was on the outskirts of a small hamlet, composed entirely of little stone dwellings where the inhabitants lived in near-primitive conditions. Water came from the village pump, and lighting was the old-fashioned wick lamp. There was one tiny church, also of stone, and the only telephone within miles was at the inn itself. The inn was the hamlet's community centre; there wasn't a cinema or theatre in miles.

The first night he was there, Stacy reflected grimly that he couldn't have chosen a better spot to be "away from it all" if he had tried. There was infinite peace in the wild beauty of the place; mountain and lake looked untouched with the mark of centuries on them. There were no roads; just flinty tracks, used only by horse-drawn vehicles. He himself had reached the place in a muck-cart belonging to the nearest farmer, who had fetched him from the railway halt, three miles away, because he happened to be collecting goods at the time. Otherwise, Stacy ruefully told himself, he would have had to walk with his bag—a fine way to start a holiday.

Some time after midnight, there was a bad storm, which in no way lessened the heat. The lightning struck a nearby tree, and in his nervy, tired state, Stacy found he couldn't sleep through the noise. How, he asked himself, had he managed to get to sleep in London? It was in the small hours before he dozed off, and he overslept. The landlord let him sleep, and it was the sound of voices beneath his window which finally awakened him.

The landlord was protesting about

something. There seemed to be a need to use his telephone, which he reiterated, had become broken down during the night. The storm, he enlarged, often damaged the wires, and the 'phone was off a great deal during the summer.

"But I must telephone! I'm stranded. D'you realize my car's nose down in a ditch a mile from here?"

Stacy frowned. He knew that voice. Looking out of the window, with his fair hair touselled, his pyjamas rumpled and his eyes heavy with sleep, he recognized Fenella.

He drew back hurriedly, and began to get dressed. His feelings were mixed. Odd, now that he had finally broken with Janine, how glad one half of him was to see Fenella. Yet the other half of him shrank from a meeting. That last time he had seen her was not pleasant to remember. It was doubtful that she would want to see him.

She was still arguing with the landlord about how she could get help for her car. He didn't hear the end of it or what happened. The girl was knocking with his shaving water. By the time he was ready to go down for his breakfast, the voices had ceased, and all had settled to that soft rural peace which had so soothed him when he arrived last night.

He wandered down to the coffee room, where the fat landlady was laying his breakfast. The aroma of freshly-fried bacon and the pungent smell of coffee came to him; the girl was taking in a plate of hot buttered toast. He apologized for being so late, but the landlady swept his apologies aside. She realized it was the storm. He was, she assured him, the only guest, so she had plenty of time to serve him when he liked. Peace, peace . . . .

He strolled into the room and sat down at the table. Just as he was going to begin, the voices started again. Fenella's protesting about intruding, and the landlady confidently assuring her that the gentleman wouldn't mind, that she did know. And then the door opened and Fenella stood there.

"It's all right, sir, isn't it?" the landlady asked.

"Of course," he nodded without realizing what he was saying. "Of course the lady can share the table."

Then they were alone.

Fenella stood leaning against the door

jamb, her face whitening. It came to him that while he had been prepared for the meeting, she naturally didn't know that he was the other person staying at the inn.

"Stacy!" she murmured in a low voice. Almost a gasp. "Did it have to be you? Why do you always turn up when I don't want to see you?"

"That isn't fair," he said. "To tell you the truth, I picked this place out as being the least likely to be patronized by anyone I knew."

His heart was pounding unevenly. She looked extremely distressed. "I thought I was fairly safe from seeing you at all," she said, "when I heard you were on holiday."

He said, without meaning to, "I've left my wife—for good. There was no point in going south for my holiday."

"I didn't go back to Richard," she answered, almost as if he had voiced the unspoken question. "Richard's no good to me—now I've met you. You've spoilt me for other men."

Spoilt for other men. And he had said to himself, not so long ago, that Janine had spoilt him for other women. It wasn't true, not in his case. At least, not entirely true.

Fenella said, again, "Stacy, why did it

have to be you here?" and slow tears ran
down her face. Suddenly she ran to him,
and automatically he opened his arms for
her. Over her bright head he watched a cat
sleepily raise its head at the unaccustomed
sound of a woman sobbing in that peace-
ful room. The cuckoo sprang out of the
Dutch clock and announced the hour, a fly
buzzed and banged itself against the
ceiling. After that first wide-eyed amber
stare, the cat stretched itself, yawned, and
curled up again against the warm glass of
the window panes. Quiet. Peace.

He held Fenella closer, and felt the
warmth of her body flooding into him,
and there was in him for the first time for
many months a cessation of that curious
unsatisfied feeling, that feeling of mental
hunger. Fenella and the peace of the inn
flooded through him, and Janine,
London, his mother and sister, everything, receded swiftly, almost as if some
part of his being that had recently been in
turmoil, shut down for a much-needed
rest. Like a somnambulist, he led Fenella
to the oak settle, and sat with her until she
was quiet again.

The landlady brought in another breakfast, and looked curiously at them, but

said nothing. That was how it was to be for the two weeks that he was there. The landlord wasn't so silent, He observed, as they went through the bar: "So you wasn't strangers after all, sir!" and went smoothly on to tell a long and involved story of how he came across the man who lived next door to him in Leeds, in his youth; they met in a dug-out in France in the first world war. It took the landlord ten minutes to tell the story, with many jabs at the air with his clay pipe, and many meaning jerks of the head. It obviously had some parallel for him with the way Stacy and Fenella had met.

They listened politely, and waved a cheery farewell to him as they went off for a walk. Out of earshot of the inn, they abandoned their casual air of friendliness to tackle the problem of themselves.

"What are we gong to do, Stacy?"

"Do you want me to give Janine her freedom?" he asked, with a frown.

"It's not what I want," she said, slowly. "It's what Janine wants, and what you want. What *do* you want, Stacy?"

It was some minutes before he replied. The roughness of mountainside and the silent strength of lake and woodland, with their air of having been there, still the same, since the beginning of time, made his little life and worries seem so puny as to be hardly worth discussing. It came to him that if Fenella had not happened to turn up, he might have worked things out naturally in this atmosphere; seen things in their right perspective. Now it was hopelessly confused. He only knew that Fenella was here, and that he liked her being near him, and it was comforting to think they had got over the initial difficulty of silently admitting their feelings for each other. Beyond that, he didn't want to go for the moment. He was not sure himself what he wanted to do, or what would be good for Janine. Although he had left her, it was not, for him, a real separation; rather a truce, a getting beyond her for a breathing-space. He didn't want to cut it right off, he still had her interests at heart, and still wanted the old arrangement of paying her weekly through his bank as a means of keeping in touch with her, too. He had himself left her, yet he had experienced disappointment that she hadn't so far written to him though he had given her the opportunity of keeping in touch.

"Let's leave it for a bit. Let's wait till the end of the fortnight, Fenella. That's if you want to stay here, that is."

"Where else can we go? At least no one is likely to see us here, no one knows us, that is—until we've decided what to do," she allowed. But she wasn't happy about it. Neither was he. Already, within the space of half an hour, it was beginning to take on the ugly mantle of the hole-and-corner affair.

She thought, with tears stinging her eyes, "He's still in love with his wife, and doesn't know it!"

He asked himself, "What's the matter with me? I don't want to live with Janine, yet I don't want to let her have her freedom. I love being with Fenella, yet I don't want to make the break with Janine and marry Fenella. Dog in the manger, I believe!" he finished, with heavy mental sarcasm.

"Is it," Fenella asked suddenly, "because of the child? A divorce would mean Janine's losing her, wouldn't it?"

"To be honest, I hadn't thought of it," he admitted. "Yes, I suppose that would kill everything, as far as the baby is concerned. And Janine wanted that child so much."

Fenella could have added that living apart from Janine would sooner or later have the same effect, but she didn't. At that point, she felt that Janine had had her chance, and hadn't taken it.

"Did she mind very much when you said you were leaving her?" Fenella asked, with hesitation. She disliked discussing another woman, but felt she had to know.

"If she did, she didn't show it!" he said, roughly. Then quickly—too quickly—"It wasn't her fault. She's tried to make a go of this marriage. So have I. It was just that we were pitch-forked into it, by her aunts. They engineered everything. If they'd left us alone, things might have been different. Very different." He thought of Hugh, and savagely decided that Janine wouldn't have married him at all, if Torrington had been handy at the time, but he didn't say so to Fenella.

"Is there anyone else that she cares for?" Fenella probed, shrewdly.

He didn't answer for the moment. Then, compromising, he said, "Well, if there is, I should have thought she'd want her freedom and ask me for it, wouldn't you?"

"I don't know," Fenella retorted. "It just

depends on how much she wants Coppernob, and . . . how little she wants you to be happy!"

He was at once angry. Fenella saw she had gone too far, by the quick flush that ran up his pale cheeks. But he said nothing, and they walked in silence for a long time. The strenuous effort needed to negotiate the narrow, rough tracks, served also to ease the tension. Sometimes he had to help Fenella round difficult bends, and over places where the paths had vanished in tiny landslides. When they reached the top of the high ground up which they had been struggling, he caught her to him without a word, and held her.

"Fenella, let's leave things like this. Let's use this fortnight to get ourselves adjusted to each other. After all, we don't know what it would be like to be together all the time. I'm a difficult devil to get on with."

"Yes, Stacy. And then?"

"Then we'll see," he evaded. "But for the moment, let's just be friends—like this."

He put his lips to the top of her bright head; then sliding his arm round her waist, he began to help her down the difficult path on the other side.

The weather was perfect for those two

weeks. A little of the intenseness of the heat went after another storm. They swam together, boated, fished, climbed. Went for easy local walks, and long difficult treks, taking their food for the day with them. There was a brightness in their manner with each other; not exactly a forced brightness, but a carefree easiness, each knowing that there were fourteen free days in which to enjoy the holiday as a holiday should be enjoyed by two people fit and strong and capable of such enjoyment.

Fenella got her car repaired, and they used that to get longer distances covered, but as a rule it was housed in the old barn at the back of the inn.

"It's the second time I've had a crash," she told Stacy with a rueful grin. "Daddy won't be pleased when he sees this bill!"

"How did it happen?"

"Damned silly thing," she said, making a moué. "A sudden flash of lightning made me jump. I jerked the steering wheel. Before I knew where I was, the old bus was going into a beautiful skid, and wham! Over in the ditch I was, nose-first! I felt an awful fool, especially having to sit there at that angle, because it was raining too damned hard to get out. A bigger fool when I realized the distance I had to walk before I got anywhere. I seemed to have been walking all night!"

"Do your people know where you are?"

She shrugged. "Yes. Why not? I told them I was going to get lost in the wilds. As a matter of fact, it was Kevin's idea. You'd like my father if you got to know him more. He gave me to understand that my nerves weren't what they were, and a rest away from everyone might be a good idea."

"Yes," Stacy said. "Your nerves can't be what they were, to let lightning upset you like that."

She shot him a sidelong glance. "Neither are yours," she observed. "What can we expect, upsetting the even course of our lives as we've done?"

Towards the end of the fortnight, a little green racer drew up outside the inn. Stacy saw it first. He was coming round from the rear with a basket of eggs he had collected for the landlady. He saw Fenella coming up the land, after posting her letters for the day.

Louise got out of the car and stood looking around. She made a picture effortlessly, in her white dress with a red scarf and belt, and little red open sandals. Her pale hair was bound down with a red patterned band, but the wind caught the long curling tendrils at the back and blew it wildly. Stacy didn't know if Louise was conscious of the perfect background the blue waters of the lake made, or whether she just naturally posed wherever she was, in the certain knowledge that she looked good whatever background she happened against. What interested him more was the way Fenella reacted when she caught sight of her sister.

She darted back a few paces the way she had come, and slipped through the gate into the yard, and round to where he stood. "Let's go back to the hen-houses," she whispered. "We don't want Louise to see us. Quickly," and she tugged at his arm.

He stood there, interested in what Louise would do. The landlord had seen her, and was coming out, but the hired girl forestalled him.

Louise said to her, "My sister's staying here, I believe. Is she in? Miss Helston."

The girl simpered. "The lady and gentleman are out, miss, but—" she broke off, as the landlord swiftly cuffed her and sent her in.

"The lady isn't back yet, ma'am, but if you'd step inside and wait—" he said, briskly.

Louise grinned. She had noticed his wary eye. Fenella couldn't be far off.

"Is the gentleman tall and thin, with fair hair?" she asked, innocently.

The landlord stared stolidly. He was obviously in a quandary. "There *is* such a gentleman staying here, ma'am," he finally allowed.

"I thought so," Louise purred, and without a backward glance, got in the little car and drove away.

"We've got to move on from here," Fenella said, urgently. "I don't trust Louise. Just for fun, she might bring her gang over, to see how uncomfortable she can make us feel!"

"I'm not hiding from anyone," Stacy said, briefly, and walked in.

"Who said 'hide'?" Fenella demanded, in a low furious voice, following close on his heels.

"That's what you want us to do, isn't it?" he returned, facing her. "Isn't it, Fenella?"

"Well, get your freedom, then we won't

have to hide! But until then, we haven't the right to look people in the face!"

It was the first time they had had a clash, and for the rest of the day Stacy was in a very thoughtful mood.

There was only one day left before they had to pack up and go. A decision had to be made. Fenella left him alone, but watched him covertly. He knew what she wanted him to say, but now that the moment had come, he didn't know how he could say it. He didn't even know if he wanted to say it. If she had gone away, used a little subtlety, he might have wanted to go after her, say anything, agree to anything, rather than lose her. But this tagging along with him, waiting, watching, rather reminded him of the way he had been enveigled into marriage with Janine. Why wouldn't these women let him make up his own mind? Did they have to keep trying to put the thoughts there? Was he a small boy, to be guided into the paths they chose?

That evening the landlady, usually so tactful, put her thoughts into words, and further added to his irritation.

They came in to the coffee-room, he and Fenella, after a disappointing day; a day that had had none of the spontaneous gaiety of all the rest of the fortnight, because of the need for facing their problem after that first clash that morning.

The landlady was fussing over the table, which had the best cloth on, the one with the coarse lace her grandmother had made. There was a bunch of their best roses in a glass vase in the middle, red roses from the central bush, the pride of the landlord's heart. The table was laid with extra care, and there was the pungent smell of roast chicken and stuffing coming from the kitchen.

"Is it a party?" Fenella asked in some surprise.

The landlady chuckled, and gave a knowing wink. "Well, the last night, you know, ma'am, though I expect we shall see you both back soon, eh?" She chuckled again, and nodded with heavy meaning at Stacy.

"I don't understand," he said.

"I fancy I can hear them wedding bells not far off," the woman said, with another chuckle, and a further wink that included them both. "Eh, ma'am? Eh?"

Fenella seemed torn between embarrassment and annoyance. "It's nice of you to go to so much trouble," she said, non-committally, "but you shouldn't have! We shall never forget this wonderful fort-night, and the way you've looked after us!"

"No, you won't forget this fortnight, that I *do* know!" the landlady agreed, as she bustled off happily to bring in the special supper she had personally cooked for them. To add to their embarrassment, the local people sang in the bar that night all the old ballads they could think of which suggested marriage and courtship, including the famous one about the bicycle made for two. At last, they had to go out and show themselves, and allow the company to drink to them.

Back in the coffee-room, Fenella said, "What's it to be Stacy?" and he noticed a half-fearful note in her voice, as if she almost anticipated that his answer would be a negative one.

He took her shoulders and turned her to face him. "My dear, let's get out of this place before we make up our minds. Now this has happened, it's impossible to think clearly. Let's just be gay, and don't let them see we've any problem to face, please—for your sake more than mine!"

She smiled brightly, but he imagined she knew the answer then. He had done what he could for her. This was her own county. He must think of her first.

They had a terrific send-off next morning. With his single bag sticking rakishly out of the boot, and a duck which the landlord had slung in for a parting gift, they went off to a flurry of hand-waving, and hearty good-byes.

Stacy felt foolish. Uneasy, too, because Louise knew where they had been staying. He let Fenella drive in silence for an hour. Then he murmured:

"This town we're coming to—is there a decent place where we can get lunch?"

She said, "The Railway Hotel's all right," and drove on.

He wondered what she was thinking, and what she would think when he had done what he knew he must do.

She parked the car at the back of the place, and joined him in the lounge. He was hastily putting his fountain-pen away, and he picked up an envelope from the small coffee-table and put it in his pocket.

"What's that, Stacy?"

"Just something I had to do, and thought I might as well get on with it while you parked the car."

"It isn't a very inspiring place for our last lunch, is it?" she said, as they chose a table as far away from the serving hatch as possible.

"Last lunch?" He looked sharply at her.

"Well, it *is* the last lunch of this holiday, isn't it?"

"Yes, I suppose it is," he allowed. "Oh, well, most hotels of this type are a bit dreary. Never mind. Let's see what they've got on the menu."

The coffee was hot, and he left her with a murmured excuse. When he didn't come back, she looked round uneasily. Then the waitress came back through the swing doors, she came straight over to Fenella's table with an envelope.

"The gentleman came away from the telephone and said he'd have to leave at once, madam. He settled the bill and told me to give you this."

Fenella took it. It was a very ordinary square white envelope, but it looked like the one she had seen Stacy put in his pocket. She tipped the girl and went out to her car. After sitting in it for a moment or two, she decided she'd go to a quieter spot before reading it. She knew what was in it.

There was no need to hurry.

She drove leisurely, almost blindly, to a spot near her own home, and opened the envelope.

"Fenella, my dear," Stacy had written. "I can't do it. I cannot bring myself to hurt Janine by depriving her of the child—as indeed any attempt to get my freedom would do. I think you knew this would be the answer, yet I couldn't bring myself to tell you. I know what you'll think of me, but I can't help it. Thanks for an unforgettable fortnight."

He hadn't signed it. He hadn't hoped that no one would know about it. He hadn't indicated that he had thought of what she would do now, or if she would be hurt or heartbroken. Just that. Just goodbye, suddenly, cleanly.

She shot up her chin, and drove home. The biggest hurt of all, seared deeply into her. Even in a private and personal farewell letter, Stacy couldn't resist mentioning his wife by name.

CHAPTER XVI

ON his return, Stacy received a letter from the Head Office of his firm, in London. They seemed pleased at his request for a transfer. Many times it had been put to him before, because he was the adaptable type who could settle down anywhere, besides being good at that particular kind of job. Many other young men were just as good, but sooner or later got tired of the eternal removal from the place where their roots began to settle, and started manoeuvring for something permanent. The letter further set out the date of the transfer and the first place to which he would be sent. He had three more weeks in Cumberland.

His relief at escaping from the Helstons' county was short-lived. Mrs. Helston sent for him.

"Mr. Conway," she began, and there was no doubt about the subject which had prompted her to invite him to see her. "Before you came to this house, we were a happy family. Your influence has been a bad one. Not only has my elder daughter broken her engagement to a most suitable

264

young man, and gone abroad without a word to any of us, but my younger daughter has now developed the same trait of secrecy. Louise has given up her young friends, and is going about with older and less desirable people. That didn't happen before my girls knew you!"

"Really, Mrs. Helston!" Stacy was moved to protest. "I'm prepared to admit that I have been friendly with Fenella, but with Louise—no! She's just a baby! Why, I hardly know her!"

"I'll send for Louise," Mrs. Helston said, and rang the bell.

Louise had dropped her air of sophistication to-day. She was indeed, as Stacy had said, just a baby. She wore a full gathered and very young-looking sprigged muslin dress, and no make-up. She looked amazingly different in this outfit, and it must have been obvious to even her mother that the girl was putting on an act, and doing it remarkably well.

"Now, Louise," Mrs. Helston said. "Mr. Conway has denied having any —er—friendship with you at all. Would you repeat again what you told me?"

Stacy wondered in exasperation and

some uneasiness what devilry Fenella's young sister had been up to now. Could she have mentioned his staying at the inn with Fenella? He hardly thought so. But he didn't understand why Fenella should suddenly go abroad, and at the same time manage to give her family the impression that it was through him. Unless Louise had told them. . . .

He shook off the idea. Why should the girl do such a thing? She had nothing to gain. Yet why had she given up her own young friends? And what sort of people were these "undesirable" ones her mother had mentioned?

"Oh, no, mummy," Louise pleaded, with a pretty air of terror lest her confidences should be divulged. "Please don't say what I told you—don't make me repeat it either. Besides, I don't want to get poor Stacy (I mean, poor Mr. Conway) into trouble!"

"So you've come to call this man by his Christian name, have you, Louise? You are aware that he has a wife in London, aren't you?"

Louise started to cry. "I didn't know, I didn't know that!" she sobbed, evidently under the impression that her mother wouldn't remember that she had been in the room the first day Stacy called at Whitestone House. If Mrs. Helston did remember, she gave no indication.

"Louise, if you please," she insisted. "I desire that you shall repeat what you told me!"

"No, no!" Louise sobbed. "There was nothing in it, I assure you! I just happened to be staying at the same place, that's all! You can go and ask them if you like—you'll find 'Miss Helston' in the visitors' book, underneath Mr. Conway's name. I didn't think anyone would know us, and anyway, it was *all right*!"

Stacy stared. Mrs. Helston's face whitened, and she clutched at the region of her heart. Stacy had no illusions about that little action. Mrs. Helston wasn't the type to pretend. That little speech of Louise's must have given her mother a very bad shock.

"I'm sorry, Mrs. Helston, but I think all your younger daughter needs is a thorough good spanking. If you don't mind my saying so, she's well and truly spoilt. All I can say is, I haven't spent a holiday with her, anywhere—which seems to me to be what she is suggesting!"

Louise gasped. "Oh! How can you say such things! Do you deny," she said, with heavy meaning, "that you stayed a fortnight at a certain inn, we know where? Do you deny that Mr. Conway stayed there with *Miss Helston*?"

She stared hard at him, and he got up and thrust his hands in his pockets in sheer annoyance. The child had got him where she wanted him.

"How would you like it if I took Mummy to see the innkeeper, then? He'll tell us who was staying there!"

And there Louise had him. Fenella was abroad and couldn't speak up for herself. So Stacy had to take the blame and get involved with Louise for heaven knew what purpose!

"All right," he said. "Where does it get you, Louise?"

Mrs. Helston flopped back on the sofa. "Sal volatile," she gasped, and Louise sprang forward to ring the bell.

"You needn't pretend, Stacy," Louise said, sadly. "For all we know, Mummy knows all about us. Didn't Fenella see us together, that night you took me to dinner?"

In the ensuing scene, with Mrs.

Helston's personal maid bending over her and someone else fetching her husband, and the doctor, and Louise standing about crying miserably, Stacy felt like a person watching a play. In his room at the inn, hours—many hours—later, he still felt a trifle dazed, and wondered what would happen next. Kevin had turned out to be a most unreal figure, dropping his vague air for once as he requested Stacy to see him in his study. There, in a stiff, even hostile voice, he had demanded to know what Stacy's intentions were, and whether he were prepared to get his freedom in order to marry Louise. The doctor had taken up the family's cudgels, from the angle of Mrs. Helston's health. It would be, he insisted, most dangerous to go against her wishes at this stage, and as far as Stacy could see, Mrs. Helston's wishes seemed to coincide with those of Louise.

When he at last got a moment to speak to Louise herself, he had taken her by the shoulders, and kept his temper with difficulty.

"Look, I've never shown the slightest interest in you, my child. I only had a friendly interest in your sister, God knows, but you—well, you're just an infant. Why you're making all this trouble, I can't imagine. Perhaps you'd enlighten me?"

She smiled, her tantalizing, slow smile that had captivated him from the first. "That's just it, Stacy Conway. You've never taken the slightest interest in me. Everyone else who comes to this house—even the stainless Richard—does, at some time or other. All except you. So—I want you!"

He stared blankly, then burst into derisive laughter. "For heaven's sake, child, I'm nearly thirty. I'll bet you're not sixteen yet! Have a little sense, do!"

"As a matter of fact, I know exactly how old you are. Personally, I'm seventeen, an old seventeen, I'm told. You'll do fine for me!"

He irritably stroked his turbulent fair hair. This, he told himself, was getting farcical. If it were Fenella in front of him at this moment, he would have some strong personal interest to keep the situation serious. As it was, Louise merely amused him in a strictly juvenile way, and the idea of getting his freedom in order to marry her was a subject for levity.

"I think I'd better get the train for London—to see my wife," he told her, in exasperation. "Anything would be better than this!"

"I shouldn't do any such thing, if I were you, Stacy. You see, Mummy might easily die of shock. She's in a tricky state of health. I'm her pet lamb. It's terrible to her to think I've been away with a wolf like you."

"What about your sister Fenella? Don't you care about her at all? What happens if I marry you, and it gets out that it was she who stayed at the inn? How does her reputation fare, in this stiff-necked district?"

Louise shrugged. "Fenella can take care of herself. We're not pleased with her because she was engaged to dear Richard, whom the parents dote on. She can go to the dogs for all we care!" she said, airily.

There may well be, he reflected, quite a few grains of truth in that statement of hers. He had noticed that Fenella hadn't been so popular with her family since he himself had appeared on the scene. It was a pity, he considered, that he seemed to unwittingly disturb this family so much. Heaven knew, he hadn't wanted to.

"Suppose I just pack up and clear out, and leave you to straighten things out for yourself?" he demanded.

Louise shrugged again. "There's nothing to stop you doing that, of course, but you'd be awfully silly. I mean, we're on social terms with the big boss of your firm. Do you think Daddy and Mummy would let you go on working for them if you upset them like this? The Helstons are a revengeful crew, believe me! On the other hand, if you married me, Daddy would settle money on you. We'd live abroad—gosh, I'm sick of lakes and fells. I want sunshine. I want to keep moving. We'd do France and the Black Forest; the Netherlands; I want to see Czechoslovakia and Yugoslavia, oh, and Cyprus. I want to stay in Egypt, too."

She was dramatizing, he thought, sourly, but she caught his imagination, just the same. To go abroad—but he'd have to be free to enjoy it. There would be no freedom with this girl. He could imagine how it would be; he would be her pet poodle on a chain. Her father supplying his pocket-money, her mother footing his hotel bills and travelling expenses. Louise going with him to choose his clothes. Louise deciding when they'd stop and when they'd move on. In fact, he'd just be Louise's shadow. And sooner or later they'd come up against Fenella, Fenella whom he had turned down on the grounds that he didn't want to get his freedom and so deprive his wife of the child. . . .

He paced his room. Somehow everything in the atmosphere here stifled him. Impatiently he decided he must get away, regardless of Adelaide Helston and her frail health, regardless of the studious gentle Kevin, who unsheathed his claws when his daughter's wishes were thwarted, regardless of the whole Helston family and their power in the district, and their beastly money.

He thought again of the possibility of going abroad, but his thoughts were regretful. Louise's offer involved too high a price, and there was still Janine to consider.

He could not leave the office until the week-end, so he resolutely refused to answer all telephone calls. A letter, which might have been written by Louise, he tore up and dropped it in a street litter basket. The week dragged on, and when Friday came, he went to Town.

His mother was pleased to see him.

273

Characteristically, she seemed to have forgotten the unpleasantness of their last meeting. Merrill, too, seemed to have buried her animosity over Hugh, and he spent a pleasant week-end in his old room.

The old influences pulled him. He examined all his books, those familiar books from which he had learned so much about the countries he had always yearned to visit. He fingered lovingly his foreign language books, the well-thumbed dictionaries, the books of travel, the classics in French and German which he had collected as a boy. His globe awakened all the old nostalgia, and he knew he'd never again be content to work at the job he had left in Cumberland. He had taken yet another step forward, a step he couldn't retrace.

"Have you seen Janine?" he asked his mother.

She was off-handed. "Of course not! You don't think she'd come here, do you?"

"I wondered if she'd been to ask you about the baby furniture," he explained, patiently.

His mother sniffed. "D'you suppose she'd want the things *I* gave her?"

He gave it up. Twice or three times he

had been on the point of looking Janine up, during that week-end, but each time, that last meeting and all its implications, came freshly to his mind, and he gave it up at last as hopeless. Why court another quarrel? She had the child. Why should she want him?

On the Monday, instead of returning up North, he went to the London office, and asked to see the director who had answered his request for a transfer. He had to wait most of the morning, but at last he was shown in.

"I want to resign, sir," he began, without preamble.

"Whatever for, Conway?"

"Oh, sick of everything, sir. I want to get away. To some other country, perhaps."

"With your wife?"

"No, sir," Stacy admitted.

"H'm." His boss frowned and studied the desk top.

"Conway," he resumed at last, "d'you know a family called Helston?"

Stacy looked quickly at him.

"Ah, I see you do! Then it *is* true," was the dry comment.

"Louise kept her word, then," Stacy murmured, half to himself.

"What d'you mean by that?" was the sharp question.

Stacy shifted uneasily in his chair.

"I can't tell you, sir, without involving others. The fact is, I'm half inclined to go back to my wife, but we can't agree over anything for five minutes. Much the best to clear out and give her breathing space. I want to go at once. I'll forfeit a month's money in lieu of notice, if it won't inconvenience the company too much."

"What are you going to do, if you leave us?"

"Oh, try and find a job abroad. There should be clerical openings going, I suppose."

"Conway, I've had a report on you and your work since hearing from the Helstons. They're friends of mine, and I'm not saying further than that. The fact remains, you're a good man, wasted in that job. I see you're no mean linguist. Have you thought of a travelling secretaryship?"

Stacy laughed. "That, sir, is the sort of job one dreams of, but doesn't actively think of."

"Well, think about it now. One of us has to attend the Brussels conference over a

276

new merger, and there's a trip over Europe following. We could do with a man who has your abilities together with several languages to act as secretary for the trip."

Stacy left the Head Office in bewilderment. He had gone there with the intention of flinging up his job, and scraping around for a new one, merely for the sake of getting out of the country and living the life he had always wanted. Now, in the space of a few minutes, he had, despite Louise's determined efforts to be a nuisance to him, landed a much higher-paid job than he had ever had before, and with it came . . . escape.

CHAPTER XVII

IT was strange, to Janine, to see Hugh coming to see someone else. At first, she couldn't believe it. He came in the evenings at first. Not every evening, and certainly without letting them know first. He just dropped in, casually, cheerfully, and always with some sort of neutral gift, which he omitted to label, and usually left it on the kitchen table. It might very well have suited any of them, and they all shared it, whether a bunch of grapes, a box of chocolates, *pâté de foie gras* or a carton of potato salad—even a bunch of mixed roses he left without saying a word.

They were happy days for all of them, on the surface. The weather that summer was perfect. There was a good public park near at hand, and a cinema frequented by them all in turn. The neighbourhood was pleasant enough, and there was a shopping centre which appealed to all three of the girls. But beneath it all, each had her problem to grapple with. Daisy with her Charlie, and the shadow of her husband for ever at hand; Yvonne with her child, who was far from strong; Janine with the searing conviction that Stacy had really gone for good.

All these elements came unobtrusively to a head one evening when Daisy came in, flushed and excited.

"Hallo, what's the matter with you?" Janine asked, with a derisive grin, as she fastened the enormous curved safety-pin into Coppernob's clean nappie. "Charlie managed to thrill you at last?"

Daisy stopped grinning and looked sheepish. "Well, tell yer the truth, I ain't bin out with Charlie, see? Don't let on, though, will yer?"

"Eh?" Yvonne gasped. "Not been out with Charlie?"

Janine put Coppernob back into her cot, and stood regarding Daisy with new attention. "What did you say?"

"You 'eard!" Daisy snapped, removing with care the new hat she had made herself, from a froth of purple veiling, two yellow roses and a bit of corded ribbon. "I've bin out with the milkman, if you must know!"

As the other two stared open-mouthed at this new and very sudden development, Daisy was moved to defend her new beau.

"Oh, well, 'e's a nice chap, quiet an' all that. Bin askin' me for ages to go out with 'im, an' I keep puttin' 'im orf, on account o' Charlie. Then I thinks to meself, well, it's like this. I don't like Charlie much, see? Always wantin' wot 'e can't 'ave—one o' them! Now Reg (that's the milkman) 'e's not like that. Leastways, 'e don't seem like it from wot I see of 'im. So I thinks to meself, well, I'll go out with 'im once. Can but try, I always say! I bin, an' it's wot I thought all along. 'E's a real nice chap. No funny business."

Janine stared at Yvonne.

Yvonne said, "Yes, he does seem a nice

fellow. Dark, rather nice-looking, quiet. Never gets familiar. He seems to like babies, too. He had a look at both of them when you were out shopping one morning, Janine."

"Yes, 'e's crazy about kids," Daisy said, happily, as she peeled off her one good pair of silk stockings, and kicked her shoes under the settee. "I told 'im Coppernob's really my kid, an' you oughter 'ave seen 'ow pleased 'e looked. Wisht I was single, I do," she finished, wistfully.

Janine said, angrily, "She isn't your child any more, and you've no business to tell such a lie!"

"Oh, yes, she is, for all the bloomin' adoption papers you signed! 'Oo you talkin' to, anyway? Come to think of it, she won't even be yourn, adopted or any other thing, if you don't get yer 'usband back quick! Reg told me all about adoption. His brother works in a solicitor's office; educated 'e is."

"I don't care a jot about the milkman or his beastly brother—Coppernob's mine, *legally*, and if I hear any more of it—" Janine shouted, her face flaming.

Yvonne interrupted, "Janine, Janine, don't lose your temper so quickly. And

you, Daisy, ought to be ashamed of yourself. You didn't want the child. You
wanted your freedom to go out to work.
Well, you've got it. You were glad enough
to pass your baby over to Janine, and you
made a bargain. For heaven's sake, stick
to it!"

"She's not going to talk to me like that!"
Janine expostulated, indignantly. "I won't
have it!"

"Janine, be quiet!" Yvonne insisted. "If
you didn't lose your temper so quickly,
that nice husband of yours would still be
with you, and there'd be no possible
danger of losing Coppernob. As for you,
Daisy, if you dare to raise the subject
again, I shall get very angry. You signed
the adoption papers, too, you know. You
signed your baby away. There's nothing
you can do now. Even if you could, you
know, you're in the same position as
Janine, here, in the sense that you haven't
a husband to support you!"

"No, but it's still my kid, my flesh and
blood!" Daisy muttered, belligerently, as
she moved off to the kitchen for some
supper. "And anyway, don't be so sure I
can't do nothin'—see?"

Janine and Yvonne stared uneasily at

each other.

"Can she do anything?" Janine asked anxiously.

Yvonne frowned. "Honestly, I'm not sure. It's a nuisance about the milkman. It's quite likely that he's got a brother who's in a solicitor's office—a clerk or something, I s'pose—and he could get hold of information like that, if he wanted it. She couldn't take the child back herself, while things are as they are, but I'm not sure she couldn't get it taken away from you, just the same! If I were you, I'd take Coppernob back to your aunts' place, out of Daisy's way."

"But she knows where they live!"

"I don't think so. Anyway, she'd probably forget about it all if you weren't here. It's seeing the baby every day that does it, I believe."

"Yes. I know," Janine said, thoughtfully. "I imagined it would be all right, her being out at work all day, and out most week-ends. But it isn't. She finds quite a bit of time in between to kiss and cuddle the child, and when Coppernob starts talking, I bet I know whose vocabulary she'll pick up first!"

Yvonne nodded. The same thought had

occurred to her, and she had been anxious about it for some time. She had even spoken to Hugh about it, but Hugh wasn't really interested in Daisy's child. It was little Georgina who claimed all his attention.

Daisy, smarting under that little scene, was biding her time to pay it back when Hugh came one Saturday afternoon. It happened that Daisy wasn't going out. Charlie was getting difficult because she wasn't seeing him so much, so she decided it would be expedient to stop going out with the milkman for the time being.

Saturday afternoon in the flat was a loathsome idea to her. She kicked around for a bit, varnishing her nails a startling mauve, then removing it for a more conventional scarlet. Then she invited Yvonne to go to the pictures with her.

"No, I don't want to go out in this heat. Besides, the baby isn't so well," Yvonne said, worriedly. "I wish I knew what was wrong with her. She seemed all right at the clinic last Monday." She felt Georgina's hot little forehead, and murmured, "I think I ought to send for the doctor."

"Oh, well, 'ere comes your 'elp an' adviser," Daisy grinned, as Hugh took the front steps at a bound.

Yvonne looked distinctly relieved. "Oh, I'm so glad you've come!" she exclaimed, sincerely, and Hugh beamed at her. Janine's heart gave a lurch as she saw the way he looked at Yvonne. Vaguely Hugh held out a big parcel to her to take, and she went to the kitchen with it, with Daisy at her heels, but Hugh's expression occupied all her attention. It was such a long time ago, that delirious summer when he had gone around with her, first in Bletchbury and then in London. Such a long time since he had looked genuinely pleased to see her. Even now, though they met at the flat not once but many times a week, he treated her as nothing but a sister or a life-long friend—certainly someone with whom he was so familiar that he hardly need look at her when he came.

"What is it this time?" Daisy wanted to know, fetching a knife to cut the string. "Coo, peaches! Fancy cakes! Eggs—lumme! Noo-laid! Don't arf do 'er proud, don't 'e? Least ways, I *s'pose* all this 'ere is for Yvonne, an' not you?" she added, slyly.

"What d'you mean?"

"Oh, nuthink—on'y I 'ad an idea you

an' 'im was thick as thieves once! My mistake, ducks!"

Yet that was enough. Daisy's barb had gone deeper than even she had intended it to. Janine saw, with startling clearness, that Hugh was hardly ever aware that she was there, so much was he interested in Yvonne. The man who had well-earned the name of play-boy and flirt, as long as Janine had known him, and whom even Merrill had come to regard as a very slippery person to put any faith in, was at last caught up in a genuine love-affair.

That night, she told Yvonne she was packing to go to her aunts'. Yvonne hardly noticed what she was saying, so distracted was she over little Georgina. The child screamed incessantly, and although Hugh had fetched the doctor, nothing had been done beyond putting the baby in blankets, with a hot-water bottle.

Janine said good-bye to Yvonne and Daisy the next morning, with the remark that she didn't know how long a visit of this sort would last, and made the tiresome journey back to the Midlands. Coppernob, at three months, was a good traveller, though a bored one. It took a lot of patience to keep her amused, as the

285

child didn't sleep for such long hours as she had done the last time this trip had been made.

It was dry and hot when she arrived. The sticky heat of mid-day had given place to the closest of late afternoons, where those people who were about the streets looked limp and enervated, and those who had no occasion to be out had made their houses look equally overcome with the heat by drawing every blind and curtain, and covering the front doors with washed-out looking striped awnings.

The station cab was out, and in disgust, she took a trolley-bus to the road at the end of her aunts', rather than wait about on the burning pavement for the cab to return.

The house was even more still than the rest. In fact, there was the stillness of death about it. A strange car was drawn up outside. Janine looked at it curiously, and decided that it must be for the house next door.

Ethel opened the door without her usual promptness. Her face was white, and she had been crying. She looked blankly at Janine, and stood back without a word for the girl to pass.

"Well, Ethel, what's the matter with you? Aren't you glad to see me?" Janine said. Coppernob's weight increased alarmingly, and Janine recollected that the pram was in London. She hadn't even stopped to have it shipped to the train, which would, she reflected now, have been the sensible thing to do.

"Yes, that I *am* glad to see you, miss, but you were the last person I expected to see!"

A man came down the stairs, carrying a little black bag. Janine's heart lurched. The reason for the stillness and Ethel's strangeness was now painfully clear. This wasn't their usual doctor, but a younger man, presumably a *locum*.

"How is she, doctor?" Ethel asked, then, conscious of Janine's prescence, "This is Miss Janine, who the mistress keeps calling for."

"Dr. Flack is away on holiday, but I have your aunt's notes. She wasn't very strong, you know. You must be prepared for the worst."

Janine said, "It's her heart, isn't it?"

He looked at her quickly. "No. Low blood-pressure. That is why it is doubtful if she'll pull through. Her age goes against her. You know she was run over, of course?"

"I haven't had a chance to tell her yet, doctor," Ethel said, and still seemed dazed.

"How funny," Janine murmured. "The traffic catching up on her, I mean. Aunt Bee always seemed to quell the drivers into slowing up for her!"

"It wasn't Miss Bee," Ethel said, in a curious dead voice. "It was Miss Agnes. She'd been ill and under the doctor for years, and we never knew!"

Miss Agnes died in the night. Janine was as stunned as Ethel. It seemed so queer that the younger of the sisters should be holding the stage. In the past, it had always been Aunt Bee who was surprising everyone. Miss Agnes stayed in the background, and somehow everyone expected her to be in the background. It suited her.

But it was not so much with Miss Agnes' death that Janine was concerned. It was with Miss Bee. The doctor said, "You know, I think you're going to lose your other aunt, too. Were the sisters very attached to each other?"

"I suppose they were, in a way," Janine said, slowly. "I mean, they agreed on everything, did the same things, even wore similar clothes. But I don't think they really *liked* each other. Why?"

"I think she's missing her sister very badly," the doctor said, with a frown. "You going to get that infant out of the house?" he continued, switching the subject sharply.

Janine shrugged. "How can I, without going back to London, and all the way back here again? Besides," she added, recalling something she had almost forgotten, "that wouldn't do. No, Coppernob will have to stay here. The girl I share the flat with has a baby, too, and her baby's ill. They didn't know what was the matter with it when I left."

He grunted. "You attending your aunt's funeral?"

"Yes, I suppose so. There are no other relatives. Ethel wants to go as well. I suppose I can leave the baby with the people next door, just for that little while."

She saw Aunt Bee after the doctor had left. Miss Bee had a curious expression on her face. She didn't seem to recognize her niece. She was fully dressed, and sitting in a chair by the window, but for all the use she was making of the fact that she was up, she might as well have been in bed.

"Aunt Bee, it's me—Janine! I've come to see you!"

Twice the remark was repeated before any light of recognition appeared in the older woman's face. Then a slight quiver ran over it, wrinkling the parchment-like skin, before it settled into immobility again.

"I robbed her!" she said, in a toneless voice.

"Aunt Bee, what's the matter? Who did you rob?"

"I robbed her," the older woman repeated. "I'll have to go and tell her I didn't mean it, or she'll never understand. Yes, that's it. I must go and find Agnes, and tell her."

"Aunt, Aunt Bee," Janine said urgently, taking her arm, but the older woman shook her off.

"I always meant to tell her. But perhaps she knew all the time. Yes, perhaps she knew ... all the time. How like Agnes to say nothing."

Janine got up to go to the door and call Ethel, but her aunt put out a hand, and grasped Janine's own, holding it in a grip of steel. The girl sat down again, and regarded her aunt uncertainly. Was this what they meant when a person was said to be "wandering"? It was frightening. More frightening than seeing, for the first time last night, a person who is dead. Agnes didn't look dead; she just looked as if she were sleeping peacefully, her pallor in death being no deeper than in life.

"I didn't know she was ill all that time," Miss Bee went on, still in that dreadful monotone. "She didn't tell me. She never told me anything about herself, after that dreadful day. How long ago? Forty? Fifty years? I can't remember, now. But it was a dreadful day."

"What day, Aunt Bee?" Janine asked, gently.

"The anniversary," Aunt Bee answered.

Janine shuddered at the word and its implications. An anniversary always seemed to be the ripest day to do something you wouldn't want to remember, and being an anniversary, the deed always stuck in your mind.

"Agnes had been secretly engaged for a year. She confided in me. I didn't like surprises. She should have known that. Besides, I was the elder sister. I should have been engaged first. She knew that.

That was why she kept her engagement secret."

"Yes, Aunt Bee?"

"I told her I'd better see the young man. She promised to smuggle him into the garden and we were to go down at seven and she was to introduce him to me. I went down at a quarter to seven. I had dressed carefully. My colouring was bold, and my features well-drawn. In those days Agnes wasn't quite so white, but my appearance made her look frail, washed-out. I cut a dash, and I knew it."

She sighed, and dipped back into the past, to her regretful memories.

"He was a very good-looking young man. The elder son of an important local family. Agnes was fortunate. Too fortunate. I decided I wanted him for myself. I flatter myself he liked me, too. Agnes was surprised when she came and found we had already met. I don't think she was very surprised when he broke with her some little while later, but she was very surprised when he became engaged to me. I don't think she thought he would come openly to the house and court me, after being promised to her for a year."

Janine listened aghast. She had never

really thought of the sisters when they were young. They were the type of elderly people of whom the young can never think of as being anything but elderly. Now, with Miss Bee's wandering confidences, between which she rambled a little, in an unintelligible way, there was a haunting whisper of the past, of lavender, rustling silks, broughams and horses, traditions and dignity long since forgotten. A world in which a younger sister stood to lose her secret beau if her elder sister were unscrupulous enough to take advantage of the inflexible rule of elders first.

"It angered me when she became ill. Everyone sympathized with her, for it appeared that her engagement, which she had thought was so carefully hidden, was not so secret from our elders. They couldn't recognize it, because I stood in the way—a handsome spinster, but a spinster nevertheless. That I should take her man struck them as being mean. Why should it?" she finished, in a low, angry voice. "I wanted him. She had no right to have him first."

"You must rest now, dear," Janine soothed, a little scared at this unfamiliar picture of her aunt, who had never been given to confidences, and had always upheld herself as a paragon of the virtues.

"But he didn't want me," she continued. "I made him compromise me. It was easy in those days. A mere matter of being alone and unchaperoned for a given time. He was even more conventional than I was. Oh, yes, he did the right and honourable thing, even to the day of our wedding."

"But you never married?" Janine asked in a puzzled voice.

Aunt Bee shook her head. "No. Fate was against me. I was angry at everyone being so nice to Agnes, so nasty to me. So I did an unforgivable thing. I fixed the date of our marriage to coincide with her anniversary."

For the first time, Aunt Bee turned and looked at her niece. "Never hurt others. It always comes back on you."

She was silent for so long that Janine despaired of hearing what happened. At last, Miss Bee made a conscious effort, and took up her story.

"He was such a strong man. I never knew how he came to have pneumonia. Some say he seemed worried, ill at ease, and walked at night in the grounds of his parents' house. He was caught in a storm one night, and was soaked to the skin. They say he stayed on in the open, in his wet clothes. He died, and was buried on our wedding-day."

Janine patted her hand. Miss Bee seemed to be near her last self. There was that strange, intangible something about her that made her seem remote, and there was a blueish tinge round her mouth and eyes.

"Let me call the doctor, Aunt Bee!"

"Presently. Presently. Where was I? Oh, yes, and so we stayed unmarried, Agnes and I. The rest of the family gradually died off and we were left alone, and you came. But I robbed Agnes. She never confided in me again. Never even told me how ill she had been all these years. How ill . . . all these years. . . ."

She was really wandering, then. The next day she lost consciousness, and died the day before her sister's funeral.

Agnes had left no will. She had little to leave, anyway. Her money from her parents died with her. Bee, on the other hand, had left all her bits of jewellery and what other possessions she had to Agnes.

"What about the house?" Janine asked

the solicitor.

He shrugged. "It's heavily mortgaged. I never could convince the sisters that they hadn't enough money to keep up the standards they were used to. They wouldn't listen. They never took my advice about investments, either. There's little left."

"Enough to pay off the mortgages?"

He shook his head. "My advice to you is, sell the house for what you can get. Clear the debts and stick to the rest. If you don't, you, as next-of-kin, will have a rope round your neck."

Janine wired to ask if Georgina was better, as she wanted to take Coppernob back to London. With the child on her hands, she could do little or nothing. The telegram was reply paid, and Janine sat back in some impatience to await its reply. Ethel was so overcome with the deaths of her two mistresses in such a short time, that she was of no help at all. This was a bigger blow to Janine than the loss of her aunts. Ethel had been such a standby in the past to all of them. Whoever failed the rest, Ethel could be counted on to do what was necessary. Now, the old woman seemed to have lost the urge to be reliable or helpful. She just sat about in a hopeless way, or did a bit of housework listlessly and indifferently. As to looking after the baby, this she refused to do, utterly.

"I wouldn't be able to put me heart into it, miss," she said, rather obscurely.

There was so much to do. Condolence letters had been pouring in. The town's newspaper had wanted copy for a lengthy obituary, as had the Vicar for the church magazine. Old papers to be gone through, and the contents of the house to dispose of or store. The sale to be arranged, and many other things. It was a further blow to Janine when the reply to her telegram arrived.

In the excitement of all that had happened since she had left London, Janine had forgotten Daisy and the reasons for her flight. It was Daisy who replied. Tersely, pithily. She said Janine could leave her kid with her if she liked, but Yvonne's baby had got "dip." and its name was "on the gate".

CHAPTER XVIII

FOR the next three months, Janine stayed at the house next door. The people had known the Stanhope sisters for some years, and a certain degree of intimacy had been reached through the mutual use of their telephone. They extended unlimited hospitality to Janine and the baby, and even Ethel was invited to stay there a day or two, until she decided where to go.

"What will you do now, Ethel?" Janine had asked the old woman, the day after the double funeral.

"I've worked it all out, miss. I'm going to have a room of me own somewhere, and I'm going to sit in the park all day, like a proper lady. I've promised meself that. I've saved up for it, too."

"Won't it be awfully lonely?"

"Maybe it will, miss. Maybe it won't. But that's what I'm going to do."

"What about your sisters? And the rest of your family? And their children you cared for when they were young?"

"All gone abroad, miss, and have been these ten years. Emigrated, that's what they did."

"Well, come with me, then. I can't offer you anything grand, but you could have a bed in my room at the flat, and you could live in with us, and look after Coppernob for me. You'd like that better than being alone, wouldn't you?"

Ethel shook her head. "No, miss. It'd remind me too much of when them two poor souls was alive. No, I'll live by meself. I've *promised* meself."

And she was unshakable.

She got a room somewhere, and wouldn't give anyone her address. She wanted, she said, to cut herself off from her memories. She wasn't even going to live in Bletchbury, but had selected a new town. She said a definite good-bye to Janine, who felt that a limb had been severed. Ethel and her aunts had been so much a part of her life. And now they had all three gone.

Those three months were lonely months for Janine, in spite of the friendly efforts of the neighbours in whose house she was staying. So lonely that she wrote an unconscionable number of letters. Mostly to Yvonne, but some to Stacy, care of his bank. As far as she knew, he was still in Cumberland, and she had a curious conviction that if she wrote to him often enough, she would keep herself in his mind and one day he would come back.

Those letters were a record of her days in Bletchbury. She wrote about the aunts and the prolonged sale of the house and the furniture—heavy old-fashioned stuff too large for a modern flat, and a life's work to keep clean and in good condition. But mostly they were about Coppernob.

The baby was altering daily. Her thatch of red hair had grown curly, a heritage from her burly stevedore father. With the pretty white outfits which Janine had knitted for her, and her own healthy firm roundness, Coppernob attracted a lot of attention wherever she went, and liked it.

She was growing into a contented child, and had a wide engaging grin that was infinitely appealing. She bounded with energy, too, and loved to lie on her back and fling up her fat legs and crow at them.

Janine asked Yvonne to send the pram by rail, and when Yvonne wrote in reply, giving the time it was due to arrive, she gave news of her own baby.

"Georgina nearly died, but Hugh had a specialist for her, a clever man who saved her. Hugh is so good to us, and Georgina adores him. She knows him, and holds out her arms to him."

Janine read it with a pang. Hugh also formed part of that old background, and he, too, was going.

Other letters contained similar remarks, all showing how Hugh Torrington was fitting himself into Yvonne's life. "Hugh took us to see his country place. Georgina likes riding in a car. Hugh's house is old and beautiful, but closed up. Isn't it a pity that no one lives there now?"

And there was news, too, about Daisy. "Charlie found out that Daisy was keeping company with the milkman, and turned nasty. He got her the sack. The milkman got her a job in the dairy, serving behind the counter. Daisy likes it, though it isn't so well paid."

Finally the house was put up for auction, and fetched very little. The furniture was auctioned, too, and at the end of it all, Janine found herself with a smallish sum of money, several hundreds less than she had expected, even after the mortgage was paid off. She settled with the lawyers, sent a small gift of money to Yvonne for her baby's account, and put the rest in the bank for Coppernob. Then

she started to look round for an un-
furnished flat for herself, with the
intention of sending to Stacy's mother for
their home with which to furnish it.

Flats in Bletchbury were not easy to
come by. It was a town of houses. Such
modern innovations as flats were inclined
to be frowned on, and the tenants of such
were hardly considered respectable. There
were many people in the place who
remembered Janine as the pretty but
rather flighty niece of the Stanhope sisters,
and at all turns Janine was hampered by
well-meaning though entirely unwanted
advice, mostly against living alone, and
always against the idea of a flat. Finally,
she capitulated, wondering if she had done
the right thing in selling the house after all.
If it weren't for the mortgage, she might
have been living there all this time, but
from her point of view it was too large, and
a rather grim house for one young person
to occupy.

When she was on the point of going
back to London to get a flat there, the
chance of sharing a small house in a cul-
de-sac came her way. A pleasant girl
opened the door, and said her name was
Barbara Vine.

302

"I'm Janine Conway; the agent who sold my aunts' house said he knew you personally."

"Yes, that's right. As a matter of fact, we're cousins. Have a look round and see if you like the place."

It was a smallish house, not very new, and entirely covered with a creeper that turned crimson and gold with autumn.

"It's at its best at this time of year, of course," Mrs. Vine grinned. "But it's not bad at other times."

There was a pleasant garden at the back, with trees, a small patch of lawn and a miniature lily-pond. All the windows had striped roller blinds against the sun, and the roof was rather like that of a Swiss chalet.

"I like it," Janine said, wistfully. "Will it be expensive to share?"

"Well, I must explain first of all, that the sharing will only be temporary. My husband's in the Far East. He won't be home for at least a year, maybe two. I want the house to myself when he comes home, naturally, but until then I'd like it kept as it is. I don't want it split up into two flats, I mean, or anything like that. Sharing's a delicate business at best, and depends on the people concerned but I think I could get on very well with you. How do you feel about it?"

She was petite and dark, rather Janine's own type. Her voice was crisp and business-like but likeable, and her skin had a brown dried look as if it had been exposed to the tropical suns.

Janine said slowly, "I feel like that too, but there are still one or two things—a question of money, for a start—"

"That can be arranged. I'll meet you if necessary," Barbara Vine cut in.

"And I've a baby," Janine added, purposely leaving the mention of Coppernob to the last.

Barbara Vine swept it away. "Oh, that's all right. I'm used to children. I've got two—six and eight. Both at boarding-school. That's why I came home first, for their education. I'm jolly lucky to have got this house, but it's rather lonely."

And so Janine found a new berth, and wrote joyfully to tell Yvonne about it, giving the address for future corres-pondence. "But for heaven's sake, don't let Daisy get hold of it, in case she wants to come here. Apart from her wanting to get hold of Coppernob, I wouldn't like the girl

I'm staying with to meet her. Daisy's all right among ourselves, but she does get a bit out of hand, and heaven knows what lengths she'd go to if she was put out over the baby."

Towards the end of the year, Yvonne wrote and said, "I wonder if you'll be surprised at my news?" and Janine felt she had sustained a blow. She guessed what was coming. Had known it would come for some time. Each letter of Yvonne's confirmed and strengthened it, until at last she put it into words.

"Hugh and I are getting married just before Christmas. We do so hope you will be able to come to the wedding. It is to be quietly in London, at a registrar's."

It took Janine a day or two to get used to the idea. Barbara watched her covertly, though Janine had given her the barest details only. In the few months they had been together a close friendship had sprung up between them, and Barbara had become touchingly attached to Copper-nob.

"Look," she said, one bitterly cold morning. "You're aching to get up to London and see that girl-friend of yours, but you can hardly take this poor infant all that way in this freezing weather. How about entrusting her to me, while you clear off and have a good time?"

"Oh, Barbara, you don't mean it?" Janine breathed.

"Don't be a silly idiot. Of course I do!"

"But won't your hands be full with your two children home for the holidays?"

Barbara laughed. "Heavens no!" She picked the baby up.

"Copper and I will make hay while you're out of earshot, won't we, my lamb?"

Coppernob crowed her approval and kicked one sock off to give some indication of what she would do when Janine's back was turned.

"I'll take you at your word, Barbara, I think," she murmured, and started packing right away.

Yvonne was out shopping when Janine knocked at the door. A buxom red-faced young woman opened it, a young woman in a blue print frock and white apron, with a baby in her arms.

Janine blinked, then recognized the grave eyes and fair hair of Yvonne in the infant's plump little face.

"That *is* Georgina Ashley, isn't it?" she said, still in doubt.

"Yes, madam. Mrs. Ashley's out, but if you're Mrs. Conway, she's expecting you."

The flat looked different. There were flowers everywhere, hot-house roses and great shaggy chrysanthemums. New cushions were about the place, and the old untidiness had vanished. The familiar rather shabby furniture was still there, but a new element veneered it. An element provided by Hugh's money and devotion for Yvonne.

It was in a sober frame of mind that Janine took off her clothes in the bedroom she had once shared with her friend. Here again there were evidences of Hugh's pocket-book. A great voluptuous satin eiderdown lay on the old divan bed, and under it was a padded quilt to match. Heavily embroidered runners were on the dressing-table and chest, and an expensive cut glass set was laid out on the dressing-table top. Even more significant, there was simply nothing anywhere to indicate Daisy's presence.

Janine wandered out again into the living-room. The maid had vanished into the other bedroom with little Georgina. Sounds of mixing food came from the

307

kitchen, and the girl came out with Georgina's bottle, and smiled at Janine as she passed. Then Hugh let himself in the front door.

As always Janine's heart bounded, on seeing him. He looked different, she noticed. His animal spirits seemed to have been curbed quite a bit. He walked with a quieter tread, and there was a quality of certain happiness on his face that Janine had never seen before.

He didn't seem in the least put out, on seeing her. He seemed to expect her. He took her two cold little hands, and searched her face.

"How are you, my dear?" he asked, and glanced around.

"No, I didn't bring Coppernob," she smiled.

"You didn't say in your telegram whether you were going to bring the baby," he explained. "How is she?"

"Huge—vigorous—cheerful—spoilt," she told him. "Georgina has changed, hasn't she?"

He sat down easily beside her, and started talking. About the baby, its frail health before the illness, and the illness itself. But mostly about Yvonne.

"I have you to thank for my future wife, you know," he told Janine. "I might never have met her, but for you. She's so different from other women I've known. She's so gentle, and kind, and *happy*—"

"Yes, that's it!" Janine agreed, remembering that old quiet joy in Yvonne's face when she had first met her. That was what struck her most. "I'm glad it's back again. It left her, you know, for a time. She was very unhappy."

"Yes. She told me. Now she's happy again. You know, Janine, you and I were crazy devils when we went around together. I think if I'd met Yvonne then, I shouldn't have cared for her. I'm ready for her now. She's come into my life at just the right time. My crazy days are over. I want a wife I can cherish, and Yvonne is just the sort of woman to make a man feel protective. Know what I mean?"

"Yes," Janine agreed softly, "I know what you mean." It was as if she, too, were seeing Hugh for the first time. He had been a great, racy hero to her, yet all the time, she now clearly saw, he had been just an overgrown schoolboy, making the most of his wealth, and flinging it around in a not too harmful way. He wasn't at all the sort

309

of person she had insisted on believing him to be. That was so clear now, as to have been absurd.

Yvonne came in flushed and rosy with the cold, and it was as Hugh had said. She was such a happy person. Her eyes glowed with it. Yet, Janine fancied, there was the slightest restraint in her manner as she greeted her.

"Come into the bedroom with me while I take my clothes off," she commanded. "I've such lots to tell you, I can't wait!"

But once in the bedroom, she was silent, and seemed preoccupied.

"You did want to talk to me, Yvonne, didn't you?" Janine said, shrewdly. "Was it about . . . Hugh?"

Yvonne appeared relieved. "Well, yes, to tell you the truth, it was."

"What about Hugh, Yvonne?"

"Well, the other day I ran into the girl who was in Hugh's flat that day—your sister-in-law, Merrill."

"Yes?" Janine breathed.

"And she said . . . well, I suppose she was just being rather spiteful, though I can't think why. She said . you and Hugh . . . Janine, you two *were* friends once, weren't you?"

310

Merrill. Open-hearted, happy-go-lucky Merrill. So she was just about as much to be trusted as Stacy's mother! Without realizing it, Janine's face froze, and the look in her eyes as she stared at Yvonne, was suddenly hostile.

Yvonne said, distressed, "Oh, Janine, I've been clumsy the way I put it. I didn't mean to upset you or be horrid, but it was so difficult to ask you without, well, probing too much into your life. Of course Merrill wasn't speaking the truth! I ought to have known that, knowing you!"

She came and took Janine's arms, gently pressing them, and giving her a little shake to emphasize her words.

"Forget what I said—if you can, Janine! It was beastly of me."

Janine smiled tightly. "It's not that. It's just that everyone—even Stacy—seems so willing to believe the worst of me, and to put the wrong construction on what happened. I wouldn't tell Stacy just what did happen, but I'll tell you."

They sat side by side on the satin eider-down, and when that old story was recounted again, Yvonne asked in bewilderment: "Then why on earth did Merrill—I just don't understand what made her say what she did!"

"I do!" Janine said, grimly. "Merrill knew I was keen on Hugh, and thought she'd lift him from me. It did seem as if she'd made a conquest. Then Hugh met you, and you can bet your life she isn't pleased to see how he feels about you! Did you tell her about your marriage?"

"Oh, yes, I had to, when she asked me if I saw Hugh these days."

"Well, then, that's it!" Janine exclaimed. "Oh, forget about her, Yvonne. I always suspected she was jealous underneath, just like her loathsome old mother."

"It's funny how a nice person like your husband came to have relations like that," Yvonne mused. "Janine, did you ever mean to tell him about, well, what you just told me?"

"Yes, I was going to, more than once, but I always got wild to think he was jealous and didn't seem to trust me."

"All men are jealous if they care enough," Yvonne said, with old wisdom. Then after a silence, "You cared for Hugh in those days, didn't you?"

"Um," Janine nodded.

"Do you—do you still love him,

Janine?"

Janine forced herself to meet her friend's eye. "Until today, I thought I did," she said, slowly. "But out there, talking to him just before you came in, I saw him as he really was." She tried to put her thoughts into words. "He's not really a swaggering, dashing hero, is he?"

"No, he isn't that," Yvonne smiled fondly.

"In fact, I think he's rather like my Stacy. Worthy, I think, is the word. The stuff good husbands are made of."

"Yes," Yvonne said. "In many ways he's like George. I suppose all really good men are alike underneath. The same good qualities, with perhaps a little variety in the exteriors. I never thought I should come to marry again. But I miss George so much, and Hugh's the only one I could ever bear to see in George's place."

"Hugh seemed so different to me, all those years ago, and in my memory since. I've been chasing a shadow, a sort of mirage, all these years," Janine said, in a far-away voice.

"Don't regret it," Yvonne urged. "Be thankful you can see it now, and get in touch with your husband while there's time." She sounded very urgent, and Janine was rather puzzled, but at that moment Hugh thumped on the door.

"How much longer are you two chatter-boxes going to be? I'm hungry!"

"We're going out to dinner, as a surprise. Hugh's favourite Hungarian restaurant," Yvonne explained. "Charlotte will look after Georgina all right. She lives in, you know. Hugh insisted on that, especially now Daisy's got a live-in job."

"Has she left the dairy then?"

"Well, she wanted more money, and I can't say I blame her for going back to be a waitress. It's the one thing she was really good at. After all, getting married is an expensive business these days."

Hugh was at his gayest that night, though Janine was amazed to see how subdued even that could be, in comparison with his crazy moods as she knew them years ago. He was still good company, but for the third person it was not such fun. He was making a point, all the time, of including Janine in every-thing, because she was their guest, but Janine felt that he and Yvonne would have been so very much happier alone.

Towards the end of the meal, when they were almost ready to go, and Janine had toasted their future happiness, a thought clicked into place resulting from one of Yvonne's random remarks. The words "marriage", "future happiness", "time" and other kindred words cropping up in the conversation brought to mind what Yvonne had said about Daisy's new job. This, in some odd way, seemed in Janine's mind to have some connection with what Yvonne had also said about contacting Stacy "while there was time".

"What did you mean about Daisy? Why should she save for marriage? Or has she got her freedom after all?"

Coppernob and all her fears for that gay scrap of babyhood suddenly overwhelmed her.

Yvonne stared.

"Haven't you heard, Janine? It was in all the papers. Daisy's husband was knifed in a dock brawl four weeks ago!"

CHAPTER XIX

STACY like his new job. He liked his new chief, too. A man of sixty, with a tired lined face, and a sparkling wit that was at all times refreshing, Noah Clynton made that trip round the world one of fascination and wonder for Stacy. It was not just a job, but an appointment. Stacy was someone. If you couldn't contact Clynton, Conway would often do just as well, at least for information. Stacy discovered, too, that he had the ingredients of the perfect male secretary. Little gifts and concessions from his new chief from time to time confirmed this.

They went to Belgium first, then Holland. After that, he flew to Cape Town with Clynton, and alone to Bombay to fix appointments for his chief before his arrival. Lightning visits, all of them, packed with a bewildering array of new sights and impressions. But the return through Europe was of necessity slower, and by the time they were back in Paris, Clynton decided they both needed a rest.

"Anxious to get back to England, Conway?"

"No, sir, I can't say that I am," Stacy admitted.

"Well, I'll want you in the mornings, but the rest of the day is yours. We'll be stopping here about a week."

This would be the first Christmas that

Stacy had not spent at his mother's house, he reflected. He had written only two letters to his mother since he left England, and they were extremely brief, and merely to let her know he was safe. He decided to send yet another note, with some gifts for her and Merrill, to explain that he would not be home this side of the New Year. She would be annoyed, he reflected, and her gentle voice would complain bitterly to Honoria Westlands about sons who were virtually dead, for all their mothers saw of them, once they were married.

He reflected that if he hadn't made the effort himself, he would never have got out of England, and all that youthful slogging with language study and travel would have been wasted. Yet he wished Janine could have been with him.

When he last saw her she was wearing a simple flower-patterned dress; no, he corrected himself, that was the time before. That last distressing interview had carried away still less glamorous memories, for she had merely worn a dark suit and plain blouse. There was a French girl sitting at his table in the hotel, whose colouring was similar to Janine's, and Stacy wished Janine had worn clothes like hers.

To-day she wore a balloon-skirted dress of white wool with thin black stripes, which accentuated her nipped-in waist and made her black hair look even blacker. Last night at dinner she had worn buttercup yellow, with tiny black dots all over the shoulders. Janine would turn up her nose at such colour-schemes and stick to her conservative suits and thick woollen jumpers, and flower-patterned crepes for dinner, because such clothes were accepted in Bletchbury as being "nice" and "discreet".

The French girl decided that Stacy was wistful and needed taking in hand. She started in on him with subtlety and before long he was calling her Anna. She had a puckish grin and a gaiety that was difficult to resist.

"You know Paris well?" she probed.

He admitted that he didn't know Paris at all, and that he intended to spend the afternoons and evenings of the rest of the week in getting to know it.

"Ah! And you intend, no doubt, to visit the Eiffel Tower, the Champs-Elysées, the Bois de Boulogne, and Notre-Dame, following on the heels of all the other

318

goggling tourists, yes?" She gave a rapid and vivid impersonation of a tourist standing gaping, while listening to the voice of the professional guide.

Stacy laughed. "That was, I'm afraid, the general idea," he admitted.

"Ah, quelle idée! Now, I'll show you Paris, the Paris of the café and the little street; I'll show you how to spend the day, and perhaps the night—eh? We shall see!"

Anna and Paris were inseparably entwined in Stacy's memories for ever. Anna in whirling, fur-edged coats, and daring bonnets; Anna wafting expensive scents delicately around her wherever she went; Anna being imperious to commissionaires of hotels, and gay and friendly with hawkers and crossing-sweepers and the greasy proprietors of wayside cafés. Anna with tears in her eyes as she showed him the beloved Seine, under a snow-laden sky; Anna in crimson, with snow in her black hair, laughing and laden with Christmas parcels.

"You love Paris, Anna. Have you lived here all your life?"

"Silly boy, I do not live here! Or why should I stay in an expensive hotel? No, I am just visiting the place where I was born.

Paris, ah, it is a wonderful place! Besides," she finished with an expressive pout, "I am also taking a holiday from my husband."

"You're married?" Stacy asked, surprised.

"Yes," she answered collectedly, "as you are, also, my friend!"

"How did you know?" he gasped.

"Because you have a restraint about you, as a man has, who already cherishes in his heart the woman of his choice. You did not want me all this so-gay week. *Non*, you wanted a little companionship, with one who knows Paris and can show her to you. Am I right?"

He nodded. "I'm sorry, Anna."

"Oh, don't apologize! I do not need that. I, too, was glad of a young man, a handsome man, beside me, this week. To-morrow I go back to Jean-Marie. He is—how do you say it?—portly." She showed him, with delicate petal-like hands, how portly Jean-Marie was. "He is a dull cabbage. He does not care to see Paris again. 'Go yourself and spend all my money' he says to me. 'But do not ask me to walk with you hand in hand and ogle at the passers-by!' Ah, he makes me sick!"

She wanted to know about his wife, and

what she looked like, and if he had any children.

"My wife," Stacy said, slowly, "looks very much like you, Anna, but she hasn't your gaiety." There, for him, was the tragedy of Janine, and himself.

"And ... children?"

"My son died," he said, briefly.

"Ah, that is indeed tragic," Anna agreed. "I have a son—so big." She stooped and showed him a place incredibly near the ground. "He has one year and is called Tou-Tou. He is fat. He will be portly like Jean-Marie when he is old. When I go back to Pleury, I shall have a daughter, I think. Yes, I should like that. And when she grows up, she will be like me. Nice?" She pirouetted for his inspection, and Stacy laughed helplessly.

"Very nice, Anna. Very nice."

"Your wife knows you are in Paris?"

"No," he said, briefly, and a lot of the fun and happiness went out of the winter's day for him. "I have left her."

Anna went home the day before he was due to go. He went to the station with her. It was bitterly cold, and she had a lot of luggage. Most of it was clothes, she told him gaily, and some gifts for Tou-Tou and

321

Jean-Marie. Gifts for the rest of the family, and for her husband's family, numbering in all, four great-grandparents, four grandparents, parents and in-laws, nineteen brothers and sisters, twenty cousins, and five small nieces and nephews.

"Only five?" Stacy grinned.

"Oh, my brothers are young—give them time. They will do better!" Anna told him seriously.

There was half an hour to wait for the train to Pleury. Anna, now that she was definitely going back home, was all of a fret to begin the journey, to be off and away. Stacy thought it was perhaps as well that Janine was a quiet soul, and then he pulled himself up sharply. What did it matter to him what Janine was like? He had left her.

And because he was digging deeply into old memories and familiar faces, it was significant, perhaps, to be suddenly aware that his thoughts were on Louise and Fenella. He remembered that Fenella had gone abroad, to Paris. Was she here now, he wondered? But no, she couldn't be still here. That was way back in the summer.

He took Anna to get some tea, stilling

her like an impatient child, and when they came out of the buffet she suddenly pointed.

"Look, who is that girl, the one with the red hair? She is staring at us. Do you know her?"

He whitened. Fenella stood amid a pile of luggage; English to the last degree in her well-cut tweeds and heavy fur coat. She took in Anna's naughty hat and bright green swagger coat, and delicately raised her eyebrows, turning away slightly.

"She does not like to see you with me," Anna said, without much interest. Already she was in Pleury with little Tou-Tou, and the Christmas tree. "You are a naughty man, I did not think it of you!"

Then Anna was on the train, and they were waving madly to each other. Gay little Anna who had made this an unforgettable week, and who would now go out of his life for ever.

He turned away rather sadly, and found himself staring into the dark brown eyes of Fenella again.

He put out his hand and she took it.

"Well, Stacy?"

"Well, Fenella?"

It was a difficult meeting. Between their

last meeting and this stood a stiff little note, saying he couldn't leave his wife, nor get his freedom. Yet here he was, seeing Anna off at the Gare du Nord at a time when he should certainly have been expected to be in England. Christmas Eve.

"Are you with someone?" he asked.

She shook her head. "I was just moving on. I've been doing that for six months, Stacy."

"Then come in the warm and have some hot chocolate with me," he said, taking her arm.

She went with him without protest. It seemed that she was no longer angry, but then she apparently no longer cared. She told him, over the steaming liquid at a table behind steaming plate glass windows, that she had been in Switzerland and Germany, and had now wandered back to Paris to spend a lonely Christmas. She didn't say it with a view to enveigling his company, and when he suggested spending it together, she was inclined to refuse.

"That girl I've just seen off was a complete stranger," he said, in a slightly rebuking tone. "Yet she took pity on me and spent her time with me, though she's

324

happily married and was going home for Christmas. Shouldn't we, who know each other so well, spend just to-morrow—Christmas Day—together if a stranger can do it?"

"It's because we know each other so well, Stacy, that we definitely shouldn't spend to-morrow together. For me, at least, it will open up all the old memories, and be a sad Christmas."

But he persuaded her in the end, and she came over to his hotel to breakfast on Christmas morning, and together they went to the cathedral for High Mass.

"Isn't Paris a lovely city, under a mantle of snow?" Fenella said, holding his arm and apparently temporarily forgetting how things stood between them.

"Yes," Stacy murmured. "I wonder if there's snow in England?"

"How long have you been away, then?" she asked in some surprise.

"I left soon after you did, I imagine," and told her where he had been.

"Do you hear from Janine?"

He shook his head. "I kicked around for two or three weeks, hoping the bank would forward a letter from her, but nothing came. It's hardly likely that she's

325

written since. If she had, then her letters will be held there till I go home."

Fenella said, "Richard's still trying to persuade me to marry him. I think I shall. A man who forgives and still wants you after all this time, is a man worth having."

"Does he know, then?"

"Yes. My dear sister Louise saw to it that everyone knew, once you'd turned her down. I don't see how you dared, seeing how it would involve me."

She was icy again. He saw now why she hadn't wanted to spend to-day with him.

"I didn't think she'd let everyone know we stayed at that hotel, Fenella. Heaven knows, it was an innocent enough holiday, in all conscience. She tried to trick me over it, and it was because of you that I didn't deny her assertion that I had stayed there with her. What could she hope to get out of it?" He was genuinely bewildered.

"You don't know Louise. She can't bear to see I've got something without wanting it. She's even made a play for Richard, but without very much hope of success. You see, Richard's known us both all our lives. He knows her, and won't stand for her nonsense! She knows that, and doesn't waste her time. You were a different proposition."

"But she knew I was married, surely."

"Oh, yes, but she's vain enough to think she could make you get your freedom for her, whereas I couldn't. Still, it doesn't matter. It's all over now, Stacy. I think I shall go back and marry Richard. He's had an offer of a nursing-home in London, poor darling, and doesn't want to take it without me. I mean to go back and finish my hospital training, anyway. It nags at me to leave anything unfinished."

"Why did you go abroad, Fenella?"

"Are you so vain that you want me to put it into words, Stacy? Because I wanted to get you out of my system, of course. What else could have made me act so foolishly?"

"Perhaps I don't understand women, but as a man, I've always found that the only way to get someone out of your system is to work, and to work damned hard."

"Have you got Janine out of your system by hard work, Stacy?" she asked quietly, and he knew she was right in her shrewd guess. He hadn't got Janine out of his system.

Fenella had been to a convent in Paris

as a child, and she expressed a wish to go back there to-night, where there was to be the nativity play enacted by some of the children, and then a party afterwards. She asked Stacy to take her.

He watched the children with half interest at first, and then it suddenly became personal. How would it be if he and Janine had had several children, children who had survived? Would it have offered the solution to that marriage of theirs?

Suddenly he yearned to know how little Coppernob was getting on. He wanted to see a picture of her. He wanted to see Janine, and it suddenly struck him that she must have had a tough time (despite all her nonchalance) bringing up a young child, even under the roof of her aunts.

There was a half-formed idea at the back of his mind, as he left the convent with Fenella that Christmas night, an idea which he decided to put into operation as soon as he got back to London. He would go to Janine and suggest to her that they try to make a new start in the New Year. The traditional time for wiping the slate clean, for turning over a new page.

He was absurdly, boyishly happy all at

once. He took Fenella's arm and marched her along the pavement above the shining Seine, where he had not long ago been propelled by the dramatic Anna.

"Fenella," he said, earnestly, "you and I are going to find somewhere very special where we can drink a toast, private and personal, to the New Year and our new beginnings. What do you say?"

Because she was anxious to approach her own future with something like enthusiasm, she did her best to fall in with his mood. She smiled tenderly at him, and nodded. He was such a boy, she thought, with a catch in her throat.

The next day Stacy sent a telegram to Janine, care of her aunts, without knowing that the house was empty, locked up, under new ownership. It had been bought by a syndicate, very cheaply, in order to use it as a lever, a very gently lever, to start converting old white elephant houses into flats. This, the syndicate felt, would be merely the prelude to a spanking white concrete block of unashamed flats in the town's centre. But Stacy didn't know this. He thought Janine would be expecting him the next day.

As it was, Janine had no idea that he

was planning to come home from the Continent to re-start his life with her, in a matter of forty-eight hours. Which was perhaps as well, considering the way things turned out.

The next morning, Noah Clynton telephoned to Stacy's room. "Come down to my suite, Conway. I've news for you!"

He presented himself to his chief, in a rather muddled frame of mind. He had been thinking of Janine, and particularly of Hugh Torrington, and that tantalizing question of their old relationship.

"Conway, you once told me you'd give your ears to see Egypt and Syria. I don't know whether the connection is Biblical, or merely one of general interest, but you'd better see about carrying out your rash promise."

"I beg your pardon, sir?" Stacy stuttered.

"We've had instructions from London, to turn round in that direction. A new deal, and a very hush-hush one."

"When, sir?"

"Right away. I'll leave you to see to the tickets as usual. Reservations have been made from the London end. You haven't long to pack."

330

His vision of Janine faded. "How long will the trip take, sir?" he wanted to know, doing rapid mental arithmetic.

"How long?" Clynton chuckled. "I thought you weren't anxious to see England yet? We won't be back this side of Easter!"

CHAPTER XX

REG, the milkman, was a quiet man. Stolid, in fact. All the girls had liked him, and trusted him. But there was about him that bulldog quality that turned his steadiness into a sullen obstinacy at times. Once he got an idea, he stuck to it no matter what effect it had on everyone else.

Yvonne mentioned this first to Janine, the day after she arrived in London.

"You must be careful of Reg, you know, Janine. He's a queer lad in many ways."

"What sort of 'queer'?" Janine wanted to know. She had seen so much less of him than Yvonne had, since Reg and Daisy had been to see Yvonne several times during the three months that Janine had been out of London. Also Reg was still serving the milk at Yvonne's flat each day.

"Well, he's the sort of man who hasn't

had very much during his life. His family were bitterly poor, and I think perhaps as a child he didn't have much of a time, and certainly no toys to speak of. When he did have things, they were poor bits he got for himself. It's made him sort of—well, what I'm trying to say is what he has he hangs on to, tooth and nail. And what he imagines is his by rights, he'll fight for."

"Go on," Janine said, quietly. "What does he imagine is his by rights?"

"Coppernob," Yvonne said, equally quietly.

"That baby's mine—I legally adopted her!" Janine burst out, furiously.

Yvonne shook her head. "I'm not going to argue with you, my dear. I'm just warning you, that's all. But I want you to know that Hugh says if you like he'll instruct his solicitor to take action for you. We'll do that, gladly. You can't afford legal help, neither you nor your husband, come to that. We'll do it, as friends."

"But what is there to take legal aid for?" Janine was bewildered. "She's mine. Daisy relinquished her. She didn't want her."

"But now she does, now that she and Reg are free to be married," Yvonne said, slowly. "Oh, I know it's backing out of a bargain, but you know Daisy, as well as I do. I think it's rotten of her, especially as she can have more children. But there it is. She wants Coppernob back, and Reg is determined to get her for Daisy."

"Well, she won't. I'll go back to Bletchbury. She won't find me there. Coppernob and I will lie low, till Stacy comes back."

"Is he coming back, then, after all?"

Yvonne was eager, too eager.

Janine flushed. "I don't know, but I hope so. But even if he doesn't come back, Daisy can't do anything. She signed the adoption papers, didn't she? Well, that's final."

Yvonne bit her lip worriedly.

"I don't think it is so final, Janine. I don't know much about legal adoption, but there are several things that might go against you, I think. You're not living with your husband, while the baby's own mother is going to have a husband who could provide her with a home. I don't know how your finances compare with what Reg makes, but I should think a Court would decide that his income was larger and more secure."

"A *Court*?" Janine whispered.

Yvonne bit her lip. She hadn't meant to say that, but it was out now, and would have to be followed up. She couldn't pretend to Janine.

"I didn't mean to tell you, but Reg is already talking of taking it to the Courts for settlement. That's what they do with an adoption dispute, I believe, unless it can be settled peaceably. Don't forget that Hugh will have it fought for you by the best lawyers if you want it, Janine."

Janine was appalled. The thought of a lawsuit over the baby staggered and horrified her.

"No, no, they're not going to do that to Coppernob. I took her from Daisy because I wanted her, but also so that she wouldn't have anything but a normal happy background. If she's going to have two camps scrapping over which side she belongs to, that's going to be worse than anything!"

"They're being married just after Christmas," Yvonne said, watching Janine.

"They can get married to-morrow, for all I care," Janine exploded. "They've got to find us first, before they can do anything!"

"They won't have to search very much," Yvonne told her friend, sadly. "I'm sorry, Janine, but Daisy knows your address."

Janine stared. "But you *promised* you wouldn't let her have it!"

"I know, but it was hardly my fault. She came one day when I was out. I wasn't expecting her. Charlotte let her in and left her in the sitting-room. She knew I wouldn't be long. Well, you know what Daisy is. Charlotte caught her at my writing-case. Charlotte's a good girl, and honest. She was furious with Daisy, and almost threw her out, but Daisy went off laughing. The damage was done. She'd found your address."

"That's about finished everything, then."

"I'm afraid so. I'm terribly sorry, Janine. Can't you go and stay with friends somewhere else? But there, I don't suppose it'd do much good, if Reg started trouble. I think they trace you with detectives. I'm not sure."

"I'll go up to Cumberland and see Stacy, as soon as I go back up North," Janine said, with a sigh. She had been hoping so much that Stacy would make a move, rather than making it necessary for her to go chasing after him at his work. She knew she had started trouble, but she had written so many letters which could have given him the lead to make the first active move.

Yvonne looked very lovely on her wedding-day. Janine was one of the witnesses, and to her surprise Callahan, the artist, was the other. He recalled the last occasion he had seen Janine, and after the ceremony, when they were all having a quiet lunch in Hugh's favourite club, the story of the muddle over Hugh's flat was gone over once again.

"It was all your fault, Henry," Hugh laughed, "for having the same initial as me!"

Janine remembered that day with wistfulness. It was such a contrast to her own wedding. Yvonne wore a soft pink crepe dress and a swathed turban of the same material, and the mink coat Hugh had given her for a wedding present. The quiet of the registry and the gaiety of that informal little lunch afterwards contrasted oddly with her own white wedding and stiff reception, with few of her own friends and a great many older people invited by her aunts.

Weddings. How different each was, and how differently they were remembered. Janine thought of her own first anniversary, spent alone in the hospital, and with something like panic she remembered the embittered anniversary of which her aunt had spoken. She wondered what her second anniversary would be like, and whether she and Stacy would be together again, and whether indeed little Coppernob would still be with them.

There were two days to go, before returning to Bletchbury, and Hugh and Yvonne begged her to stay in town for a complete rest before she returned up North. They told her she could stay in the flat, for when Hugh and Yvonne returned from France they were giving it up, and going to open up the country house. They were leaving little Georgina with the capable Charlotte.

Janine waved good-bye to them on the platform, and decided to go and see Stacy's mother and sister. The idea was an obnoxious one, but the only alternative seemed to be to spend the rest of the day with Henry Callahan.

"Oh, come on, old girl," he said, "I hate the aftermath of a wedding. Let's go

337

somewhere and get tight. Let's have a good time on our own."

"No, honestly, I can't," Janine laughed, finding his persuasion tactics rather amusing.

"What're you going to do? Go back to that 'palling furnish-flat and mope. Mope! All on your own! No, you come and keep little Henry company. Much the best thing."

"You've had too much wine already, Henry. Go back to your studio and do some work. That's best for you."

"Studio—good idea! Come back with me and see some pictures. See my latest picture. Best thing I've done in years. Come on, I'll call a taxi."

"No!" Janine said, firmly, but laughingly, and shaking him off, she got a taxi for herself, and gave the address of Stacy's mother. Henry stood sadly shaking his head on the pavement edge, and the last Janine saw of him out of the back window was when he stepped off the curb and leapt back in time to avoid a passing motor-bus.

The taxi swung down the long main road and turned into the district which she had first come to, as a bride. Memories crowded back on her. The little basement flat, where she had prepared for her baby son, amid the high tension of visits to and from Stacy's mother, and the loathsome visits to the clinic at intervals for examination and check-up. Somewhere, among her things, were little half-finished night-gowns and dresses that she had made herself, and tiny white woollies. Somehow she couldn't bring herself to put Coppernob in them, and now Coppernob was too big. At seven months, she was as large as a year-old baby, and as bonny.

The cab passed the hospital, with all its memories, and for no reason at all Janine thought of the ginger nurse, who had seemed to want to talk to her, but had never quite come to make the effort. Janine wondered if the girl had had troubles of her own. There was that something about each of them that had made the other feel instinctive dislike. Janine didn't know enough about Fenella Helston to realize that her home was in Cumberland, and it is doubtful if she would have connected her with Stacy.

By the time they had reached the top of Mrs. Conway's road, Janine experienced a revulsion for all the memories the place brought back. Suddenly she knew she couldn't face Stacy's mother without letting the old dislike show very clearly, and that wouldn't help matters. Besides, Merrill would be there, and she had not seen Merrill since Yvonne had told her what the girl had done to try and prevent Yvonne and Hugh from going through with their marriage. For that, Janine decided, she would never be able to forgive Merrill, nor ever be pleasant to her again.

"I've altered my mind, driver. Turn back," she said, rapping on the glass.

Back at the flat, she found Charlotte getting Georgina ready to go out for a short walk. The day was fine though cold, and the child was so wrapped up that only her little button of a nose and her two bright blue eyes showed above the blankets of the pram.

"I shall be back in an hour, madam," the girl said, as she wheeled the pram out of the entrance hall.

Janine was disappointed. The flat was large and lonely. Here the three of them, Yvonne, Daisy and herself, had rattled round after leaving Hugh's luxury place, and although she herself had been there a few days only, it had a nostalgic quality about it. She didn't like it without the other two.

As if in answer to her thoughts, the doorbell went, and she found Daisy and Reg standing there. Daisy very cock-a-hoop in a brand-new and rather flash outfit in brown and yellow check with a shiny brown bag slung jauntily from her shoulder, and shiny patent leather shoes with precariously high heels. Reg looked sober, but determined. It was Reg's determined look that disturbed Janine most.

Daisy said, "Well, ain't you goin' to ask us in?" and pushed by without waiting for an answer. Reg followed without removing his bowler hat.

"I knew you was 'ere," Daisy went on, without looking at Janine, and wandered over to the mirror above the mantel where she stood titivating her face and hair. "I see Charlotte up the road with Yvonne's kid."

"I see."

" 'Course, Yvonne's too 'igh an' mighty to invite us to 'er weddin'. She's too much up in the world for the likes of us, now. But we're not the sort to take offence, are we, Reg?"

"That's right," Reg said, sitting down

uninvited in one of the arm-chairs.

"So we thought we'd come along an' wish 'em luck, 'fore they went orf, like, didn't we, Reg?"

"That's right."

"But Charlotte says they've gorn. 'Ad a bit of a do and scarpered. 'Well,' I sez, 'No sense in callin', then, is there?" But just then I sees someone git out of a taxi, an' blow me down if it isn't you! Recognized yer, I did, all that way orf, right from darn the end o' the road. Didn't I, Reg?"

"That's right."

"So we sez, well, we'll look in on old Janine while we're 'ere, then it won't be a wasted journey."

"That's right."

Janine still stood staring across at Daisy, who was making herself as at home as if she still lived there.

"Doesn't Reg ever say anything but 'that's right'?" she asked, tartly.

"Oh, yes, when it suits 'im," Daisy said, looking fondly across at the man she was going to marry. "'Eard my noos?"

"Which ones?" Janine asked, cautiously.

"'Bout Reg an' me. Goin' ter be married termorrer. Want ter come?"

"I'm afraid I shan't be here to-morrow," Janine said, suddenly making up her mind. This pair were going to be more formidable than she had realized.

"Oh, goin' back to see Daisy's kid, eh?" Reg put in, smartly.

"I'm going back to my child, my legally adopted child," Janine corrected him.

"We'll see about that," Reg said, licking his lips. "Know where your 'usband is?"

"Of course I do!"

"I bet!" he said, derisively. "All right, then, where is 'e?"

"Mind your own business!" Janine said, angrily, "and bearing in mind that I didn't invite you here, I think you two had better go. You're getting offensive!"

"In good time, in good time," Reg said airily, waving a stubby hand at her, and making no attempt to move. Daisy, scenting trouble, moved forward, looking indignant, but Reg frowned at her to say nothing.

"It's my belief," Reg said, with emphasis, "that you don't know where your 'usband is. You're separated, that's what!"

"How dare you!"

"All right, then, where is 'e? All you

343

gotta do is just say where 'e is! Course I can find out for meself, if I want, an' between you 'an me, I shall want, pretty soon!"

"How can my husband's address possibly concern you?" Janine asked, furiously.

"I want 'is address to give ter my s'licitor," Reg said grandly. "Thought I couldn't afford to go to the law, didn't yer? Well, I've got a bit of money saved fer this an' that, an' I sez ter Dais, we're 'avin' that kid o' yours back, an' I got the cash ter git 'er back. Easy as kiss yer 'and."

"Daisy signed her over to me. It's all legally arranged and there's no going back!" Janine told him.

"Oh, isn't there? D'you think they'll let you keep the kid, you wot's livin' away from yer 'usband? I should shay sho! What, tell the Court a woman whose 'usband left 'er because of a certain fella whose name we won't mention—"

"Now look here, that's going too far!" Janine said, two bright pink spots glowing in her cheeks.

"Don't you get uppish with us—we know what we're torkin' about!" Daisy shrilled. "We bin ter see your mother-in-law!"

344

"Shut yer mouth!" Reg said, in a savage undertone, but the damage had been done. A visit from Daisy and her Reg would be all Mrs. Conway would need to bring about an event which would lead to Janine's hold on Stacy being broken for ever.

"It isn't true," Janine said, "and anyway, you've no proof."

"Mud sticks!" Reg said, his eyes gleaming with something near triumph. "We're gittin' that kid back. You can't stop us. Why, you don't even know where yer 'usband is!"

Janine shrugged. "That's also where you're wrong. It happens that I naturally know where he is. He hasn't left me at all. He's where his firm sent him—in Cumberland."

Reg looked surprised, and more pleased than ever. He turned to Daisy. "In Cumberland, she says." He winked broadly and laughed aloud. "Cumberland, eh? That's a good 'un!"

He got up suddenly, and took Daisy's arm. "Come on, gel, there's nothink more to keep us 'ere," he said, and firmly walked her to the door, without so much as a look in Janine's direction.

Daisy was inclined to stop and argue further, and perhaps to gloat over Janine's situation, but Reg wouldn't have it. He knew when to make his exit, and made it before Daisy spoiled it for him.

Janine stared at the door, and listened to them banging the front door behind them. For sheer bad manners and utter effrontery, she had seen nothing like it. Their visit had been extremely disturbing, too. They were too swaggering to be just bluffing. They knew something, or thought they did. She was anxious about that remark about Cumberland. Had Stacy been moved, and told only his mother, and if so, had she been unwise or spiteful enough to tell Daisy and Reg?

Janine wished she hadn't altered her mind about seeing his mother now. She would have missed this very unpleasant visit, on such an otherwise happy day, but following on Daisy's visit to the Conway house, Janine's reception might not have been so pleasant, after all.

Janine made up her mind that the only thing to do was to get to Cumberland as soon as possible. The bank was closed, so she couldn't ask them for Stacy's address, and doubted if they'd give it to her anyway. There remained only Stacy's mother, to whom Janine had been going to apply all along, but had put off the asking, in the vain hope that Stacy himself would write. At last she realized there was nothing else to do but telephone, in the hope that Mrs. Conway would not object to telling her where he was now.

She dialled Mrs. Conway's telephone number, and Merrill answered.

"It's Janine. Merrill, I want you to help me!"

"Oh, it's you," Merrill said, the disappointment in her voice suggesting that she had been expecting someone else, probably a new boy-friend.

"Merrill, I'm in trouble and want to contact Stacy quickly. Where is he staying now?"

There was a tiny pause at the other end. Janine could imagine Merrill doing a bit of quick thinking. Then:

"D'you mean to tell me you haven't got his address?"

"That's none of your business," Janine said. "If you won't give it to me, I can get it from somewhere else." She bit her lip angrily as she said it, and wondered why she had always felt impelled to quarrel with Stacy's sister, for Merrill avoided open breaches where possible. It was her boast that she was too good-natured to quarrel with anyone.

Merrill said, pleasantly, "Then you'd better get it from somewhere else, dear, hadn't you?" and hung up.

Janine replaced the receiver. What a silly thing to do, she told herself furiously. But it was doubtful from the first, whether she would have got it from that source, whatever had happened. If Stacy's mother had answered the telephone, the conversation might have been a good deal more unpleasant.

She packed her week-end case, and by the time Charlotte returned with the baby she was ready to go.

She kissed the chubby mite, and told Charlotte she was leaving for home, having suddenly changed her plans. The girl accepted it as one of the many vagaries of her employers and their friends, and watched her go without curiosity. Janine reflected that not long ago she had been very, very sorry for Yvonne in her unenviable position. Now Yvonne had everything, even a thoroughly reliable girl to look after her baby.

It was necessary to go back to Bletchbury first, and tell Barbara what had happened to make her change her plans, for not having Stacy's address in her possession she didn't know how long she'd be looking for him.

Barbara was sympathetic, though hardly surprised. "I wondered how long you'd be able to go on like this," she said. "What are you going to do now?"

"In my things upstairs there's a list of the branches of my husband's firm. He shouldn't be far from the Cumberland branch, should he? Anyway, I'll start off first thing in the morning, and if I have difficulty, I can always telephone the branch when I arrive, can't I?"

"Yes, I suppose so. Look, Janine, I don't want to pry, and all that, but . . . well, are you all right for money?"

Janine turned swiftly, and her eyes glowed. "Oh, Barbara! I wouldn't borrow, even if I needed it, but it's terribly sweet of you to think of it, and to ask!" She hugged the other girl and turned sharply away, blinking fiercely. Barbara was one of her newest friends, and one of the staunchest.

She booked to the terminus, and took a local train to the town where the Head

Office was. It was a bleak morning, grey of sky and landscape, with snow in the air. Suddenly Janine realized that this was Christmas Eve. If only she were in time to contact Stacy before he went south for the holiday, she might be able to patch things up and spend Christmas with him.

She felt heartened at the thought. Last Christmas had been a bitter one, spent between their own flat and Stacy's mother's house. There had been acrimonious remarks within earshot about her home-made gifts, and Stacy had felt that she had made them herself because she was ungenerous towards his people. He had reminded her that she had only to ask him for more money if she wanted it. He would, he had said, rather go without himself than have his mother feel that she was being slighted by poor quality presents. Janine, who had worked very hard on making the things, and given up time on the baby knitting to do it, had been angry and hurt. How many times had she been angry and hurt through Stacy's mother!

Most of the staff had already packed up for the holiday, at the Head Office, when she telephoned, but she finally found someone's secretary who vaguely remembered that Stacy had been transferred to a smaller office. Janine made the next journey by hired car, because time was running out.

There she had more luck. She learned from the cleaner (the rest of the staff having gone already) that he was staying (as far as she knew) at the Fisherman's Arms.

Janine, tired and cold, began to feel elated at last. The Fisherman's Arms. An attractive name for a pub, and not a bad address to have over Christmas. She thought wistfully how nice it would have been to have had Coppernob with them, but that wasn't possible now. Perhaps she could persuade Stacy to go back to Bletchbury with her to-morrow, and meet Barbara Vine, and her two children, Nancy and Peter. Barbara, she had no doubt, would be so pleased to see her back with her husband, that she would have him in her house over the holiday without a murmur.

The inn was gaily lit. There were paper decorations festooned across the ceilings of the bars, and tiny electric lights draped all over a miniature Christmas tree. In the public bar, where Janine rather hesitantly ventured, was a crowd of people, all singing gay Christmas songs, and filling their glasses with hearty regularity. Some were local people, but most of them were young, well-dressed and obviously together in one large party.

Janine elbowed her way to the counter and asked the barmaid if a Mr. Eustace Conway was staying there. The girl was new, and referred Janine to the little bald-headed shirt-sleeved man beside her, who was serving bitters at a terrific rate and talking fast at the same time.

No, he told Janine, there was no one staying there at the moment, and he knew of no such party as Eustace Conway. Had she got the right pub? Janine explained in desperation that she had been sent there by Mr. Conway's firm, and that he certainly had been staying there. The same stream of negative replies came, and she turned away.

All of a sudden she was very tired and alone. It was as if Coppernob had already been taken from her. She started to push her way through the crush of people when she felt someone touch her arm. It was one of the party of young people. A pretty fair-haired girl with a soft over-red mouth, and hard blue eyes.

"I think I heard you asking for Eustace Conway, didn't I?"

Janine turned eagerly to her. "Oh, yes, do you know where I can find him?"

"Oh, yes," the girl said, easily. "Come and join our party and have a drink."

"No, I can't, really. I'm in a hurry. I must see him at once. It's urgent."

The girl laughed, easily, with a suggestion of a wink at the others. " 'Fraid you can't see him at once," she said, and ordered another round.

"What d'you mean?" Janine asked.

The girl studied her, coolly, insolently. "I suppose you're Janine."

"I'm Mrs. Eustace Conway. If you know where my husband is, do tell me. It's vitally important that I contact him."

All round the people surged, made merry jokes about the season, drank and spilt their drinks, and in one corner joined arms and began to sing noisily. Janine's head began to ache. The blonde girl was talking but she could hardly hear what was being said.

"Can we go and talk somewhere?"

"Yes. Why not? Come on, gang, let's go

353

to the parlour."

"No, alone, if you don't mind. It's rather private."

"Private? Stacy Conway private? Don't be silly. Everyone knows him here. Not very *au fait* with your husband's movements, are you?"

One of the young men with the girl's party shifted uncomfortably. "Don't be a cad, Louise. If you know where the chap is now, say so."

"You're spoiling it. Roddy," Louise drawled. "When did you last see Stacy?" she asked Janine.

Janine turned to the young man. "Do you know where my husband is? It's terribly important to me. They're going to take my little adopted baby away if I can't get in touch with Stacy."

That sobered them a little, even Louise. She seemed a little resentful that Janine could find something to say to sober them. It spoiled the fun.

"Adopted baby? Stacy? That's a good one!" She started to laugh, and demanded another drink.

The young man said, "You'll get nothing out of her—she's drunk. If it means anything to you, she's Louise

Helston, and Conway's been to their place a lot, seeing her sister Fenella."

"Helston? Fenella Helston?" Janine wrinkled her forehead in an effort to remember. The name was familiar but she couldn't recall where she had heard it.

Louise said rather shrilly, "Roddy, you're a beast! *I* was going to tell her that, only much more dr'matically. Why shouldn't he be friends with us? Met my sister Fenella in London. She only wanted fun—that's what she went to be a nurse for. Wish I was a nurse. Much more fun."

A nurse. Helston. The two things clicked together, and made a composite picture of the ginger nurse who wanted to talk to her, but didn't. Had it been about Stacy then? Had she and Stacy—? No, no, not that, Janine's mind clamoured. Not Stacy. Not Stacy.

"Where is my husband—if you really know?" she heard herself saying.

Louise laughed again. "Surprise! He's on the Continent. Gone 'broad. Been 'broad six months." She closed one eye in an attempt to look knowing, and only succeeded in looking gloriously drunk. "But then so's my sister Fenella."

CHAPTER XXI

NOAH CLYNTON was pleased. The trip had been outstandingly satisfying. London was pleased. Noah was pleased with Conway, and so was London. Everyone was pleased, it seemed, but Conway himself.

"What's the matter, my boy? Syria and Egypt disappoint you?"

"No, sir. Not in the least."

"Well, cheer up. I've news for you. No, don't look alarmed. We're not going anywhere else. We're going home —immediately. We should be back by the end of March. Ah, that pleases you, I see!"

Stacy cablegrammed his mother to say he was returning, and he let the bank know, with instructions to tell Mrs. Conway in case she asked. He had instructed his bank to hold any letters from Janine until his return, and now he found himself wondering with ill-concealed eagerness whether there would be any there.

On a sunny, but wild day towards the end of March, he walked into his bank. He was, if possible, thinner than when he went away, but now he was a reddish-brown and his fair hair was bleached almost white. But there was a subtle difference about him that was not lost on the people in the bank. He dressed in a different manner. From a wandering clerkship he had jumped to the important post of secretary to Noah Clynton. He was, in himself, a different man.

He took away with him a bundle of letters, and his heart leapt as he recognized Janine's handwriting. He read them over lunch, and because the last one was addressed from Bletchbury, he took the afternoon train to the Midlands.

It was not easy for a stranger to find Barbara Vine's house, and it was late when he arrived. His feelings were confused. The torrent of emotions on being in England again were mixed and intermingled with the events listed in Janine's letters. The last letter, dated the end of December, had put the thought of visiting his mother, out of his mind.

"I've been to Cumberland," Janine wrote, "to find you. It wasn't easy, but because it was so terribly important to me, I somehow tracked you down. I don't know how, but I did. No wonder you told me to write via the bank! You didn't want me to know where you were or what you were doing! And I was coming round to believing what a fool I was to let you go, because you were such a good man! I was right to let you go, and I'm glad. Anyway, the reason I wanted to see you, doesn't matter any more. By the time you get back to England it'll be too late. Much too late."

Barbara opened the door to him. "You're Stacy Conway," she said, looking him up and down with her shrewd grey eyes. "I've heard all about you. Come in."

He followed her into her pretty sitting-room.

"I was hoping to see my wife. Is she in?"

"You won't see *her*," Barbara told him, severely. "She saw you coming. She went upstairs, and said I was to tell you she was out."

"It's awfully important," he stressed.

"No, that won't do," Barbara said, and sat down, at the same time pointing to an arm-chair facing her. "Now look here, Stacy Conway, there's been a lot going on between you two that needs clearing up, and I'm going to stick my neck right out and undertake to do it. Janine and I have become close friends. I like her. She's a damned nice child. But a silly child and an obstinate one. I rather fancy from what she's told me that those two adjectives might easily apply to you, too."

Stacy frowned, but it was impossible to be angry with Barbara. Also, dimly inside him, he felt that Barbara was what they needed most. A friend who didn't mind sticking her neck out, in order to clear up things between them.

Barbara went on, "Janine thinks you've been carrying on with some woman up north, and were fool enough to go abroad with her. Now, you may well say that it's none of my business, but the fact is, I don't believe any such thing. I don't think you've got it in you."

She gave Stacy a verbatim account of what happened when Janine went to Cumberland. He snorted, and got up and paced the room, and got off his chest what he thought of Louise, and, in fact, the whole Helston family.

"Fenella's all right. I shouldn't have been friends with her, I suppose. Platonic friendships never work, and in this case it made her get silly and chuck up her own fiancé. God knows why. I was selfish enough to like being with her, talking to her—mainly about myself and Janine, it's true. She seemed the sort of woman a fellow could be friendly with, just talk to, I mean, without her getting any silly ideas. I seem to have been mistaken."

Barbara shook her head, with a wise, sad smile. "There isn't a woman on earth who can give a man just that, Stacy Conway—not a young woman, anyway."

"But honestly, I never had the urge to be anything but friendly with her," he protested.

"I can believe that," Barbara agreed. "Because you've got Janine under your skin. I can see that. You're the sort of man who'll never want anyone else while Janine's around."

He paced the room in silence, like an angry beast in a cage. "I wonder what she wanted to see me about, when she went to Cumberland?" he muttered. "She said in her last letter that it would be too late by the time I got home."

"Can't you guess?" Barbara murmured.

He swung round to face her, appalled. "Not...not the baby? It isn't...nothing's happened to it?"

"Oh, no, no, nothing like that. A

healthier baby never breathed. How like a man to jump to the conclusion that it was ill or dying. No, much worse than that. The mother's taken it back again, that's all!"

"How can she? The woman signed it over to us." Stacy was at once surly, caught out on the wrong foot as he had been.

"Stop pacing up and down. You're getting on my nerves. It's a long story. I don't know whether you know it, but Janine was foolish enough to keep on a sort of friendship with this little Cockney. Oh, quite an excellent creature in herself, no doubt, but quite a pest where the baby was concerned. Naturally. No mother should have access to her child after she's given it up. There should be a complete break. For a time Janine even shared a flat with her—three of them, there were."

"Yes, I know. I suppose Janine knew what she was doing."

"I'm not so sure she did. However, the woman's husband was killed accidentally, which left her free to marry again. A most belligerent sort of fellow, I believe, who divined that his new wife wanted her child back, and frightened the wits out of poor Janine. She didn't stand an earthly... with you away heaven knew where. The Court allowed that she'd been deserted."

"Court?" Stacy frowned incredulously.

"Oh, yes, the precious pair who've taken that poor child over, decided they'd be really nasty and get a legal ruling. The child's own mother, with a step-father who was on the spot and presumably not lacking for money, were more acceptable than a foster-mother on her own, with a small allowance from the absent foster-father."

Stacy sat down and buried his face in his hands. "Oh, lord, it's all such a mess. I haven't deserted Janine. She knows that. But I've only just had all her letters. I thought it was all right instructing the bank to hold them for me. I didn't know where I'd be."

"If only you'd written to her, just once, she could have used the letter as proof that you were still together," Barbara murmured regretfully.

"I know, I know. I've been a damned fool. How's she taken it—about the loss of the child, I mean?"

"Very well, on the surface. Underneath, pretty badly, I imagine. I thought she was going mad, the day they took the child away from her. The baby seemed to know it was a final good-bye, too. She screeched and sobbed, poor mite. But now Janine's settled down pretty calmly, though she's bitter."

"Yes, she can be bitter when she likes."

"Do you blame her in this instance? The only children she can bear the sight of are my two. She met them at Christmas, and I think they helped to take off the disappointment and upset she sustained in Cumberland. The kids are pretty fond of Janine, you know, and I think children are a good judge of people."

"Can I see her now?"

Barbara shook her head. "I can't let you go upstairs when she's said she didn't want you to know she was in. I'll see if she's changed her mind, if you like."

A small boy, with dark wavy hair and a brown skin like his mother's, poked his head round the door. "Mummy, Janine's crying," he said, in a distressed voice. Then, catching sight of Stacy, he exclaimed, "Oh, sorry Mummy, I didn't know there were visitors!"

He hurriedly backed out, but Barbara called him back. "Go and fetch Nancy. I want to present you both to Janine's nice husband."

When the boy had gone, Stacy said, "Yours?"

Barbara nodded. "My husband's still out East. I brought the children home to England to school. They're home now for Easter, so the house isn't what it was."

"He looks a nice lad," Stacy said, wistfully.

Peter came in with Nancy, who was an inch or two taller and had fair straight hair, done in two ridiculous short plaits that persisted in turning up at the ends and gave her a rather rakish appearance. She had a wicked grin, freckles, and a front tooth missing.

"Skinny, aren't they?" Barbara grinned. "It's the climate out there. They'll pick up in this country. At least, I'm hoping so."

Peter said again, "Mummy, Janine—" and broke off to look uncertainly at Stacy.

"Stay and talk to Mr. Conway, while I go up to her," Barbara said, and hurried upstairs.

"Have you got any children?" Nancy demanded at once.

Stacy admitted that he hadn't, and omitted to say that they had, once.

Nancy wrinkled her nose. "That's a bad job."

"Oh. Why?" Stacy asked, smiling.

"Well, because I think you're wasted. You'd make rather a nice Daddy."

"And," Peter added, breathlessly, "Janine'd make a *smashing* Mummy!"

"I see. Well, have you kids got any pet animals?" Stacy asked, adroitly switching this rather delicate line of conversation, and succeeding in interesting the children with comparisons of animal life in the East and England.

Presently Barbara came down. "Well," she said, in an exhausted voice, "I've worn myself out in your cause, young man, but I've achieved the apparently impossible—Janine says you can go up and see her. But for heaven's sake, watch your step!"

Janine had powdered her nose and combed her hair. He thought she looked very tired; almost like a person getting over an illness. He stood inside her door, hesitating even though she had called out "Come in" in answer to his knock.

"Janine?"

"Come in, Stacy," she said, in a non-committal voice.

He shut the door, and sat in the one chair, a small arm-chair, and looked at her. She was on the side of her bed, and wore an unfamiliar garment; a house-gown. He looked hungrily at her, and noticed that her hair was brushed up in a style that made her look older, and that she had cut a short thick fringe that made her look slightly provocative, rather like Anna, the girl he had met in Paris.

"I've just had your letters. This morning, in fact."

"Yes. Barbara told me."

"Did she tell you that it wasn't true, what Louise hinted? That time you went up to Cumberland?"

"Yes. She told me."

"And you don't believe it?"

She considered the point, and shrugged. "What does it matter what I believe? You and I are finished, anyway. You're free to do as you like."

"Are we finished?"

"It looks like it, doesn't it? You haven't bothered to get in touch with me, though I've written loads of letters to you. I wanted you to come back, when I needed you so, but now it doesn't matter any more."

"I didn't know where I'd be, Janine, that's why I told the bank to hold any letters for me."

"But you went away without saying anything."

"How was I to know you wanted me to say anything?"

"What d'you mean, Stacy?"

"I saw the way you looked at that fellow Torrington, Janine. That was enough. You can't care for two men like that. You've never looked at me in that way."

"There you are!" she said, as though proving her point. "That's why we're finished, because you never trusted me. You were always jealous about Hugh. You believed what everyone else said. You never asked for my version."

He got up and went to the window. "I was just friends with Fenella Helston. I started being friendly with her the day I asked her, while you were in hospital, to talk to you, try and find out why you were so queer, so strange towards me. I could never get at you to find out. That damned visiting hour was too short. When you came out of hospital, we quarrelled the minute we started talking. We always quarrel."

"So that's what she wanted to talk to me about," Janine murmured. "I wondered."

"Did she ever speak to you, then? She told me she didn't."

"No," Janine said. "I wouldn't have liked it if she had. But she did seem on the point of speaking to me once or twice. I thought perhaps she had troubles of her own."

"Well, that's all my so-called affair with her was. She insisted on being friends in Cumberland where her home was. She threw over her fiancé and of course her parents immediately decided it was my fault, and her young sister made a damned nuisance of herself. I decided I'd get out of the place and go abroad. It was when I went to ask for my release that I got the offer of this good job. It was too big a chance to turn down. D'you blame me?"

She shrugged again. "Why not make money when you can?"

"It was more than that, Janine. It was getting experience, getting foreign travel, a chance to use my linguistic knowledge. More than that, it was to try and forget you. But I couldn't." He came and sat down again. "I wanted you, my dear."

"Despite Hugh Torrington?" She smiled, a little crooked smile.

His face was tortured. "Despite Hugh Torrington."

"I can't believe that, Stacy. You never even asked me for my side of that old story. You believed your mother. And that's what'll happen again and again, whatever the subject—you'll always believe your mother against me."

"Is that fair? Well, then, give me your version now."

"No. Why flog the dead past? Let's leave it as dead as it's always been. I'd prefer you to believe the worst of me. At least I know you're being honest."

She stuck out her lower lip, and together with that little action he remembered so well from their courting days, and the saucy little fringe, she looked like a mutinous though provocative child. He wanted to take her over his knee and spank her seat, and at the same time he wanted to take her in his arms and kiss her as passionately as he had never dared to do in all the time he had known her.

He suddenly got up. "Janine," he said, "you're like a damned silly school-kid, who wants to fight and makes something to fight about. It's damned well time we cleared up this old story, and we're going to, here and now. Come on, out with it!"

She said, a glint in her eyes, "That line won't get you anywhere, Stacy!"

"No?" He pulled her up, suddenly, and held her tightly to him, pressing his lips down on hers with a grip that hurt. She struggled, then suddenly gave in.

His heart was pounding when he let her go. "I've never kissed you like that before, Janine. I should have done."

She looked at him in amazement. Her lips quivered a little. "Yes," she whispered, "you should have done, Stacy."

Downstairs the cheerful rattle of tea-cups mingled with the sudden shrill scream of a whistling kettle. Barbara never got the tea on her own while the children were on holiday. They loved to help, and she encouraged them in this. There were special little fancy cakes from the French pastrycooks in town and little name-flags stuck in the sandwiches to show the different kinds of fillings. This, too, was for the children's benefit, as a special treat because they were home from school. And home-made jam tarts.

"Is Janine's husband home from the East?" Nancy wanted to know.

"Why, yes, I suppose he is," Barbara

admitted, pleased that the children had found their own simple solution to Stacy's absence.

"Will you cry like that when Daddy comes home?" Peter asked, anxiously.

"I don't know," Barbara said, a little shakily. "Well, no, perhaps not, because I've got you two."

Peter said, "Mr. Conway said he hadn't got any children. Didn't he know Janine had got a little baby last Christmas?"

Barbara looked nonplussed for a minute, then, as always, she plunged quickly and unerringly into a convincing explanation before Peter had time to press his point to awkward lengths.

"I've told you all about that already, both of you," she said, severely. "She only *called* it her baby, because she wanted one so badly. It wasn't really hers. It's gone back to its real mother. She was only sort of minding it."

"How rotten for Janine," Nancy said. "I wouldn't have given it back. Would you Peter?"

"No, I'd have hidden it," Peter said, stealthily removing a jam tart from the top of the pile, and biting into it before his mother noticed and made him put it back.

"I bet no one would have found Coppernob if she'd been mine."

"I'm rather of the opinion that I should have done that too," Barbara muttered, turning away quickly to make the tea.

But it was not of Coppernob that Janine and Stacy were talking. It was of the old story of Hugh Torrington.

"Like everything else, there are two explanations," Janine sighed. "The right and the wrong. You heard the wrong, naturally. It's so much more satisfying to say that a girl you don't like stayed out all night with a man, miles from anywhere, whether you know the truth or not. As a matter of fact, I think I'd rather you hung on to that idea than have you know the true story, because the true story's so damned silly. I should feel an awful fool, telling you."

"Don't you think I ought to know the true story, Janine? Don't you owe it to me?"

She shrugged again. "All right. But promise not to laugh. You see, Hugh seemed so exciting in those days. All the girls wanted him. I was so thrilled when he seemed to want to go around with me. He was big, dashing, rather devil-may-care, and he had a lot of money to sling around and he wasn't mean. It was fun being with him."

"I can see that," Stacy put in.

She leaned further into his arms and snuggled her head on his shoulder. "I thought I was in love with him. It never occurred to me (believe it or not) to wonder if he was in love with me. I just took it for granted. Well, the night that everyone loves to remember, we had been out in his new sports model. We'd got miles out in it, and didn't know what to do next for fun. Suddenly Hugh said, 'I know, let's look at some houses for my mother. I love looking over empty houses.' It wasn't a trick. He really did like doing that. So did I. He honestly wanted to look out for a house for his mother—she's too silly to go house-hunting, anyway."

"So I gather," Stacy said, drily.

"We went to a country agent's and got the keys to a manor not far out. The agent was closing, and said, when we'd finished, put the key through his letter-box. Well, we went out to the place, and looked it over. It was all right, but not so exciting inside as outside, and pretty solid and Victorian. Hugh got bored, and so did I.

He said we might as well do the attics and then clear out and put the key back. That's where we went wrong. A draught slammed the attic door and it jammed. Damp, I suppose. We couldn't get it open."

Stacy's face darkened. "And you were both there all night—together?"

Janine dropped her eyes. "That's the damned silly part of it. Everyone has decided we were, and presumably spent a very hectic night. As a matter of fact, Hugh was so wild when he found we were trapped, that he spent the rest of the night getting out—climbing out of a dormer window and scaling the roofs! He worked like a nigger, and when he did get down to the front door and let himself in, he couldn't get me out because the door couldn't be moved from the outside. So he went back to the town and knocked up the fire brigade, and got them to bring an escape to get me out!"

Janine's face was flaming. Even now, the memory made her boil with rage and humiliation.

Stacy said, "I owe the fellow an apology."

"What about me?" Janine cried.

"You need a spanking, mostly for being

disappointed that he went to such lengths to protect your honour."

"Anyone'd think I was poison, being so feverish to get out of the place."

Stacy kissed her again, laughing. "You—child!" he said, fondly, shaking her. "You silly child!"

Barbara called to them that tea was ready. She sounded half-fearful, as if she were intruding.

"By the way," Stacy said, watching Janine comb her hair. "What happened to Torrington?"

"He married Yvonne, the fair girl I was living with in his flat that time. You remember her?"

"Good lord!" Stacy said, understanding at last.

"Yes. It was a bit of a shock. I didn't like it at first," Janine said, with engaging candour. "But when I went up to their wedding, just before Christmas, I saw Hugh as he really was. D'you know, Stacy, he's not exciting at all!"

He laughed, and took her down to tea.

On the bottom stair, she stopped, and looked up with a new expression in her eyes. "Not nearly as exciting as you are, Stacy!"

CHAPTER XXII

BARBARA VINE reflected that the children's school holidays came round too quickly. It seemed such a little while ago that it was Easter, and the children going mad over Janine and Stacy Conway being in the house, and taking them out. That was a crazy holiday.

The summer holidays had been more sober. Janine and Stacy had not been with them then. The only thing that had made the children go wild over that holiday, apart from their rather sober two weeks by the sea, was the bi-weekly letter from the Conways, who had bought a small house just outside London, handy enough for Stacy to go into town each day, in his capacity of secretary to the big shot in his firm. Janine had two maids, which seemed to Nancy and Peter the height of wealth.

"Why can't we have two maids, Mummy?" Peter wanted to know.

"Because your father is only a poor planter and not a company director's secretary, my pet," Barbara explained without rancour. Impossible to explain to the children that every penny the Vines had was being sunk into a fund for college and university, at a later date, for the children were destined for medicine and the law.

"Has Janine got any more babies?" Nancy wanted to know.

"Not yet," Barbara grinned, with an eye on Christmas.

That was in the summer. Now December and preparations for Christmas was upon them, and the children were clamouring to know if the Conways would be coming to stay, and if not, why not?

"Not this holiday, darlings. Easter," Barbara said, writing envelopes for Christmas cards.

"Have they sent us any presents?"

"Yes. Christmas morning, and not before, it says on them. And that's how it's going to be," Barbara told them severely.

"I sent Stacy some bicycle clips," Peter said.

"Has he got a bicycle, then?" Barbara asked in surprise.

"No, but if he ever gets one, then he's got the clips for his trousers already," Peter explained.

"I sent Janine a baby's rattle. It was pretty, and ever so cheap," Nancy said.

"Wha-a-t?" her mother gasped, looking up sharply.

"Well, it was all right, wasn't it? She wants a baby, and if she gets one, she won't have to buy a rattle," Nancy said, imperturbably.

"Bless my soul, what have I done to get such offspring?" Barbara exclaimed, slapping a hand to her head, and laughing till the tears came. "Oh, well, perhaps both your presents will come in handy before long," she gasped.

"What, is she going to have a baby?" both the children shrilled, together.

"Oh, lord, now it's out, and she'll think I told you!"

"We won't breathe a word, Mummy, but when? When's it coming?"

"Well, as a matter of fact, pretty soon now."

"Before the hols. are over, Mummy?"

"Yes, before you go back to school you'll know what it is—a girl or a boy."

But Barbara was sorry she had let the cat out of the bag. Every day there was a stampede to collect the letters and to take any incoming telephone calls. Her life was pestered with the eternal question: "Have you heard from Janine yet? Has the baby come?"

In Janine's own household the subject wasn't mentioned. Stacy merely asked her each night and morning how she felt. With this child, she had been ill. Ill from the third or fourth month, and with this contrast to the first, both Stacy and Janine had experienced a new anxiety.

"I wish it was all over," Janine said, one morning after Christmas. "It's like the weather. The snow's holding off, threatening. This business is over-time, and holding off. If only it would happen."

"Janine, I don't know how to tell you, but I've got to run over to Paris for a few days. I tried to get out of it, but I couldn't."

"Oh, Stacy!"

"I don't know what you'll say, but I've sent for Yvonne. I thought you'd like to have her with you. She's coming willingly. Torrington doesn't mind a bit. He's running her over this morning as a matter of fact."

"Oh, I'm glad. I'd like no one better. The girls are all right, of course, but they're in the kitchen most of the time. It'll be nice to have a friend with me. I wish Barbara lived nearer."

"I think you'd find Barbara's children a

bit exhausting, wouldn't you, darling?"

"Perhaps. Is Yvonne bringing Georgina?"

"No. She thinks it wiser not to. Charlotte will take care of her."

"I wish it were all over," Janine whispered again.

"Well, don't forget. The moment you feel unwell, get Yvonne to ring the nursing-home. Wilkins will have the spare car standing by in the garage. You'll be all right. It's under an hour's journey by road. That's if you're sure you won't go now, to be on the safe side?"

"No. No, I don't want to go too soon." Stacy hesitated.

"Janine, you do feel all right about the nursing-room? I mean, about it being Mayo's?"

"What you really mean is, do I mind Dr. Mayo being Fenella's husband, don't you? Oh, Stacy, you are an old idiot. Every so often I catch you looking at me with that uncertain look. Why didn't you ask me that before?"

"Well, as it was your idea, I hardly liked to."

"It's because of any number of reasons, darling. First, I didn't want to go back into that hospital. Second, though I didn't tell you, Fenella came to see me. She wanted to make sure she hadn't caused irreparable damage between us, I think. She seemed relieved when she saw how happy I was."

"Why didn't you tell me, Janine?"

"Well, she asked me not to. It doesn't matter now. She's married to Richard Mayo, and everything's all right. But just then she wanted it to be between just us. When I told her I was going to have a baby, she asked me to have it in her fiancé's nursing-home, just to prove that I had no bad feelings—and I rather rashly promised."

"Rashly?"

"Well, rashly because I didn't talk it over with you first. I was glad afterwards, though, because I heard that Dr. Mayo was a first-rate obstetrician."

"Yes, he'll look after you all right," Stacy said, but he still seemed worried over her condition.

"So will Fenella," Janine said, with conviction. "She happens to be quite happily married, working with her husband."

Stacy went to Paris with a sinking heart. He had tried hard to get out of this trip,

381

but it was important. There was no shelving it. He flew, and all the way he had the same dead feeling in the pit of his stomach as he had that night when he had first met Fenella, and she had told him his boy was born dead. It was a queer feeling, conjuring up that picture of Fenella in her uniform, and her red hair flowing under one of the dimmed corridor lights, and all the sounds and smells of the hospital around him, and that dead grip of grief in his inside.

The business finished more quickly than he anticipated, he had a meal in a brightly lit cafe and left it unfinished because an organ-grinder brought his box and monkey into the door-way and played that same tune, that gay little dance-tune which had once been so popular both in England and on the Continent, the tune that had been played outside the hospital on that tragic April night.

Little odd memories came back. His mother, with her gentle voice, and the triumph in her eyes. She had wanted him to have a son by Janine. She hadn't wanted him to have Janine. She had dropped corresponding with him since he and Janine had come together again. He had an odd swift memory of Mrs. Petts launching into her favourite theme, the strange births and deaths she had witnessed—that on a night when he least wanted such reminiscences. And Mrs. Westlands calling him "proud father" without recalling that his child hadn't lived.

At last he flung his papers together in his brief case, and took the earlier plane back to England, instead of taking the one booked for him by his firm.

The telephone was out of order when he rang his home. The recent gales had broken down the outlying cables. Torn with anxiety, he rushed for the next train, and missed it by a minute. He fretted and fumed up and down the platform, conscious that there was an hour to wait.

At last, he decided to telephone the nursing-home, just in case they had heard anything of Janine. He dare not think what might have happened if she had needed to telephone after the cables had blown down.

It was cold in the callbox. He was cold inside him. For no reason at all, he thought of Janine leaning forward in her hospital bed, asking him what the day was.

The anniversary he forgot. His son's birthday. And the anniversary last April, in contrast.

That was a happy one, that last one. He had awakened early and caught sight of a calendar on the wall. It was the 31st March. It hadn't been pulled off yet for the new day. He had kissed the tip of Janine's nose, and as she sleepily looked up at him, he had murmured: "Good morning, darling. What's to-day?" and he had teased her because she had been the one to forget. In their happiness, she had told him about Aunt Bee's anniversary. Three anniversaries. What would the next one be like? A cold little voice inside him whispered: Will there be another?

He shut his eyes, and listened resolutely to the burr-burr of the telephone ringing in the nursing-home. A brisk voice answered, and he heard himself asking shakily if he could speak to Mrs. Mayo or the doctor, whichever was available. Fenella came to the telephone, after an unconscionably long wait.

She was breathless, as if she had been running.

"Stacy? You've hardly given us time . . . how did you know? I thought you

384

were in Paris."

"I came back early. What d'you mean, Fenella? Is everything all right?"

"Yes," Fenella sang. "Janine's fine. She came through with flying colours. May I be the first to congratulate you. *It's a boy*."